WALKAWAY

MARK ARENS

This is a work of fiction. All characters, names, incidents, dialogue, and plot portrayed in this book are either products of the author's imagination, or are used fictitiously. Any resemblance to real people, living or dead, or to any company is purely coincidental.

Published by ThumbPeople™ Books, Inc.
14400 W Burnsville Pkwy
Burnsville, MN 55306
www.ThumbPeople.com

www.WalkawayBook.com
www.MarkArens.com
Printed and bound in the United States of America.

First printing 2007
Second printing 2011
Third printing 2017
ISBN 978-0-9801606-3-5

OTHER BOOKS BY MARK ARENS

Thumbuddy You

Thumbuddy Special

Thumbuddy Goes to School

Thumbuddy, Thumbuddy I Love You

Thumbuddy, Thumbuddy Oh What You Do

I'll Always Love My Thumbuddy

You Are Thumbuddy

For my wonderful family!

I love you so much!

Prologue

October 27, 2004.
Boundary Waters Canoe Area, Minnesota/Ontario Border

Around the bend, the river narrowed. There, the water moved fast before flowing into a deep gorge of rapids. Mike Montane paddled hard, roughly a canoe length from the Canadian shoreline. Two other canoes followed, shadowed as dark reflections in the rainy afternoon mist, barely within sight. Adrenaline pounded through his body. Sweat dripped from the long sleeves of his concealed wetsuit onto his cold, bare hands.

The river turned. It was time.

With one sweeping stroke, Mike heaved his canoe sideways against the choppy current so the others could see its full length.

Now!

Placing two fingers under his tongue, his whistle pierced across the water. At the same moment, he stood in the canoe and thrust his paddle in the air. The others stopped paddling and peered through the haze. He pointed the blade toward the Minnesota shoreline and signaled them to look. Four heads turned, and Mike imagined the strain in their eyes as they refocused on him, then back to the empty shore.

Still pointing, he deliberately stepped onto the back edge of the canoe. Water poured over the side. Seeming to struggle for balance, he flailed his free arm, then grabbed all the air his lungs could hold, pitched his paddle chaotically into the sky, and fell backward into the icy river.

The arctic water wrapped its grip around him. It burned his face, like fire engulfing a match. Cold bore into the thin wetsuit with penetrating stabs of pain. But he had no time for pain.

He swam underwater as far as his breath could take him, knowing the others would be racing to his rescue. His lungs exploded as he pushed himself, eyes wide open – one, two, three strokes beyond his desperate need for air.

Bubbles burst through the water as his lips strained for the surface. He gasped and dove again. A few more strokes and he'd be past the bend.

The drag of his fully clothed body fought against his pulling arms. His feet splayed against the soles of his boots trying to turn anchors into fins. Fear of being caught controlled every nerve, forcing him to push. Push. His hand hit a rock, then silt – he was near the shore.

Heaving chunks of air, he scrambled, almost fell onto the rocky shoreline, somehow wary not to break any branches, overturn any stones, or leave any trace except the water trail that would soon blend into the already-wet rocks. Bending low, trying to stay invisible among the giant boulders, Mike sprinted silently. He needed to make it over a small hill about forty yards from shore to an area overgrown with thick brush amidst the twisted trunks of fallen trees. There, in the man-sized briar patch, he'd vanish like a deer in the woods.

Anxiety overpowered him. It wasn't the fear of a hunted animal. Rather, it was the calculated, self-imposed terror of being caught. His beating heart tried to betray him while every pulse throbbed inside his throat. He crouched motionless in a hollow of torn roots and wet leaves. Shutting his eyes, every sense, every cell of his body focused in order to listen.

By now the others rounded the bend. He heard them yell against the howling October wind. They hollered loud. Again and again he heard his name in panicked cries. They felt close. Too close. He dropped flat to the ground except for his heaving chest, unwilling, unable to look.

Mike knew they'd be scared. Temperatures hovered barely above freezing. Water this cold could kill in minutes. Worse still, they were alone, at least two days from the nearest road and well beyond the reach of any cell phone. He was their leader, the one who had brought them to this lonely place. No one else had a map to guide them home.

As they approached his overturned canoe, he heard Kelly's voice scream above the rest. His wife shouted in anguish, each time louder, more fierce than the last. "Mike! Mike!!! Mike!!!!!"

Despite years of premeditation, he wanted to cry out. But seasons of pent-up wrath held his tongue in numbed resolve. Fury transformed itself into resolute silence as his lips mutely mouthed the words that tore through his heart. *I'm here . . . I'm sorry . . . I love you.*

As their search moved down river, their yelling slowly faded, while his anger simmered into silent rage. He wanted to look, to see where they were, but his own heavy burdens forced him to the ground.

Time passed. Despite the wet cold gnawing through his muscles, he remained motionless. He knew the forensic detectives from Platinum Insurance would come back to the woods – probably with helicopters and an army of people. All to look for him. Their own private investigators would overturn stones to prove he wasn't dead.

But they would find nothing. No body. No clues. Nothing.

Nothing but speculation that a former Platinum agent might have tried to commit life insurance fraud.

No one else could be a part of this deception. His wife had to *know* he was dead to have the strength to battle the monsters who had destroyed his life and taken his soul. Mike had counted the cost, and had given back the change.

In the end, he'd show Platinum. And he'd get their money, too. His body grew static and numb to pain as he waged war with his enemies. And waited.

Waited.

Waited for the others to give up.

He pressed himself into the bitter wet ground for hours. All the while a cold wind sliced through the damp wool clothes he wore on top of his eighth-inch wetsuit. Shaking cold and throbbing nerves ravaged his body. When he finally had the courage to move, his rigid muscles trembled in shock. Slowly, silently, Mike peered over a fallen log, then froze. There, so close, a silver-skinned

Alumacraft canoe had been left behind.

Without moving his head, his eyes slowly scanned. Back and forth. No one. The others were gone. He assumed they had left the canoe along with his pack and extra gear to lighten their load for the long trek to find help. It would all remain untouched by him.

Crouching low to the ground, he inspected every twig, piece of grass, and clump of dirt to be sure he'd left no trace, then silently tiptoed toward the water. When he got to the river's edge, he gazed across to the Minnesota shore.

Still wet and fiercely cold, he made a final check of his wetsuit, adjusted the zipper buoyancy belt filled with soft weight, and stepped back into the frigid water. A lot of work lay ahead.

Just then, the sun pierced through the clouds.

Chapter 1

Seven years earlier: June 1, 1997
Rocky Mountain National Park: Ten miles southwest of Estes Park, Colorado.

At 14,155 feet above sea level, and only one hundred feet from the top of "The Diamond," Mike Montane clung to the sheer granite wall. Twenty-five feet above his wife Kelly and her twin sister Alex, Mike had been lead climbing the black rock face on the eastern side of Long's Peak since an hour before dawn. Now it was noon.

The hot summer sun bore down, stabbing the big slab of stone. Heat transformed its frozen outer shell into a vertical desert. Veins of milky-white perspiration trickled down Mike's wrists from his chalk-covered hands. Wetness altered his blond hair to a shade of sandy brown.

A relentless wind streamed four thousand feet up the sheer rock face. Mike's dark green tank top flapped on his muscular frame, and gusts lifted fists of hair off his head. Thin air made him breathe fast and hard. His arteries pushed more adrenaline than oxygen through his taut body and his bloodied fingers clenched inside a small rock fissure.

The wind grabbed at Mike. It had already tried to throw him off the mountain, and the blasts grew stronger with each new pitch. It pulled at his psyche, and threatened to push beyond his limits.

The mountain began to move and spin as Mike's old childhood fears dredged their way through his consciousness, as if he sat in the stands of the Hubert H. Humphrey Metrodome at his one and only Minnesota Twins game. The third grade outing was supposed to be fun. Then Mike found himself on the upper deck in the cheap outfield seats. The whole dome spun as the green turf mixed with the blue bleacher seats. The queasy feeling gnawed at his guts. The crowd cheered for the game, oblivious to his rising fear.

The concrete steps pretended, almost taunted, a disappearing act over the field. Looking down became impossible. Mike squirmed, then crawled under his seat until an usher carried the boy to the safety of the mezzanine. The other kids jeered. The memory seared into his psyche.

Mike pushed the image from his mind. He remembered instead how, with Kelly's encouragement, he had faced his fears head-on as he went rock-climbing on their first date ten years ago. His confidence and abilities had grown until they squashed those horrid feelings into submission.

He thought the terror had vanished. Thought with the hundreds of hours spent climbing, the dreaded thing had been swept away, a part of his long-forgotten past. Now that old enemy was back: the vision of spinning helplessly in space . . . the unbearable anticipation of the moment of impact . . . fear so overwhelming he almost wanted to submit to it . . . to somehow end the clammy dread.

Fear whispered; *You're not good enough to make this move.* Mike's legs trembled. His calves burned, a cramp twisted his muscles tight. One blue climbing shoe extended far to the left and squeezed against a small crystallized outcropping no larger than a thumbnail. His right leg stretched in the opposite direction to a pencil thin ledge. A multicolored rack of carabiners and slings dangled off the back of his harness above the abyss. He did the splits on a plumb wall of nothingness.

His ring and middle fingers dug inside a narrow crevice. He twisted them into a pretzel shape. The force formed a torn wedge of flesh just strong enough to support his weight.

As his tenuous grip became harder and harder to hold, Mike's left forearm and wrist burned with fatigue. He couldn't hang on much longer, but the next handhold remained out of reach. Any move up seemed impossible. The only way down, to fall.

But the fall was too great. Too long. The run-out to the last piece of protection stretched twenty-five feet below. Like the full swing of a pendulum, a fall would drop him a total of fifty feet.

Then the rope would slam to a halt. The jolt alone had the potential to break his neck. Paralyzed by fear, Mike was, as climbers call it, "installed" on the mountain.

"You can do it, Mike." Kelly Montane's voice vainly masked her worries as she watched on belay. Her feet pressed tight against a ledge the length and width of a ruler while she hugged the wall the same way her sweaty red tank top clung tight to her body. Her right hand gripped the purple rope, ready to lock it with a downward tug. Her eyes glued upwards, and a sixth sense caused her to inhale Mike's fear.

"Go for it." Urgency penetrated Alex Richter's words. She glanced at her twin sister, then refocused on Mike. Alex "sat" in her black climbing harness, clipped into two separate fixed pitons, ten feet to the side of Kelly. A second rope snaked seventy feet down the vertical cliff before coiling back to Kelly. The flat slate wall gave no footholds, so she literally hung from her harness.

Gravity held their lives in its hands. If Mike fell onto Kelly, the force would probably throw everyone off the mountain. The "safety" ropes literally tied everyone to the same fate.

Kelly tried to make herself small as she inched as far to the left as her sling allowed. The green webbed nylon sling connected her to a metal wedge stopper inserted into a tiny crack in the mountain.

"Do it. You know you can."

"I'm scared, Kel."

"I know, Mike. But you've got this move. See it in your mind." Kelly closed her eyes. "You have to go for it."

"Kel, I can't hang on, let alone go up." A strong gust of fear blew up the mountain and tried to peel him off. Suddenly all the plans, preparation, and practice on their local Minnesota cliffs seemed wholly inadequate. These were the big leagues. The real thing. Life or death.

"Listen, Mike," Kelly commanded. "You have to get off your left foot and bring it into the same crack where your left hand is. When you wiggle your toe in there, you have to pull your hand out. Mike. Listen! You've done it before in the gym. It will give you the reach you need to get to the next ledge."

"Climbing." Mike tried to sound determined.

"Climb on." Tension sounded in Kelly's voice.

Mike used the power in his right leg to push as he pulled with his left hand. His body moved upward and he tentatively brought his left foot up an inch at a time. He held his balance against gravity. Slowly, slowly, his foot crawled up the wall until his toes pointed at the edge of the hold his hand occupied. Now, somehow, he had to jam the rubber nose of his climbing shoe into the hole while removing his hand at the same instant. It seemed impossible.

Kelly crouched far to the left and held her breath.

Mike struggled to believe.

Do it. Or fall.

Little by little, with unwavering balance, Mike removed his bloody fingers from the narrow crevice and dug in with the black rubber tip of his climbing shoe. Only the friction of rubber on rock held him on the crag.

The palms of both hands opened against the flatness of the smooth slate. His hands glided slowly up the surface toward the next handhold, as a trickle of blood mixed with the white chalk on the back of his hand. His body melded into the wall.

"I got it," Mike silently shouted – knowing he dared not breathe aloud. His heart pounded. Nerves ratcheted tension. Tighter. *"Stand up and reach. Do it. Do it."*

As Mike's body moved upward, the angle of pressure on his climbing shoe changed, and because the crack was wet with perspiration, his foot slipped out. In desperation he lunged for the next handhold.

And missed.

Chapter 2

Mike plummeted off the mountain. Kelly felt the wind as her husband hurled within inches of her face.

They all shrieked in terror. Like the cry the instant before a blow. Chaos.

The force of the fifty-foot fall was too much. The rock surrounding the fixed piton exploded. His body plunged past his expected stop. A rush of horror, compacted into a moment of eternity, tore through his soul. Reality merged with every terror he had ever imagined. Mortality blended with immortality.

Twenty more feet and less than a heartbeat later, the rope caught. The backup safety wedge that secured Kelly to her belay position held firm.

The impact slammed Mike against the harness. Then the first recoil thrust him back toward the sky. He dropped again. Smashed once more into the straps of webbed nylon that wrapped around his legs and back. The vibrating, twisting rope tossed his limp form.

Because of the overhanging angle of the climb, Mike's fall carried him out and away from the mountain. As the rope recoils slowed, Mike was left rocking back and forth – seventy feet below his wife and fifteen feet out from the cliff. He hovered in mid air.

The violent force against the rope catapulted Kelly three feet up and smashed her hard against the cliff. Like a human splat-ball shot against the wall, her torso flattened into the granite while her arms and legs extended horizontally. But despite the impact and contortion, she still held the rope with her brake hand.

"Hang on, Kel!" Alex yelled.

Kelly's grip never wavered. Only a tiny metal wedge inserted in a crack of rock kept them all alive. Her eyes darted down at Mike, back to the wedge, then over to Alex. Her wide-eyes locked on the tiny stopper that still held firm. She called down to Mike. "Are you okay?" There was no response.

"Mike?" This time, Kelly and Alex both yelled.

Mike's lungs heaved and his body shuddered as he fought to catch his breath.

"Are you okay?" Kelly's voice screeched against the wind that howled and sucked the rope and man away from the mountain in a taunt of power.

Kelly's heart raced.

Wind filled everything but his lungs as he fought for even a whisper. He tried to nod.

Then the wind let go. It spit him out and slammed Mike back into the wall like a tetherball on a string.

Kelly tried to call out, but her voice didn't work.

For an eternal moment nothing happened, as if time itself stopped to watch.

Then a new gust pulled a tear from Kelly's eyes. Her body remained pinned against the wall.

She could only wait.

And wait.

Finally, Mike lifted his hand and signaled by raising his finger as if to say: "*Give me a moment.*"

The wind carried him away from the cliff for another round.

No words.

Only wind.

The dangling puppet looked up at his wife, then glanced over at Alex. Barely loud enough to hear, Mike expelled a sort of snicker. Then, even as he fought to breathe, his shoulders began to shake and he exhaled, "Big air."

Just as Kelly and Alex registered the words, Mike said it again. "Big air, Kel."

"We've got to get down." Kelly's voice shook.

"Nothing but air!" Mike's face transformed into the image of a man who had fought death, and won.

"This isn't fun anymore." Kelly yelled at Mike then looked to Alex for support.

"I'm not scared, Kel." He held his arms out, hanging in his harness like a bird hovering in one spot against the wind. "No more fear."

"Stop it, Mike."

"I'm wired."

"Please get back on the wall. You're scaring me."

"Kel, you've got him." Alex raised her closed fist and pounded into her other hand.

With renewed strength and a new fearlessness, Mike rocked his body back and forth to create momentum. His actions, more than any words, told everyone he would never back down. "I'll never be afraid again, Kel."

"I'm scared," Kelly refused to look.

"Kel, when we get to the top we're going to celebrate. You'll never want down."

Mike needed to swing hard to propel himself the fifteen feet back to the cliff. Once he reached the wall, he would have to snag a handhold and climb back up, past his wife.

He swung harder. Arching farther and farther out from the mountain, each swing brought him closer, then farther, closer, then farther, back and forth. He needed to grab the rock, and never let go.

************ *********

"Piece of cake," Alex yelled into the wind. She scrambled up another fifty feet before stopping for the view. "Hey, Kel. I thought this climb was supposed to be a challenge!" She winked at Mike and Kelly who sat with their legs dangling over the top ledge some forty more feet above her.

Mike snapped a picture, while Kelly belayed her sister. Alex's shoulder length blond hair fell behind her, while her hyper-inflated muscles bulged against her maroon tank top. Only a tiny mole on her left cheek distinguished Alex from Kelly.

"Did you miss me, Al?" Kelly leaned over to touch Alex's hand, now only one easy move from the top.

"More than ever." Alex smiled.

When she stepped on the summit, Kelly yelled, "Arriba, Arriba, Arriba!"

"Oooohhhh, Oooohhhh, Oooohhhh!" Alex joined in, making coyote cries.

"Yippee, Yaaahoooo, Yeeee-haaaa," cried Mike for all the wannabees of the world.

Within a few seconds, it became a contest to make the weirdest uninterrupted sounds. The snorting, quacking, barking, woofing, high-pitched squeals, and belching noise continued beyond a minute of insanity, until they broke into hearty laughter.

"All right for the Richter sisters," Mike shouted, as Kelly met him with a kiss and Mike wrapped his arms around both twins in a full-body hug.

The threesome finally sat down, only inches from the ledge. Their purple ropes coiled against the rock outcroppings like snakes winding down the cliff, while the racks of slings and carabineers dangled from their harnesses.

They soaked in the scenery of the vast mountain. The jagged peaks stood as sentinels guarding the beginning of time. Down below, what appeared an arm's length away, the little village of Estes Park lay nestled into a sea of evergreens. The trees resembled a green velvet carpet crawling up the mountainsides from the valley floor.

After ten minutes of quiet reflection, Mike unstrapped his Kelty pack. "I've got a surprise." He pulled out a bottle of champagne along with a red Platinum Insurance jackknife.

"I can't believe you hauled that bottle all the way up here," Kelly said.

"Yeah. I can't believe I did either." Mike grinned and held the bottle above his head in victory. Then with both hands, he shook it hard.

"And that stupid knife of yours must weigh two pounds," Alex said.

"You never know when it might come in handy." Mike dug the corkscrew end of the knife into the top of the bottle.

"Did you pack some business cards with you too?" Alex crossed her eyes, opened her mouth, and stuck her tongue sideways.

"I love this knife."

"I can tell."

"If it makes you happy, I have three of them!"

"Is that all?" Alex snorted.

"I won them selling life insurance for Platinum," Mike said.

"Whatever." Alex rolled her eyes with a feigned innocence.

"Yeah, I love my job," Mike's voice turned edgy, "and have a lot of pride in my work – just for the record."

"Whattt – ever." Alex's head cocked toward Mike, then flung her eyes out into space.

"No one's cutting down your job." Kelly's voice remained calm as she shot a stare at Mike.

"What?" He mouthed the word, rifled a disgruntled stare back at Kelly, then raised his hands and turned away. His job had nothing to do with it. But Kelly had a history of refusing to examine any deeper issues, and now wasn't the right time.

"You got to hand it to him, Al." Kelly patted her twin sister on the back as if nothing was wrong. "The boy sure likes his little knife!"

Mike walked to the cliff's edge, unleashed the cork and a stream of champagne sprayed twenty feet into the mountainous sky before dropping into the gorge. "Look at that cork go!"

Chapter 3

As the threesome lingered on top of the Diamond, the blue sky transformed into pillows of clouds. Mike began gathering the gear. "It looks like a storm is heading our way. Let's get outta here while the rock is still dry."

"It's a beautiful day, and I want to stay for awhile." Alex protested.

"We deserve this, Mike." Kelly seconded her sister and Mike immediately felt discounted. It seemed whenever he and Alex disagreed, Kelly took sides with her twin no matter what.

"I don't want to argue." Mike stared at the twins who continued to look out over the mountain, virtually ignoring him. "But we know that summer storms can flare out of nowhere. These mountains create their own weather, and we need dry rocks to make a safe rappel out of here."

Alex didn't move, and Kelly glanced at Mike but shrugged her shoulders. Then she too, looked away.

"You know we had to work as a team to get up here. As your teammate, I'm asking you to listen to me."

"We're listening, Mike." Alex's body, head, and eyes remained fixed in an immobile stare.

Kelly said nothing.

"Okay. We agreed to climb fast and light. No extra gear except the champagne we all enjoyed, my *stupid* jackknife, and a couple of lightweight poly tops."

"The champagne wasn't too smart." Alex quipped. "Now you got an empty bottle to haul back down, too."

"We're scantily dressed and have no jackets or raingear. These mountain storms can cause temperatures to drop by fifty degrees in an hour. In the valley, it might be warm, but it could be snowing up here. Wet rocks make for a dangerous rappel and an even more treacherous hike out. We agreed to play this day safe, and I'm asking you to honor that."

"You win." Alex jumped up without looking at Mike and hauled Kelly up by the arm. "I'm sorry. I wanted to enjoy the view, but I guess you're right."

"I don't want to be scared any more today." Kelly let out a sheepish laugh to break the tension.

"I'm sorry, Mike." Alex walked over and punched him lightly in the shoulder, then flashed her little smile.

Mike felt the twist dig inside him. And worse than being mad at Alex, he felt sad that Kelly could have so easily sided with him, yet refused. He forced his lips to smile back at Alex.

They coiled the extra rope and strapped it onto Mike like a backpack. Then they wrapped two slings filled with carabiners, draws, wires, and cams across his chest like a giant X. Behind all the gear, Mike's shoulder and arm muscles swelled from the day's exertion. "I knew you guys brought me here for a reason. You wanted a pack mule."

Kelly volunteered to be the first one over the edge. Using her air traffic controller to slow her descent, she performed a controlled drop as she pushed away from the cliff. In less than a minute, she plunged 140 feet below the others.

With her right hand, she brought the rope tight under her butt as she came to a stop. Her feet splayed out on the rock in front of her, and she sat in her harness with her torso three feet out from the cliff.

"Whew," Kelly exhaled. She hadn't realized she'd been holding her breath the whole way down. No matter how many times she had rappelled in her life, going down still felt scarier than climbing.

With her left hand, Kelly pulled a sling off her harness and clipped two carabineers into the fixed pitons marking the rappel station. Then she added a wedge stopper for extra security.

"Off rappel," she hollered up the cliff as she let the ropes swing free.

Loaded with thirty pounds of gear, Mike went next.

"Hi ya, honey!" Mike smiled as he swooped down the mountain and tied off next to Kelly. "You're incredible."

"Hi ya, back!" Kelly carefully leaned over to kiss Mike.

"How many other guys get to rock-climb with their wife?"

"You always say that."

"It's true."

"I'm glad we're going down." Kelly sighed.

"It's been a big day." Mike looked intently at Kelly, hoping she might sense his earlier need for support. His mouth gaped slightly open and his eyes locked into hers.

Kelly knew all his little clues by heart. "Thanks for bringing Alex with us." She didn't know what else to say, and simply didn't see any need to apologize.

"How couldn't I?" Mike tried to keep his voice level, knowing Kelly could read every verbal and non-verbal octave. But while his voice stayed calm, his mind involuntarily reeled. He knew how Kelly and Alex's unity, almost a oneness, went far beyond being twins. He'd seen the home movies a *dozen* times. He heard *repeatedly* how, as toddlers, they would sit side by side on the living room couch. Their feet weren't long enough to reach the ground, so they sat deep into the sofa. Then they would rock. Back and forth and side to side, heads down to their knees. Their rocking moved back up and pounded the back of the sofa. Back down, up, to the side – always in sync. Day after day, they'd rock, go play, then come back and rock some more. When one got out of step, the other would stop, wait, and then they would start again.

Maybe two dozen times. Before they learned to speak, the girls communicated in a language of their own. The movies showed the girls, barely old enough to walk, babbling to each other. The little people carried on a conversation, even made joint decisions, before racing off to play.

No matter what, they were *always* together. Soulmates.

Mike had never met a friend or relative from the twins' childhood who could remember them being apart.

Then came the car accident that killed their parents. They had no choice but to move to Minnesota to live with their uncle. Because he traveled for weeks at a time, the thirteen-year-old girls learned how to cook, do the wash, and get around on their own. They had no one to rely on but each other.

When it came time for homework, Kelly helped Alex with history and writing, while Alex helped Kelly with math and science. Teachers and students alike struggled to tell them apart, but it really didn't matter, because they were rarely apart anyway. Instead of saying, "Hey, Kelly!" or "Hey, Alex!" people said "Hey, Richter!"

There was no question of who they were, or what they were about. They shared the same friends, watched the same shows, ate the same food. They liked it that way. Instead of saying "I," the girls said, "we."

They were identical. Identical outranked identity.

Even after Kelly and Mike were married, Kelly and Alex continued their mystical connection, many times making Mike feel second to Alex. Often they would phone each other, but the phone never rang, because they had dialed simultaneously. Conversations began without any warm-up chatter. Each was a simple continuation of the previous conversation because the twins stayed in touch several times each day.

What was he supposed to feel? Jealous?

The negativity toward Alex had a habitual way of boring an ugly hole out of Mike's subconsciousness, right out into the open. Even here on the mountain, the "twin-thing" was something he couldn't escape. "Off rappel." Mike barked, almost hissed the words, up the mountain to Alex.

The hard sound made him catch himself, and he bit his lip before stealing a glance at Kelly. "Sorry, Kel." He looked down to beg a moment of forgiveness for his tone, thankful that she couldn't read his mind, then smiled sheepishly, and tried to move on. "We're going to be on the ground in a couple hours and I can already taste that ice cold beer."

"Beer sounds awfully good." Kelly agreed to the unspoken game plan. "I want to taste it now!"

Two minutes later, Alex's silhouette appeared against the sky. Within seconds she dropped down, almost as if she'd flown on a Bungee cord.

"This is fun!" A giant grin filled Alex's chalk-covered face.

"I only saw a black spandex ass descending from the sky!" Mike said with a half snort half laugh, trying to be funny.

Both girls laughed at the snort, but Mike thought they appreciated his wit, so he joined in with another snort/laugh and now the girls howled. Alex jiggled up and down on the rope as she tried to contain herself.

Finally, Alex used her sling to tie off next to Kelly and Mike. Now, all three stood together on a yardstick dimensioned ledge, totally separate from the rope, while the edge of the cliff disappeared below them.

"Imagine being an eagle." Alex held her arms out.

"What a gift to fly as high as a mountain and have no fear." Kelly too, put her arms out as a stiff breeze blew up from the valley floor.

"Let's think about raptors some other time," Mike barked. "That wind felt cold, and the sky is getting darker. We need to keep hustling. I'm going to pull the rope through our rappel sling now. When it comes down, it's going to whip. Keep your body next to the wall and cover your head."

As Mike pulled on the rope above them, Alex pushed the slack through another set of carabineers in preparation for the next downward pitch while Kelly snaked the rope down the mountain, trying to keep it untangled below them.

Although they worked together and moved fast, they proceeded with painstaking care. If a rope hung up on the rocks above them, it could require one of them to make a potentially dangerous climb to free it. On the other hand, if one strand of rope snagged in a hidden crevice below, it could force the rappel to stop short of the next rappel station. At a couple thousand feet above ground, the consequences of a casual mistake could easily mean death.

Working fast, proceeding with enormous respect for the mountain, they took two long hours to rappel to the base of the climb. By then, the sun hovered on the other side of the mountain. Giant cumulus clouds filled the voids in the blue sky and the shadow of the peak chilled the air.

"What a day," exclaimed Kelly.

Alex's face appeared stuck in grin mode. "Best day of my life, times ten."

************ *********

Two hours later, the victorious threesome drove into Estes Park thirsty and hungry. With their climbing gear stowed in the back of the van, they each dressed like Indiana Jones in khaki pants, oversized safari shirts, and cowboy hats to cover their dried, sweaty hair.

No longer climbers, these tourists were ready to do the town until they dropped. Given the day's events, and with all their adrenaline spent, Mike hoped they could last until sundown.

"Talk about great timing. We have fifteen minutes to kill before our dinner reservations!" Alex laughed.

"And to think you made me run the last mile to the van." Mike smiled.

"You're the one who wanted to race," Kelly said.

They parked on Elkhorn Avenue, across the street from a furniture store that displayed burlwood tables on a large open porch. Twisted, gigantic roots of redwood trees created the burlwood and the gnarled look intrigued Kelly who blurted, "we gotta do some window shopping."

"We deserve it." Alex seconded the motion before Mike had a chance to object. Kelly and Alex started across Elkhorn, while Mike checked the van to make sure they had locked the doors.

"Take a look at that huge couch on the porch." Kelly pointed toward a polished birds-eye burl whose cross section formed the back of a massive couch.

"I've never seen such beautiful wood." Alex's enthusiasm echoed half way across the street when suddenly she looked up and saw an oncoming car racing through the red light.

Instinctively, Alex shot out an arm and pushed Kelly out of

the way. Kelly sailed from the force of the shove. She tripped over the curb and sprawled onto the concrete sidewalk.

The black car cruised through the intersection.

Mike turned away from his van just in time to see a big Buick slam full force into Alex. The car struck Alex in the thighs. She buckled forward onto the hood. Her face slammed into the metal. Her thighbone snapped. Flesh smashed, then tore in the same instant. The car tossed Alex's body high into the air, as it shot across the intersection. The picture blurred as the sounds blended into chaos. Alex slammed onto the roof of a car parked twenty yards down the street. Her body crumpled. Then it slithered off the roof, and slumped to the ground.

The brake lights on the Buick flickered for a moment – like an afterthought. Then the car sped off. Mike didn't get the license number, but an unmistakable bold, red fluorescent sticker on the back of the car broadcast to the world: PLATINUM INSURANCE.

Kelly looked up from the sidewalk and saw Alex's cowboy hat crushed in the middle of the road. Kelly hurtled off the ground and raced toward Alex. Mike was already at her side.

A small red puddle pooled around Alex's head. Blood hemorrhaged from a huge gash across her forehead. Her blond hair and white bandana soaked up the deep red. A tiny stream of blood and spittle oozed from her mouth. Her thighbone protruded from torn pants like a piece of shattered wood. The leg twisted grotesquely outward from half way up her thigh. Alex didn't move or respond to Kelly's cries.

Mike raced to his van to call 911 on his cell phone, then quickly returned while a crowd gawked in a circle around them.

Kelly gripped her sister's hand. Tears flooded Kelly's eyes and rolled down her cheeks. Her face turned toward heaven. Her mouth opened. Indistinguishable prayers filled the air.

Chapter 4

June 1, 1997
St. Louis County Courthouse, Duluth, Minnesota.

Harley Crane sat on a hard oak bench in the first row of the mostly empty courtroom. He hadn't been to church in twenty-some years, since his late teens, when he decided religion wasn't logical. Still, the benches reminded him of pews and invoked a disjointed sense of piety.

"The great halls of justice," his voice echoed. He didn't care that people turned to look at him. Glancing up at the twenty-foot ceilings, he admired the etched plaster, then noticed the marble floors and intricate woodwork touching every curve of the walls. "This is where the destiny of man is decided."

Within a couple weeks, a jury would undoubtedly agree, on national television, that he had his man. Harley Crane was about to win another victory in the battle against insurance fraud. And with his triumph, Harley would be promoted as the youngest Claims Vice President in the history of Platinum Insurance.

"Hi, Mr. Crane." A fresh-out-of-college WCCO Television reporter scurried up the aisle and sat next to Harley.

"Nice to see you, Jack." Harley flashed his steel-gray eyes and smiled. "You've done a helluva job handling this Thorson case."

"Between you and me, we both know all the credit belongs to you."

"I only provided a few clues. Your eagerness led the yokels to all the right places."

"The sheriff's office followed the leads, just like you said. Thorson's guilty, that's for sure." The reporter grinned. "My boss is *very* happy how the station stayed on the exclusive edge of this case, right up to the end. And now we're the lead on a national ticket."

"National..." Harley lavished in the word for a moment before continuing. "I understand your job is to objectively report the facts, but nonetheless, I sure appreciate the positive spin you've given Platinum in this trial."

"You helped a raw rookie uncover a great story," the reporter said.

"There's big news potential when someone kills their own mother. Especially with a life insurance motive."

"And we get a chance to sensationalize it when the fire burns the arsonist's mom while she's sick in bed," the reporter added.

"What is the world coming to?" Harley glanced the other way to signal his waning interest in the conversation.

"Yes." The reporter sensed the departure. "I just don't get one thing. How did you know it was arson when no one from the fire department could find the cause of the fire?"

"Well you see, that's where the difference is. It's a law of life. It's all about enthusiasm, and zeal." Harley paused to exhale and to replay what he had just said. "In a word, it's about passion."

"But the yokels, as you call them . . . they didn't have a clue."

"Passion – I'm telling you. Why do you think I picked you?" Harley stared at the freshman.

"I don't get it, Mr. Crane. You'd think the police, or at least the fire department would've . . ."

Harley clasped his hands together. "You see son, if the fire department gets it right or wrong, no one really cares. But Platinum has to *pay the bill* if someone commits fraud and gets away with it."

"Passion." The reporter whispered the secret word.

"It's my job, my reputation, my future, and my self esteem to catch the bad guys. *I live for it.* It's my *passion* to catch a rat – especially when it's been hiding and no one else can find it.

Chapter 5

Duluth, Minnesota

"Why me?" Sitting in the county jail, on the other side of a glass panel from his wife, thirty-year-old Chad Thorson stared at the floor. His bald head rested in the cup of his big hands while his dark eyes saw absolutely nothing. Despair had reduced the six-foot-eight, three-hundred-twenty-pound giant to an image of hopelessness. The barren, concrete room matched the empty feeling in his gut.

The fluorescent lights hummed as they cast a brooding shadow. Neither spoke. A crackling hiss vibrated unevenly through the phone line.

More silence.

Thorson barely lifted his head. "Remember when Pastor told about the people with Moses? The ones who died in the wilderness. Remember?" He waited for a reply, but none came. "Serpents killed them. They complained that God led them into the desert to die."

"So?"

"Elsie, I don't like it. Both good and bad people died. The serpents didn't care who they bit. Mosquitoes are the same way. They bite everyone." There was a long pause and Thorson continued his empty stare. "Doesn't matter if you're good or bad."

"Chad."

"I've been bit." He put one hand on the glass. "Listen. You gotta know I love you. Loved you from the moment I met you. Tried my best to be a good husband."

Elsie didn't respond.

"Tried to be a good son, too." Thorson's lips trembled, and his chest started to heave unevenly as he fought his need to cry.

Elsie watched, knowing she wanted to see him break. As it became apparent that there would be no tears, her thoughts turned. "Yeah, your mom knew you loved her, all right. Don't know how many boys would give money to their lazy mother so she could buy a run-down dump."

Thorson closed his eyes to shut out the anger. "It was only a couple thousand dollars." He remembered his mom's tender look when he had handed her the cash. How she cradled and caressed his hands the same as when he was a little boy. It made him feel whole, appreciated, and somehow better about himself.

Elsie's voice rose, "We could've used that money to start a family. I would've been able to stay home and–"

"Stop. Please. We agreed to help Mom with that house. We were going to wait–"

"Yeah well, look where we are now. Your mom's house is gone, along with our chances of having a family–"

"I haven't been convicted–"

"I feel like a damned widow."

"They're twisting the facts." Thorson dug his fingers into his temple as his teeth ground against each other. "I'm bit, I'm telling you. And Mom was bit."

"I've been bit, too." Elsie spit poison while her tongue flickered on the roof of her open mouth.

Thorson couldn't look at her. "Someday you'll know I'm telling the truth."

"Who's going to make our house payments now? How'm I going to make it?"

"We've talked about these things before. We'll appeal if I lose."

"What'm I supposed to think? No one even knows where you were when the fire started."

Thorson's big hands turned into fists. "You know I always left work so I could have a quiet lunch at the lake. Why's that so hard to believe?"

"But all the facts point–"

"Don't let some hard-ass prosecutor do your thinking."

"When you left work, everyone saw you turn north toward your mom's house, and the lake is the other way–"

"It was a nice day. I planned to bring Mom to the lake with me. I only went a few blocks before I remembered she was sick. Then I turned around. Elsie, we've been married for six years. You know what kind of man I am. How many times do you want me to repeat my story before you'll believe me?" He didn't know what else to say. The dirge that resonated deep inside his guts liberated itself in the form of a weary laugh.

Elsie stood. "Why are you laughing?"

"Elsie..." Thorson motioned her back to her seat. "What do you want me to do? All I can do is laugh. No matter what I say, you don't believe me. I can't cry and I'm scared."

"I'm scared worse than you."

"Let's try to laugh."

"I can't."

A guard approached the couple. "Time's up." He put his hand on Thorson's arm. Thorson shrugged off the hand in rising. Towering above the guard, Thorson ignored the request to move. Like a granite pillar, he stood before his wife and looked at her face one more time.

Elsie's sagging eyes and down-turned lips showed her story. She undoubtedly believed he had killed his mother. The gravity of the situation, and the pale cast of the fluorescent lights drowned her face into a hardened frown.

Thorson burned the vision into his mind. Then he turned and walked away.

Chapter 6

The June 20th thermostat read ninety degrees outside the St. Louis County Courthouse, but the fresh breeze off Lake Superior made it feel much cooler. Inside the crowded courtroom, Harley Crane cursed the moldy smell and the under-equipped air conditioner. Reporters and film crews sweated in the old building as they milled around in the stuffy marble halls, waiting for the jury.

Everything in the trial had gone according to Harley's plan, and now he envisioned the glory of his future: the big desk, but not just big . . . the enormous desk on the 28th floor of 900 N Michigan Avenue. How he'd be able to look out his window to see the sailboats on Lake Michigan. Maybe he'd take an afternoon off and take the "L" to Wrigley Field and watch the Cubs play.

Most importantly, he imagined what his dad would say. Harley would finally be able to prove he had what it took to succeed. Harley remembered how his dad had made him kneel down in the dirt, with his glove hand ready and his other hand opened. His dad, standing fifty feet from Harley, threw baseball after baseball so they slammed into the ground directly in front of him.

Sometimes the ball rolled hard and flat across the dirt. Harley's official Rawlings leather mitt flashed out and the ball smacked tight in the webbing. "Good job, Son. Way to keep your eye on the ball."

The next ball might skip, and Harley's glove would snag it out of mid air. "Use both hands, Harley."

One after another, Harley's dad threw thousands of grounders in his quest to turn the boy into a major leaguer. There was no room for fear. The pursuit of excellence did not allow it. His dad taught him how fear was nothing but unchecked, illogical emotion – the kind of emotion that led to failure.

Occasionally the ball would hit a rock or pebble. Faster than an eye twitch, the ball would sail past Harley's outstretched glove and slam into his body, even his face. "That's it, Son. Stay in front of the ball. Use your body to block it."

By age seven, Harley had memorized his dad's number one rule: crying had consequences. "If ya want to play with me, Son, ya'd better dry those tears." His dad walked off the field, grabbed a Marlboro, and started to pack the car.

"We just got here, Dad." Harley's voice and little body trembled to fight the tears, even as they streamed down his face. His cheeks streaked with dirt where his dirty hands wiped the wetness away.

"I ain't playin' with a boy who cries. Babe Ruth and Mickey Mantle didn't cry when they got hit by the ball." Harley's dad slammed the Rambler's trunk shut. "Get in the car."

Broken nose and all, Harley Crane exemplified a man who stayed in front of the ball. Someone who finished the job long after others gave up. Someone with *passion.* Even at the cost of his marriage, the quest for success drove him. Not that Harley didn't try in his marriage. By the time he'd been married three years, he and his wife had been through two therapists each. Then a marriage counselor declared that Harley's ex-wife was a "human being" while he was a "human doing." Driven to excel, Harley couldn't spend time watching the clouds, or lie in bed past 6AM to cuddle.

Now Harley sat in the front spectators' row, on the opposite side of the room from Chad Thorson, waiting for the jury to come in. Harley stared at Thorson's monstrous shoulders. The big man looked out of place next to his petite, fresh out of law school, court-appointed attorney.

But for Harley, Thorson's shaved and polished scalp stereotyped him into the same junior subcategory as a professional wrestler. Harley noticed sweat roll off the bald man's head. Thorson's collar looked like a wet towel wrapped around his neck.

Thorson's size represented a walking opportunity for Harley, who suspected the media would jump to the same conclusions he had. Harley figured it was almost impossible not to believe this giant freak of nature had murdered.

"Such a big man. Burning his own mother while she's sick in bed," Harley mouthed the words with disgust and began to think of the big boys in high school, the kind who picked on little people. Their unjust bullying required someone brave enough to stand up to them. One time in eighth grade, when Harley had camped at the Boy Scout's Spring Jamboree, a group of bigger, older boys from his troop dragged Harley out of his tent in the middle of the night. Four of them held Harley to the ground while a fifth smeared peanut butter all over Harley's immature body in the "right of initiation."

They were so far into the woods that no one heard his "girly voice" scream. No one except the other small boys who hid in the woods until the adults in charge came back from the bar. "Boys will be boys." That's what one of the Scoutmasters had said.

Harley never liked the woods since then, but over the years he'd learned how one good blow could drop most long-armed pansies. Someone had to be brave enough to stand up and fight the lard asses of life.

Yes, Harley thought, there were plenty of reasons to dislike Thorson. Besides, Thorson was stupid. It was a clumsy, bungled murder. Anyone dumb enough to kill should at least be smart enough to do it right or create an alibi.

None of the jurors looked at Thorson as they walked in. Thorson turned toward Elsie, but she stared at the ground. Harley smiled. The theatrics swelled his imagination as he envisioned himself the hero in a play. The antithesis of the Henry Fonda role in *Twelve Angry Men* . . . but still the man who used his brains to guarantee victory. Only this time, the bad guy would go down. He glared at Thorson. To think Thorson had once asked Harley to "do him a favor" and help the police investigate other possible suspects. Thorson's obvious guilt made Harley sick at the thought.

The plump, middle-aged foreman stood holding a sheet of

paper, waiting for the judge's orders. When the judge asked for the verdict, the foreman stared directly at Thorson. "We find the defendant, Chad Thorson, guilty of murder in the first degree."

"Guilty!" a reporter crashed out through the courtroom door.

As the foreman finished announcing the verdict, Thorson dropped. His head struck the table, and his giant body sprawled on the floor. Elsie never even budged. It took six men to lift Thorson into a wheelchair. They handcuffed his arms to the chair and used duct-tape to keep him from flopping around, then wheeled him off to the local jail to await sentencing.

Harley's play had a perfect ending.

Reporters swarmed around him. Harley crinkled his broken-nosed face, knowing what it took to create a charming smile. "I want to express my sincere appreciation to the media for your fair and impartial reporting of this trial." Harley's grin beamed as cameras flashed across the room. "At Platinum Insurance, our goal is to save the honest guy a buck. We want to wipe insurance fraud off the map, and make insurance affordable for everyone."

Chapter 7

Harley loved getting off the elevator on the twenty-eighth floor. The textured carpet felt plush under his Bruno Magli wingtips. The mammoth lobby and the mahogany woodwork spoke of wealth, privilege, and corporate splendor. But the one word on the sign said it all: EXECUTIVE.

The big boys played here.

To Harley's right, his private office nestled among the twelve other vice-presidential offices. To his left, the presidential suite's eastern view expanded panoramically over Lake Michigan.

Throughout the Labor-Day weekend Harley's signing bonus, a black Mercedes 5600, and three janitor's pickups were the only vehicles parked in the company parking lot. But that working weekend had prepared Harley for his first one-on-one extended meeting with the boss. Today, Harley took a left and entered Roger Phillips's massive office.

"Hello, Harley. I hope you're not working too hard. You know, you've got to take some time in life to enjoy the view." In his medium size gray suit, which matched his speckled gray hair, Roger floated across the floor, extended his hand, and gave Harley a warm smile.

As much as Harley appreciated the friendly welcome, he was distracted by Roger's thick-framed black glasses. Harley bit his lip to prevent a smirk, simultaneously imagining his boss wearing a pocket-protector under his suit.

"Roger." Harley shook hands with his boss. "You promoted me because I work hard. I'm not about to change. The view is nice, but I intend to prove that you chose the right man." An arrhythmic flash passed through Harley as he realized how his own need to impress had shifted from his father to the man in front of him.

The two men moved across the expansive room to a large oval shaped conference table where they sat diagonally from each other, their backs to the window.

"Harley, you indicated you wanted to discuss strategy."

"The way I see it, Platinum is heading down a slippery slope in its dealings with the legal community."

"Why do you say that?"

"Lawyers think Platinum is an easy mark. I have a whole briefcase of examples that say practically the same thing. Let's look at a current case where one of our tenured adjusters wrote a check for a hundred thousand to the claimant. Our policyholder's car slid on an icy road and hit a fifty-year-old homemaker on the sidewalk. The woman sustained a broken leg and needed a dozen stitches on her forehead. We should've paid her a maximum of forty thousand, but her lawyer threatened a lawsuit for grief, loss of sex drive, sleep deprivation and anxiety. We ended up paying an extra sixty thousand, all the way to the policy limits, simply to avoid litigation."

"It's a common problem, not just for us, but for the entire industry."

"And we have to solve it. We have to let arrogant, intimidating lawyers know that Platinum is not afraid to go to court." Harley sat on the edge of his chair.

"Then our legal fees will double."

"Only at first. These lawyers are smart. They'll figure it out," Harley said.

"Figure what out?" Roger played the role of encouraging skeptic.

"That you don't mess with Platinum, and you don't mess with Roger Phillips. They'll explain the process of a drawn out, expensive lawsuit to their clients. Most attorneys and their desperate clients won't have the wherewithal to fight us." Harley flashed his politically correct smile.

"Word of Platinum's resolve will quickly spread throughout the legal community," Roger added.

"That's right. In the long haul we'll save billions. Our public line will be the same. Platinum Insurance pays what it owes. But our private battle cry will be subtly different. We will only pay what we owe, not a cent more. If a claim is questionable, or we feel pushed in any way, we'll fight those lawyers until they prove we owe."

"It's a hard line."

"These are hard times, Roger. Hard times need hard lines."

"What do our claims people say?"

"That I'm right. It's time for us to take a stand." Harley stood for effect. "Our claims actuaries estimate that in the last year alone, we paid six-hundred-thirty-seven million dollars more than we should've on bodily injury liability claims. It's all right here." Harley held up a four-inch thick binder. "We threw away sixty grand on the one claim I just mentioned. Imagine how many more are out there."

"What's our potential savings?"

"Enough to drop our operations ratios by 7%. But we have to take a tough stance on each and every claim."

"Six hundred plus million dollars." Roger exhaled the number like a whisper.

"We owe it to our stockholders."

"You've got my support."

Chapter 8

"Elsie, it's good to see you." Chad Thorson reached out to give his wife a hug in the special "Greeting Area" at the Minnesota Correctional Facility in Stillwater. The black striped lines on the concrete floor marked the only place where inmates could touch visitors. But Elsie shrugged her husband away.

The barren room matched Elsie's demeanor as they walked in silence toward the two rows of chairs. Inmates sat in the row to the left, and their guests across from them. A guard walked up and down the middle of the row.

"Elsie, I've missed you terribly." It had been over a month since Elsie last visited the prison.

"I've been thinking a lot, Chad." Her eyes glued to the floor.

"I can tell."

Elsie looked at her husband and said nothing. She ignored the fresh two-inch laceration, complete with three butterfly bandages, on the front of his chin. Thorson tried to smile and leaned his head onto his hand in a futile effort to hide the cut.

The day before, one of the other prisoners had held the dull knife next to Thorson's chin, while a half-dozen others held him and took turns punching him. By the time the guard arrived, the knife had sliced all the way to Thorson's chin bone. Everyone in prison had a friend, but no one wanted to be friends with a mother killer.

One of the men who had cornered Thorson sat right next to him and talked across the aisle to his sixteen-year-old daughter. The girl's smile flashed as she shared her latest stories. Thorson turned sideways in his chair, careful not to even appear to look at the man's daughter, worried the creep next to him might take any glance the wrong way.

After closing his eyes, he refocused across the aisle onto Elsie's forehead as she continued to stare blankly at the floor. Chatter from the other inmates and their guests filled the room, but the Thorsons only heard silence.

"Please let me help you, Elsie."

"I can't take it anymore."

"What's wrong?"

"I can't make the house payments. I'm so far behind in my bills. They're calling me all the time–"

"Who's calling you?"

"The bill collectors. They call at six in the morning and at midnight. I hate them."

Thorson let out a weak smile. "You know they don't call at those hours."

"Would you shut up!" Elsie's voice screeched like fingernails on a chalkboard.

"Honey, you can get caller ID to screen the calls." Thorson reached across the row toward his wife.

"Thorson. No touching." A guard came close, and Thorson pulled his giant hand back.

"Caller ID won't help me pay the bills." Elsie shouted and everyone in the room turned.

"Please don't yell, Honey. I want to help you."

"How can you help me when you're in here?" Elsie's voice remained high.

"I'm sorry. You know I've been in contact with a new lawyer. He believes my story, and thinks he can help prove my innocence."

"How do I know that?"

"Elsie–"

"I want to believe you. But the judge said you're here for life. And I feel like *my* life is over."

"Elsie–"

"I'm over my head."

"Have you tried to get a couple of renters like we talked about?"

"Yeah, Chad. I have."

"And?"

"When they call on my ad in the paper, and find out who I am, they're not interested anymore. Everyone in town treats me like *I murdered my mother*. They stare at me on the street. People in the grocery store look the other way when I come down the aisle. I can't take it anymore."

Thorson tried to reach across the aisle to touch his wife, but the guard brushed his hand away. "Thorson, you bring your hand across the line again and you'll go to isolation." The sign on the wall said it all: NO TOUCHING. NO EXCEPTIONS.

"I'm so sorry."

Elsie got up and turned from her husband. "I can't wait for you. I can't pretend nothing happened. I have my own life to worry about."

"Honey, please. Let's talk."

Elsie silently gazed at her husband's pleading face. She stared at him with a menagerie of pity, contempt, and emptiness. Then she turned, and walked away.

Chapter 9

Built in the early 1950s, the Montane's south Minneapolis home was a square, 1½-story house that mirrored half the houses on the block. The main level barely contained enough room to squeeze in a tiny kitchen, two small bedrooms, a half bath, and a cramped living room. The long, narrow room upstairs had a low, angled ceiling designed for kids.

The home sat a half block from Minnehaha Creek and four miles south of downtown. Mike used to love to canoe the creek, but today his favorite stream rested as a solid mass under an endless blanket of winter snow. In the same way, life as the Montanes once knew, seemed frozen beyond possibility of thaw.

Two full months had passed since Platinum Health Insurance stopped all payments for Alex's health care from the accident. Although the policy brochure advertised "lifetime, no ceiling coverage," the fine print made it clear that convalescent care was not covered. Since Alex was no longer under a threat to die, and because she had stopped improving, Platinum abruptly ended all health coverage – irregardless of the protests from Kelly and Mike.

Alex occupied the master bedroom. "Al's room" became the only clean place in the house. Mike and Kelly had moved their bed upstairs, while their clothes remained scattered in various closets and laundry baskets around the house. Dishes filled the sink and surrounding counter area. Some stayed dirty for weeks at a time and the few clean ones still needed to be put away. Unpaid bills and stacks of mail heaved like a small cairn on top of their refrigerator. Dust, dog hair from Alex's dog Scooter, and dirt tracked across the carpet and collected with the spiders in every corner of the house.

The clock read 7:15 AM and Kelly had pushed herself until her eyes turned upward, crossed, then shot open as her head bobbed down on her chest. She had been up since three caring for Alex. "Mike, I can't make it another forty-five minutes until the nurse gets here. Can you please watch Al until eight and go to work a little late today?" Her drained voice pleaded, fighting the need to cry.

But Mike had already done his "shift." Go to work at eight, come home at six, take care of Alex till three in the morning. Drag himself out of bed at the last minute, every day living on four hours of sleep. His muscles ached constantly, and he'd lost twenty-five pounds since the accident. His casual slacks and long sleeved polo shirt hung limply off his scarecrow frame.

Kelly's plea zapped what little strength he might have had. "Sure, Kel," his voice trailed with despair. He would have done anything to escape the dreadful boundaries of the little house. Now he felt trapped – again.

He walked into Alex's dark room and looked out the window onto another dreary winter day. Alex lay on a special recliner/adjustable bed, and as he entered, she turned her head and stared blankly toward him. "Hi, Alex. How is my friend?" Although certain she understood nothing, he tried to keep his tone gentle.

For the first weeks after Alex had been brought to the Montane home, friends had sat through the night to help suction her phlegm. But everyone knew they would eventually stop coming by. Now, only Julie Jewel, Alex's former law partner, still found time to help, but even her visits had become increasingly rare.

As they ran out of volunteers, Kelly and Mike tried to hire home health nurses to spend nights with Alex. Even so, Kelly kept a baby monitor next to the bed so she could listen for the gurgling. The monitor broadcast the noise of the television while the nurses watched. Kelly heard the nurses talking on the phone, eating, belching, and sighing, but her subconscious minds tuned in for the special sound of the gurgling.

The gurgling.

Many times Kelly woke to the gurgling, raced down the stairs, and found the nurse sleeping. She suctioned the spittle that oozed out of Alex's twisted mouth and fired the nurse on the spot. Then she spent the rest of the night alone with Alex, sleeping for ten minutes, then suctioning, sleeping, and suctioning. Together, Kelly and Mike became programmed machines, and they never – *never* – missed the call to suction Alex.

Now Mike stared for the thousandth time at Alex's permanently disfigured twist on the left side of her face. Her facial skin pulled up as if she were trying to hold her left eye in a cringe, while the right side of her face drooped lifelessly. Her jaw dropped so her tongue stuck out and her lower lip perched outward as if it had no muscular attachments.

Paralysis of Alex's left side had locked her arm in a frozen position near her chest. Her left hand had withered into a gripped, half-closed fist in the shape of a claw, like an old, arthritic hand. Except for moving her head and a staring void, her body remained limp.

As Mike looked at Alex's comatose form, he wondered what hope Kelly hung onto. If it weren't for Kelly's undying faith in her sister and her desperate need for his support, he would have given up on Alex a long time ago. He would have let her die.

Mike was certain Alex would have wanted it that way. He remembered a year before the accident when they canoed in the Boundary Waters. They had been with a group of college friends, and everyone sat around the campfire sharing dark stories. Alex's story said it all:

> When I have nightmares, I dream of myself tied up, unable to run. Even worse, I'm unable to shout no matter how hard I try. I open my mouth, but I can't make any sounds. There's a lump in my throat and it chokes me. When the bad dreams are at their very worst, I can't move at all. And something horrible is coming at me, I don't know what it is, but I know it's going to get me, it's coming, and keeps coming in slow motion, and I can't do anything about it.
>
> Then I wake up drenched in sweat, my mouth is dry, and I find myself panting. My heart is racing

> and I finally break free. I bolt out of bed. It shakes me up so bad, that I have to turn on the TV no matter how exhausted I am just to try to get my mind off of it. And it won't go away. I usually remember the next day, and it haunts me. I hate that nightmare, and sometimes when I'm sleeping I know I'm falling into it, and I try to wake up. But I feel handcuffed to the bed by the weight of the covers, and I can't escape reliving that same horror. I get this terrible dream about once a month, and no matter how many times I've had it, it still scares me to death.

On the strength of Alex's dream alone, Mike remained convinced that Alex – if still cognizant – would wish for death. Somehow, Mike sensed that her vacant eyes pleaded that he should end her nightmare.

For the first several months after the accident, Mike had spent countless hours scanning the internet for articles about coma recovery. Once he found a story of a paralyzed man who could not move or swallow on his own. Still, the man could hear, understand, and communicate by using an alphabet card and a pointer. Someone would point to a letter on the chart until he blinked. The first thing he spelled was "kill me."

"Kill me." Mike said it out loud.

He stared at the pitiful waste in front of him as Alex started to gurgle and watched the spittle as it bubbled in the pouch of her lower lip. Then he closed his own eyes to try to hide the rage that burned behind his lids. "Kill me."

For the millionth time, he leaned forward to place the suction tube in Alex's mouth, only this time, he didn't care if he was a little rough. "You're the one who's killing me."

Chapter 10

The clock showed 3:35 AM. Mike and Kelly both slumped in chairs across from Alex. The nurse hadn't shown up once again, so they found themselves alone to suction Alex's phlegm through another long night. Mike's glazed eyes fluttered open, then closed as he tried to look at Kelly. "How many days in a row have you worn those striped pajamas?"

"Three," Kelly responded matter-of-factly, causing Mike to burst out in a laughing spasm. Kelly snorted when he laughed, and they laughed all the harder.

"I gotta stop. It hurts!" Mike tried to take a deep breath and hiccupped so they started to laugh again.

When the laughing finally stopped, Mike looked at Kelly's exhausted face and compared it to the wretched, twisted features of her identical twin. No one could possibly tell they were sisters anymore. A huge poster picture of Alex climbing "The Diamond" hung above Alex's bed. In the picture Alex looked awesome, powerful, and full of life's energy. Her face radiated courage, confidence, and determination.

But now... Mike simply couldn't look. "Kel, I'm dying, but I can't sleep."

"Go to bed and close your eyes."

"Honey, look at what's happening to us."

"Now isn't the right time to discuss anything."

"Kel, we never get a chance to talk, and we haven't made love in months."

"I know." She paused and looked down. "I miss laughing with you." Her face puckered into its serious look.

"Remember when we went to the Virgin Islands at Christmas two years ago?"

"How could I forget?"

"Remember how we went sailing with Captain Buck on that racing catamaran?"

"Of course. The swells swallowed the sail." Kelly smiled.

"One second we were on top of a crest, and our bodies leaned straight out over the water. The next we were down in a canyon surrounded by waves. Then the wind stopped for all of a second."

"We'd submerge in the ocean before the sail would catch the wind and heave us back into the air."

"We rode up and down and our bodies moved in and out."

"Like we had sex with the wind."

"Yeah," Mike said, "those swells must have been twenty feet high."

"But the best part was being alone." Kelly winked.

"Just the two of us in a secluded cabin overlooking Trunk Bay."

"I remember sun tanning off our deck."

"I remember watching you suntan."

"I knew you were watching me, even when I had my eyes closed."

"The best part was that bottle of suntan lotion."

"We went through a lot of lotion."

"Yeah."

"I miss that smile." Mike touched Kelly's face and leaned forward to kiss her.

"Mm, your lips are soft," Kelly purred, "do that again."

They kissed a long, slow, tender kiss. Their lips moved gently, and their tongues lightly touched. Mike moved closer and wrapped his arms around Kelly, pulling her body next to his.

"I miss you." A tear formed in the corner of her eyes. "I'm sorry."

"Kel, we need to get away by ourselves."

"I know."

"Don't you think we could find someone to watch Alex for a few days so we can regroup?"

"I'd sure like to. But when I call people and ask for help, I feel like it's such a burden."

"Honey, we can find some volunteers. There are lots of people who still care about Alex and us. They'll understand."

"Mike, I don't think I can leave Al for even a day." Kelly's real reasons stepped forward. Alex gurgled again and Kelly released herself from Mike's arms, then stood over her sister and gently allowed the machine to carry away the saliva. "As much as I want to be alone with you, I can't leave Al."

"Sometimes I feel so unimportant."

"I'm sorry, Mike, but I can't."

Silence permeated the dark room. A small table lamp in the far corner burned as the only source of light.

"You look exhausted," she said. "Please go to bed. It's not doing any good for both of us to be here."

Mike rolled his head. "I can't sleep. I keep thinking."

"Why don't you write it down. It'll ease your mind."

"I've already done that. I have a list. I memorized it." His voice raised.

"What list?"

"Let's start with home health care, the recliner bed, wheelchair, ramp on the house, medications, doctor visits, the physical therapy–"

"Okay. I get it. Stop with the list." Kelly closed her eyes and put her hand in the air to signal time out. "Tell me what you're thinking."

"We're broke."

"Then why did you bring up the idea of going on a vacation?"

"Because we need it. I'd rob a bank to be alone with you."

"How broke are we?"

"We've used up all our savings, and I've cashed in our IRAs. We're over thirty grand in credit card debt and all we have left is the equity in our house."

"I don't get it, Mike. The drunk who hit Alex had a million dollars of liability coverage, plus her car insurance. Why hasn't Platinum paid us yet?"

"They tell me they're waiting to see Alex's final outcome from the accident."

"That's insane." Kelly instinctively threw her arms into the air.

"I know. I've never felt this powerless in my life." Mike

stood. "I told the liability claims people that Platinum's health insurance division gave up on Alex. If Alex's condition isn't going to get any better, then they need to pay the claim now."

"Those hypocrites are hoping Al will die. That way they'll get off with a tiny accidental death payment."

"I checked with the claims department, and they said an accidental death had a typical value of $150,000."

"So if Platinum thinks Al might die," Kelly's voice rose to exasperation, "why did they take her out of the hospital?"

"I told claims there were only three options. If Alex gets better but never fully recovers, they'll owe her the full million liability settlement. If Alex stays the same as she is now, they still owe a million. And if Alex gets worse and dies, we'll sue them for pulling her out of the hospital, and they'll still pay the million."

"So why haven't they paid?"

"Kel . . . I don't know." Mike dropped his arms, then fell to the floor to demonstrate his exhaustion.

"I hate Platinum." Kelly sighed, then got up and suctioned phlegm. "I feel like they've ruined our lives."

"I can't believe it's been ten months." He swung his foot straight into the room and clenched his fists. "I feel like they're purposefully trying to get me."

"Platinum has turned away from us, Mike."

"I don't know what to do." Now he knelt and held his arms out as if in some anguished prayer.

"Get the money. Even if you have to sue them. Use all your contacts. Call the Commerce Department and the president of Platinum. Do what you need to do. We need financial help before it's too late for Al."

"If it's the last thing I do. I'll get the money."

Chapter 11

On a bright April day of 1998, Sheriff Mason Crow from Lake County, Minnesota gave Harley a call with some news. "I'm calling about your friend, Chad Thorson."

"What about him? I'll bet those bad boys have knocked him down to size a few times. Mother killer." Harley held a portable phone and strode across the plush carpeted office in his stocking feet and looked into his telescope.

"He didn't do it, Harley."

"What do you mean? The jury found him guilty."

"It's a long story, but we found the guy who burned the house down. You'll never guess who."

"Who?" Harley felt a lump forming in his throat.

"Your friend, Harley."

"I don't have friends like that."

"When you write big checks, it's easy to make friends."

"What are you talking about?"

"The contract-for-deed holder."

"I can't believe it." Harley's knees turned weak.

"You better start believing. We got a signed confession from the guy. He has a long history of arson. He's been torching two houses a year for the past ten years."

"The CD holder?"

"Yep. Looks like your insurance company database on contract-for-deed holders doesn't extend across state lines. The guy used to be a claims adjuster for one of your competitors. He knew the system."

"You're not kidding?"

"You catch on quick, Crane. He bought run-down houses for practically nothing, then sold them to people like your buddy Thorson – people with poor credit. He sold them a house at a super-inflated price, but with almost no interest. When the poor homeowner fell behind on the house payments, he torched the house to make it look like the homeowner committed arson. And you morons from the insurance company paid off the contract."

Harley sank into the oversized leather couch. He hardly listened. A vision of Thorson appeared, begging him to investigate other areas. He could see the exchange of looks, and remembered his own smirk of contempt at the big man.

"The *real* bad guy has netted over $800,000 with this scam," the sheriff continued, "When Thorson bought the house for his mother and she fell behind in her payments, it was the perfect setup."

Harley breathed heavily. The phone dangled in his hand, somewhere near the side of his face.

"Ya there, Crane?" The sheriff's voice boomed across the line.

"Yes."

"Meanwhile, imagine what *really bad men* do to a guy who killed his mother. You know, Harley, no one likes a mother killer." The sheriff had openly disliked Harley's methods during the investigation, and now Harley remembered the sheriff's sarcastic tone.

"Where is Thorson now?"

"He's out. He gave interviews to the local television station and the newspaper. I'll send you a copy of the paper when I get it. I know he mentioned your name, said something about seeing you, and that's why I'm giving you a courtesy call."

"Some courtesy," said Harley.

"I didn't have to call," the sheriff snapped.

"What did he say in the interviews?"

"I wasn't there, Crane. You're going to have to read about it."

"And you don't know where he is?"

"Nope. We don't keep track of law-abiding citizens," Mason said.

"We've got to find him."

"You mean, *you've* got to find him. Crane, you'll be real lucky if this doesn't make national news."

"I'm not worried about the news." Harley slammed down the phone. He felt weak and rested his suddenly aching head on the back of the big leather couch. He closed his eyes, while his pounding heart moved to somewhere near his throat.

Thorson had promised a visit.

Chapter 12

George Slayton had been Mike's General Manager at Platinum for eight years. For as long as Mike could remember, Slayton ended each of his monthly meetings with the same words: "Call me anytime. I'll always do whatever I can to help you."

The older agents told Mike that Slayton was a multiple faceted liar capable of eyeballing a crowd for prominence, while entertaining the masses and subtly destroying someone's reputation, all at the same time. Heeding their warning, Mike worked hard and kept a low profile in order to avoid the GM's dark side. But today, May 1, 1998, was the day of reckoning. Now was the time to see the real Slayton.

Mike and Kelly dressed in their most respectful Sunday clothes, and in an attempt to please his boss, Mike even got a haircut so both his ears showed. They sat silently, holding hands, waiting in the foyer of Slayton's Minneapolis office. They sat for nearly an hour.

Finally, Slayton's two-hundred-fifty-pound frame rumbled into the office mumbling something about a late lunch. Mike couldn't help but notice the distinct patches of silver hair that streaked like waving flags across the temples of Slayton's otherwise dull mane. Kelly had only met Slayton once before, and had asked Mike if Slayton dyed his hair that way on purpose. The silver swirls and Slayton's small, squinty eyes dominated his otherwise big jowled face.

Once inside Slayton's office, the manager took his time organizing his desk, and shuffled a few papers back and forth, while the Montane's watched, not knowing what to say.

"Nice to see you again, Kelly. Sorry about your sister's situation." Slayton spoke rapid fire and never looked at them. "We're here today to discuss the Alex Richter claim, but before we do that, I need to show you something."

Mike and Kelly sat on the far side of Slayton's oversized desk.

Slayton walked over to a row of filing cabinets and pulled out a three-foot long file drawer. As if he held a baby in a cradle, he gently set the drawer on his desk in front of the Montanes. "Do you see what that drawer's label says?"

"It says Mike Montane," Mike said.

"This whole drawer is full of complaints and problems we've had with you since you became an agent. If you think this file is big, the dope they have on you at the home office takes up a whole cabinet. Mine is only one drawer."

"What complaints and problems?" Mike felt his face flush, but tried to stay calm. "We've always been able to work through any problems with a simple phone call in the past."

"These are things we took care of for you. Mostly poor judgment on your part. The company chose to look the other way. I'm sure you'll remember some of them."

"We came here to talk about Alex. I'd be glad to discuss my mistakes with you at a more appropriate time."

"I'll be the judge of what's appropriate."

"I don't believe this." Mike gritted his teeth, and dug his fingers into his own thighs under the desk.

"You better believe it. You're the kind of guy who has a lot of pride, Montane. Sometimes you think your ways are better than Platinum's."

"Sometimes my ways might be better in a particular situation!" Mike snapped. "Platinum didn't hire me to be a drone. If they want the French fries to come out of the grease after exactly thirty seconds, then they better put a timer in the grease. If they want agents to stop making decisions, hire a computer to do the job."

"You've got a bad attitude."

"I don't think so." Mike's voice rocketed upward. "Why are you dredging the river to find things that have been long forgotten?"

"I'm bringing these to your attention today because they'll use these against you if you continue to pursue the Alex Richter claim. It's a conflict of interest for you to be involved in her claim settlement anyway. Alex is a claimant against the company."

"What do you mean?" Mike sensed Kelly's strain to keep her

voice level.

"It means Alex is trying to collect money from Platinum, not as a policyholder, but as someone on the outside," Slayton said.

"But she is a Platinum policyholder."

"I know. But in this case, she is trying to get money out of someone else's liability policy, and therefore we treat her claim as an outsider – and we call her a claimant."

"Look," Mike interrupted. "Whether she's a claimant or a policyholder is irrelevant. The bottom line is she got hit by a Platinum-insured drunk, and Platinum needs to pay this claim in good faith."

"Don't take that tone with me. I'm here to help you, before you get in trouble and lose your job over this. Now, as I said, it will appear to be a conflict of interest if you try to collect a claim payment for a claimant. Furthermore, Platinum won't think twice before they use that as an excuse to get rid of you, especially considering your history of problems."

"Show me one of the complaints against me. Any one."

Slayton pulled out the very last file. It represented Mike's first month as an agent. "Do you remember a client Peter Mackinac?"

"Other than his name, no." Mike said.

"Mackinac is simply the first example."

"Example of what?"

"How you insured a car without inspecting it."

"How do you know that?"

"Because you insured him on August 3rd and he had a broken windshield claim on August 10th."

"I can't believe this!" Mike's mouth gaped open.

"Believe it, Montane." Slayton growled. "We called Mackinac to verify the date his windshield broke. He stuck by the August 10th story."

"So what's the problem?"

"Then we checked with the guy who sold him the car. He confirmed what we suspected. The windshield had a break when he bought the car, before you insured it."

"It was my first month on the job," Mike's voice raised.

"If you only had one little deal, I wouldn't worry about it." Slayton smiled as if he enjoyed this. "But we got a whole file." Slayton's hands rubbed the metal drawer.

"I can't…." Mike started to protest.

"It's guys like you that teach customers how to commit insurance fraud."

"I collected twenty dollars a month from Mackinac for two years, until he paid for that windshield, then forwarded his payment to Platinum. It was no big deal ten years ago. And now, you act like I'm a criminal."

Slayton glowered at Mike in silence, then reached into the file and pulled out another case. Then another.

Like inverse magic, junk that had disappeared years ago suddenly reappeared under a microscope. Management had never mentioned most of these issues.

They spent four hours at Slayton's office.

Kelly fought off tears, while Mike's face and temper steamed hot.

At the end of the meeting, Slayton reminded them, "I've met with you today to look out for your best interest. You may not like my methods, but the company will make me look like a pansy when they finish with you. You've worked long and hard to build your agency. You've invested serious time and money, and I'm telling you if you want to keep your job, you better stay out of the Alex Richter claim."

"What are you going to do, fire me?"

"It's as simple as turning off your computer, my friend."

"Then you'll blackball me." Mike's guts tore a hole into his throat.

Slayton smiled sickly.

"Maybe you'll find a way to yank my license." Mike stood with his fists clenched. He took a giant step toward Slayton, and struck his finger out across the desk pointing into the man's fat face.

Their eyes locked.

Mike yearned to climb over the desk and tear Slayton's tongue out of his head.

Instead, Mike grabbed Kelly's trembling hand, and fled out the door.

Still within earshot, Slayton hollered. "Remember who controls the switch."

Chapter 13

Harley's mind spun as he reevaluated his position. Surely Platinum would understand a judicial error, and not blame him. After all, a jury had convicted Thorson, and Harley simply did his job – maybe too well.

The phone rang again. "Hold all my calls and cancel my appointments for the rest of the day," he snapped across the expansive room to the intercom.

His mind reeled. Thorson would never blame the jury. Thorson was free, and was coming to get him . . .

What went wrong? He looked at a gigantic portrait of his favorite stallion, Secretariat, the essence of power, speed, and greatness. Harley stared at the painting and tried to think. To remember.

When Harley was only three years old, his dad had begun preaching. "Son, you're either a plow horse or a racehorse. Ya can't be both and ya can't make one into the other. Whichever ya are is in your blood."

Harley used to lie awake in bed and worry about being a plow horse. What did it mean to be a racehorse? Why didn't his dad like plow horses? Why was this so important that his dad said it so many times?

On Harley's fifth birthday, his dad took him to the races for the first time. They walked near the stables to see the horses up close. They were so big, muscular, and powerful. One of the horses, a roan with three socks named Man-of-the-Hour, got excited and reared while the trainer tried to keep him steady. The horse snorted loudly, and people scurried to get out of the way. The horse's giant nostrils and scorching eyes scared Harley, but his dad laughed.

When Man-of-the-Hour won the race, the man behind the counter gave Harley's dad a lot of money. His dad told him that the fire in the horse's eyes showed the spirit of a true racehorse. "The other horses were plow horses compared to that stallion, Son. Just plow horses."

Harley pondered every word, memorized every gesture, and constantly studied his dad. He developed into the perfect student, practicing the mannerisms, words, and attitudes. When people clichéd, "That boy is a chip off the old block," it made Harley feel very, very good.

Harley gradually learned to recognize plow horses. The kinds who were clumsy, weak, and stupid. They were the ones who drove slowly in the left lane. The ones who counted their change, read the instructions, and followed the rules.

He learned to judge others, the same as his dad. Fast and harsh.

Harley stood at his window and looked over the big lake. He had moved up the ladder on the back of an innocent man.

"Thorson was no saint." The words involuntarily escaped from Harley's mouth. The trial had uncovered plenty of problems in Thorson's character. He couldn't even find a friend willing to stand up for him. *Nobody who worked with Thorson defended him either.* "Even his wife thought he was guilty," he screamed through the glass, slamming his fist against the giant pane.

Now Harley had to face the fact that maybe he'd been wrong. No maybe. He was wrong. Thorson hadn't killed anyone.

Plow horse. Racehorse. Harley felt sick.

Thorson would come calling.

Chapter 14

Over the long July 4th weekend, Mike arranged to sell or give away all of Alex's personal property. Paying rent on a storage garage had proved to be a waste of money, one he should have taken care of long ago. Denial and Kelly's emotionally collapsed condition had prevented him from acting earlier.

He took it upon himself to clean out her desk, go through her files, and tie up any loose ends. As he went through Alex's paperwork, he rediscovered how orderly and meticulous his sister-in-law had been. Labeled and dated pictures filled her scrapbooks. Color-coded hanging files, sorted in alphabetical order, occupied each drawer.

As he went through the very last drawer, he pulled out a folder marked "LIVING WILL." No one had ever mentioned a living will.

How could Alex have signed a living will without Kelly knowing about it? After helping dozens of his Platinum clients with living wills, he was quite familiar with them. He opened the booklet to the last page, the signature page.

Sure enough, Kelly's signature sat at the bottom.

It was dated only a few months before the accident.

Each page looked totally complete, making it clear that the lawyer portion of Alex Richter wanted to leave nothing to chance. It was all done in Alex's handwriting:

> *I, Alexandra Richter, want to make my wishes known regarding keeping me on any type of life support. I have always felt that life is for the living. There is a huge difference in my mind between breathing air, and being fully alive. I have lived my life as a person who is fully alive. I have enjoyed the outdoors, enjoyed taking risks, and enjoyed laughing and crying with*

> *Kelly and my friends. I love to run, canoe, bike, climb mountains, and read good books. In my mind, this is what it means to be fully alive.*
>
> *I do not want artificial life support of any type – except under the most extraordinary circumstance whereby it is a temporary measure only – and then there must be a very strong and reasonable expectation of a full recovery. If full recovery is not readily and clearly foreseeable, then I ask to be relieved of pain, and allowed to die. I have lived a full life, and I want to be fully alive.*
>
> *Alexandra Richter*

Mike's mind spun like the blue bleacher seats in the Metrodome. Alex had been on a respirator for more than a month after the accident. Surely, the suction machine constituted artificial life support. It didn't matter that living wills had no legal basis. Kelly should've told him.

Even the most optimistic person in the world couldn't possibly visualize a prognosis of full recovery. Alex would never climb, hike, or bike again.

He sat alone in Alex's empty apartment.

Then read the will again.

************ *********

Later that day, Mike found Kelly sitting in Alex's room, holding her hand and reading a story. Kelly wore a pair of her favorite jungle green baggy pants, with an oversized cotton army shirt. Alex lay in bed wearing the exact same clothes.

For Mike, no amount of dress, no amount of pretending would ever make Alex and Kelly look alike. *Never again.* "Hey. Kelly." Mike's voice snapped.

"What?" Kelly shot her response back at him.

"We have to talk, and I mean now."

"I don't want to talk," she spat saliva across the room. "I'm busy." Her grimace begged for a fight.

"What about Alex's living will."

Kelly's fighting stance fell as if she'd been shot in the heart. She choked unable to look, and started to sob.

No matter what, Mike had given himself permission to explode. To lose his mind. To swear and curse and rant about Kelly's lie. He stood with his entitled arms crossed in front of his chest, ready to do battle.

But Kelly only cried.

And faced with Kelly's tears, he said nothing.

Kelly continued to cry for the next five minutes.

Alex gurgled with saliva, and Mike suctioned her, while the crying continued.

"I don't know what to say."

"Why didn't you tell me?"

"I couldn't." Kelly blurted, almost bleated, out the words.

He moved toward her and tenderly took her hand. They collapsed in slow motion, ending up on the floor, lying next to each other. Mike crossed his legs over Kelly as her back shuddered into massive heaves with each breath.

"I'm sorry," her voice trembled. "I've thought about that living will every single day since the accident, but I just couldn't tell you about it."

"Why?"

"I was afraid of what you might say. I wanted to tell you, but after a while, I was scared."

"What were you afraid of?"

"I couldn't live without Alex." She paused. "I'm so selfish." The tears swelled again.

Mike dropped his head. "But Kelly–"

"Al saved my life."

How many hundreds of times had he heard those words?

"I . . . I meant to tell you."

"Why didn't you?"

"Because I couldn't let her go. I still can't."

"Alex wouldn't want to live like this."

"I know, but I can't let her die. She means too much to me."

"Honey, you owe it to her to honor her wishes."

"I can't. I've thought about it over and over . . . And I can't." She dabbed her tears as she spoke.

"But Kel, even if Alex recovers enough to talk with you, she'll probably be handicapped. She'd need a wheelchair, or a feeding tube, for the rest of her life. That's not what she wants."

"But I don't think we thought things out," she paused. "Remember the woman who wrote the book *Miles to Go Before I Sleep*? An airplane hijacker shot her in the head, then dropped her out of the plane onto the concrete. Now she goes around and gives talks. I don't know if she ever climbed mountains with rock-climbing shoes, but she certainly climbed her own personal mountains."

"But Kel–"

"I don't deserve… I was wrong not to tell you about the living will. I don't deserve you."

"Kel–" Mike struggled to think. What words could he say to fight the arguments that she had obviously rehearsed for so long?

Alex gurgled, and Kelly got up. When she had finished the suctioning, Kelly sat in the chair away from him. "There'll be new mountains for Al to climb. And when she recovers, she'll still be Al. She'll still have the same personality, the same love and passion for life." Kelly turned her face away. "There is a lot of life out there."

The discussion had ended. Kelly would fight to the end to save Alex's life.

And I'll be the one who dies.

Chapter 15

They found him in a soup line. He wore blue jeans and a heavy wool sweatshirt to fight off the late November chill. The sweatshirt wore streaks of catsup and mustard stains. Dirt and grime covered the sleeves while the armpits bore rings of human stench soaked through.

An army duffel bag sat on the floor next to him. Inside the bag, the man carried a thick down jacket, long underwear, and an extra pair of boots. Rumor had it that he also packed a loaded 44-magnum pistol. From the way he wrapped his leg around the canvas strap, one couldn't be certain if the man protected the bag, or if the bag protected him.

Harley's men found Chad Thorson in the warehouse district north of the Loop, exactly where the Chicago police said he'd be. One of the police "regulars" had informed them of a giant bald man from Minnesota "looking to hurt someone."

Thorson pushed back his chair, ready to go for a second helping, when two suits from Platinum strolled in and sat next to him.

"Chad Thorson?"

"Who's asking?"

"We're from Platinum Insurance." A balding, skinny man, somewhere between sixty and ninety tried to make his frail voice sound official.

"Then I'm not interested." Thorson stood. Before he could pick up his plate, the elder Platinum rep put his hand on Thorson's tray. "You better move your hand," Thorson growled.

The man's trembling hand never moved. "Mr. Thorson, we're here to offer our apologies and to pay what is rightfully yours."

Thorson sat down.

"Thank you." A drop of sweat rolled off the top of the old guy's head and slid down his face, but his voice remained steady.

"Tell me what you got," Thorson said, "then leave me alone."

"First, we want to express our sincere apology. Platinum Insurance realizes the terrible magnitude of its mistake, and regrets it had any part in what happened to you."

"What about your golden boy?" Thorson asked.

"We have a letter of apology from Mr. Crane, and another from the president of Platinum." The insurance rep set two sealed envelopes on the table. "We cannot begin to appreciate your anger toward the people who wrongly imprisoned you."

"You mean rage." Thorson glared.

"What?"

"Rage."

"I'm sorry." The suit from Platinum tried to move on. Even with the support of his companion in a public place, the confrontation with Thorson scared him. "I would like to explain the checks we have for you. First, your mother's life insurance policy had a death benefit of $150,000. Although we've already paid this to her distant relatives, we are going to pay you again. $150,000 plus $18,365 interest since her date of death."

Thorson looked expressionlessly at the check.

"I also have a check for $90,000 plus interest for her personal property destroyed in the fire, and–" the Platinum rep felt his Adam's apple bob in his throat.

"And what?"

"And I have an additional $250,000 from Platinum as a gesture of good will. Again, Platinum offers its sincere apology."

"So all together I get over a half million bucks, and you hope I leave your golden boy alone."

"We all want to move on."

"I could sue you for ten million dollars."

"I'm sure you know that Mr. Crane was only a part of your conviction–"

"He led the charge."

"The State of Minnesota and a jury of your peers convicted you as well, Mr. Thorson. I'm sure that by now you have met with several attorneys who have advised you that such a lawsuit would be difficult to win, and would consume many more years of your life."

"Your money is bad."

"It still spends."

"Tell Crane I'll never forget."

The men got up to leave.

"Don't forget. *Never.*"

Chapter 16

The weatherman promised the July 4th 1999 holiday would be a near perfect 85 degrees. When Mike opened the windows in Alex's room, she turned her head to look outside and listen for the chirping birds. Now she even watched TV and wiggled her face at some funny parts of the reruns of her favorite shows, *Seinfeld* and *Cheers.*

Doctors monitored her brain waves and measured her emotional/physiological response to words, suggestions, and phrases, but other than the unusual face movements, no communication existed yet.

Mike heard the sound of his own teeth grinding. Again. His jaw ached from the continuous pressure as he bit down to suppress his torment. He longed for a normal day when he had time to walk, bike, or climb with Kelly again. They hadn't made love for six months.

Now he weighed forty-two pounds less than he had two years earlier while climbing the Diamond. His clothes hung off him like big brother hand-me-downs, because they could barely afford *food.* Lack of sleep left him so ragged that he only shaved after his facial hairs turned back into his skin.

One lonely wish repeated itself. *If only Alex had died back in Estes Park.* Her life would have ended on her most glorious day. A day of victory, and bravery.

He rationalized. If she couldn't communicate, had no memory, no future, then what was the difference anyway? Her life was <u>not</u> worth living. It would not be like a baby, who had the potential of life before it. It would not be like an elderly person who had the memories of yesterday to share with others.

Mike looked at Alex in mockery saying, "I don't think, therefore I am not."

Thoughts of smothering Alex . . . Putting her – and himself – out of misery seemed to fly in and out of his dreams. Even now, wide-awake, the thoughts pounded through his skull, despite his attempts to make the ugliness go away.

How can I live with myself? "Help me." Mike dug the palms of his hands into his eyes trying to wipe the thoughts away. Then he stared at Alex's twisted mouth. "You pathetic thing."

She stared at him with blank eyes.

"You've cheated me." He stared back with a mocking, empty look in his eyes. "I'm married to woman who abandoned me, all because of you."

Alex started to gurgle.

"Today I saw a guy in a wheel chair crossing the bridge over 494." His eyes squinted. "Is that how you want to live someday?"

Then he started to sneer. "Alex this. Alex that. What do you think, Alex?" Mike's face puckered and his lips bleated poisonous sarcasm as he stared at the woman who could not answer. His teeth bore down as the unfairness of life cast its shadow over him.

The gurgling continued as some spittle ran down her face.

Mike whipped his hand across his own mouth to remove the frothing saliva. *I'm a rabid animal.* "Help me," he yelled while his body trembled.

Then, with as much tenderness as his shaky body would allow, he moved to the side of her bed and placed the suction tube into her mouth for the five hundred and eighty seven thousandth, trillionth time.

But this time, he gritted his teeth especially hard.

Chapter 17

Mike knew he'd be late for work. Even so, he had to stop for a cup of coffee and a roll. He had always hated coffee, but now the addiction owned him. Without it, headaches pounded him to submission, and he couldn't afford to be sick.

Thirty people had crammed into Starbucks. When Mike got to the cash register, he pulled out his wallet. The clerk was a college-age girl who practically lived there. "Two dollars and twenty-eight cents," she chirped.

"All I have is a credit card today," Mike said.

"No problem." The girl took the card and swiped it through the computer on the cash register as Mike waited.

"Excuse me, sir."

"Yes?"

"The machine says your credit card is invalid." The girl's voice seemed louder than necessary.

Mike flushed as he looked at the girl. Though he dared not turn, his peripheral vision told him everyone in the room stared at him. "There must be a mistake."

"No, it says your account is closed. Can you pay some other way?" the girl offered.

"I don't have any cash with me. You know I come here all the time. Can I come back and pay you later today?"

"I'm sorry sir, but the store policy – "

Mike slammed his fist down on the counter. The store grew silent. "Look, you know who I am. For the sake of a long-term customer, you can't trust me for two dollars?" Mike pleaded as everyone watched.

"I'm sorry, sir."

Mike punished his van on the way to work. He slammed on the brakes at the stop signs. Then pounded the accelerator. His mouth shrieked, "two years!" "Two Years!" His thoughts whirled as his van darted between lanes.

"Damn you, Slayton." He bore down on his teeth, and the side of his mouth got in the way. His lips coated with blood.

If they didn't get money soon, Alex would be forced into a nursing home. Mike remembered the image of his dying grandma in the nursing home.

How they had strapped her to the wheelchair.

How her head bent over all the way to her chest.

How she drooled onto her own lap hour after hour.

All day long in the same horrid posture.

By the time he got to the office, Mike's head pounded. Pounded. Pounded with every breath. Like pounding on the door when no one was home. He clenched his fists, unclenched them, then bore his fingers into the top of his scalp. *Platinum is never wrong.* "Never."

"So George, which is it today?" Mike mocked to the empty office. "Is it a sin if I don't wear a coat and tie?" He filled his mouth with saliva and swallowed five Advil. "Or do we suddenly have a new casual dress policy?"

He got on the phone with the claims superintendent in charge of Alex's claim. "I want to offer Platinum a win/win proposition," he tried to force a calm voice.

"I'm listening."

"If Platinum will reimburse me for my out-of-pocket expenses to date, we could wait on the outstanding liability settlement until Alex's condition is conclusive."

"I don't think it's in our best interest to pay a partial liability settlement."

"Think about it." Mike pleaded. "Platinum will be able to keep the vast majority of their money. Platinum can earn interest without a demand for payment, and without need to employ any legal staff."

"How does that help you?"

"We need the money. Desperately. We've got nothing left, and Alex is going to have to go to a nursing home if we don't get some money soon."

"I'll have to make some calls, and we'll get back to you."

"I'm running out of time."

Chapter 18

The white-haired old man walked slowly with the aid of a cane. When he got off the elevator on the twenty-eighth floor, he appeared lost and unsure which way to turn.

"May I help you, sir." An attractive young receptionist stood behind the mahogany desk.

"Yeah, the name's Crane, and I flew here to see my boy," he mumbled.

"I'm sorry?" The receptionist held her hand to her ear.

"What're ya sorry about?"

"I didn't catch your name."

"John Crane. I'm here to see my boy."

"Oh. Please have a chair, and I'll see if he's available." She knew Harley's schedule better than her own, and a visit with the elder Mr. Crane wasn't on the agenda. She walked down the hallway and knocked on Harley's door.

"He's here?" Harley's eyebrows raised in surprise, then he smiled. "Please cancel my appointments for the day, and tell him I'll be right out."

Harley straightened up the already immaculate desk, then walked over to his stallion pictures to tweak them perfectly on the wall. *"Dad is here!"* The excitement of seeing his dad pulsed through him. More than anything in the world, he still wanted the approval of the old bull. He'd begged him to come to Chicago to see his office. Now he was finally here.

After checking himself in the mirror, Harley strode down the hall. "Hi, Dad!" Harley reached his arms out to embrace the old man.

"Hey, Son. Nice place ya got here."

"You're looking good." Harley lied with a smile. "Come on, I'll show you my office."

"Did I surprise ya?"

"I'll say. It sure's good to see you."

The old man hobbled next to Harley as they slowly walked down the plush hallway and into Harley's office.

"Holy cow, would you look at Lake Michigan. You can practically watch the girls in those sailboats with this stinkin telescope."

"I'm so glad you came."

"Thought ya'd take me to a Cubs game, and maybe we could see that new Comiskey Park where the Sox play, too."

"I haven't been to a ball game in years!" Harley smiled.

"I want to see some real baseball. The Twins stink this year."

"Ah, Dad. They won the Series a few years ago."

"I know. Maybe I'm just fickle, but the dome is practically empty, even when the Yanks are in town. But enough about baseball."

"Do you like my office?"

"Harley, it's a fine thing ya've accomplished, and I'm proud of ya." The old man reached up and put his hand on Harley's shoulder. "But remember one thing."

"What's that?"

"Ya don't become great by winning one race." He pointed his cane at the picture of Secretariat. "It's one thing to make it to the majors, and another to stay there."

"Dad." Harley's voice dropped.

"Like I said. No one even watches the Twins anymore."

"But–"

"Hell, I got faith in ya, Harley. Always did." The elder Crane squeezed Harley's arm. "Show me where the bathroom is. Then ya can show me the town."

Chapter 19

Almost three full years after the accident, the May 20, 2000 trial docket showed Alexandra Richter vs. Platinum Insurance. At 7AM on the day before the trial, attorney John Jacobs called Kelly and Mike into his office.

Jacobs, in his late fifties, had a full head of black hair, not an ounce of fat, and a chiseled look to his face that spoke of experience. As the Montanes sat in Jacobs's office on the forty-first floor of the IDS tower in downtown Minneapolis, the normally upbeat man looked different. His eyes wore big shadows of gray under them, and his tight lips turned into a frown.

Mike sensed the effort Jacobs made to make his face smile.

"What's wrong?" Kelly wore a baseball cap over her unwashed hair. She crossed her arms in front of her and refused to sit.

"We aren't going to trial tomorrow, and may not for a while."

"Why not?" Mike bleated.

Kelly hollered, "It's been three years."

"I don't know how to tell you this news." A long pause ensued as Jacobs sat, then stood, unsure of how to proceed. "Okay." He gave a deep sigh of resignation.

"Okay." Kelly's voice cracked with impatience.

"Platinum informed me that they paid the drunk driver $80,000 to release them from covering her on the day of the accident."

"They can't do that!" Mike screamed and flew out of his chair.

"What does that mean, Mike?" asked Kelly.

Mike paced the floor.

"Platinum gave money to the drunk," said Jacobs. "In return, she signed a form stating she wasn't insured by them on the day of the accident."

"Impossible," Mike spit. He strode across the room and swung his foot up in the air as though kicking an invisible enemy.

"I'm on your side. But at this point, the judge has ruled to dismiss our case against Platinum."

"On what grounds?" Mike yelled.

"On the premise that Platinum didn't insure the drunk on the day of accident, therefore Platinum has nothing to do with it anymore," Jacobs repeated.

"I've never heard of anything so insane. Of course Platinum insured that drunk." Mike whirled and shot his arms into the air.

"Some clever whore stayed up all night to put this one together." Jacobs shook his head. "We've got a team of lawyers who have been on the phone and studying all aspects of this case since we got the call yesterday. I wanted to wait a day to tell you, so I could explain things properly and let you know our options."

Kelly muttered, "I don't get it."

"They're trying to bog us down and will do everything they can at this point to delay or cancel a jury trial. They want to avoid heavy punitive damages."

"But Al's in a nursing home," Kelly cried. "Everyone's given up on her, and our mortgage company wants to foreclose on our home. I can't take this anymore."

"Kelly, I–" Jacobs started.

"You said a jury might give her seven to ten million dollars."

"I still believe that, and undoubtedly, Platinum does, too." Jacobs' hands gestured through the air. "But now they know we'll have to fight them on a whole new round of legal technicalities before we can ever bring Alex's case before a jury. I think they planned this all along and are trying to push you into settling out of court for their original offer, without punitive damages."

"We can't accept that," Mike ranted. "After subtracting your fees, and paying all the debt we've already incurred for Alex, she'd have practically nothing."

"Platinum's money is too late to help Al recover. Where were they when we really needed the money?" Kelly moaned.

"Platinum needs to be taught a lesson." Jacobs paused. "Get this. The drunk already spent her eighty grand to buy a house, and has filed for bankruptcy."

"There's no way she could have moved that fast by herself,"

Mike yelled and turned toward the big window. His ears burned from the pressure that surged through them. He put his hands above his head and leaned heavily on the glass. Somewhere deep in his mind, he wished the glass would explode so he could fall to his death and end the nightmare.

Kelly rocked back and forth in disbelief. She held her head with both hands. Tears streamed down her face. She never blinked. The baseball cap shrouded her pale face in darkness.

Jacobs stood, covered his mouth with his hands, and turned away from the Montanes. His body wobbled. "We'll nail them." Everyone heard the hopelessness.

"I don't get it?" Kelly séanced her new mantra.

"This sort of thing happens all the time, but usually only when it involves two parties, and not an injured third party. For example, suppose you had a life insurance policy worth $100,000 when you died. Suppose you had a terminal illness and needed money right now to pay your medical bills before your death. Some insurance companies allow you to make an agreement with them that essentially 'releases them' from paying any death benefit, in exchange for a lesser amount of cash right now."

"So the drunk driver released Platinum from their obligations, in exchange for a smaller amount of money?"

"That's right."

"But that drunk didn't have money coming to her in the first place." Kelly's voice sounded like a child's plea.

"You're right."

"And we get nothing?"

"I'm sorry."

"It's bullshit." Mike yelled.

"So why did Platinum do that?" asked Kelly.

"Because someone in their top brass realizes someone in their claims department made a mistake. They know they should've paid out the million plus dollars within a few months of the accident. Even if Alex had recovered at that point, she would probably suffer lifelong disabilities. When they didn't pay the first time, it was a routine business practice. They hold onto the money as long as they can – you know, to let it collect interest."

"This can't be legal." Kelly cried.

"It's immoral, Kelly. But we're trying to find a way to make it illegal. No one's ever thought of it before. There aren't any laws in Minnesota to prevent it," said Jacobs.

"They don't have laws against drinking toilet bowl cleaner either," Mike quipped.

"If it's all right with you guys, I'd like to call a press conference. We could use some public support and let the media know what a monster Platinum is."

"Do it!" Mike slammed his fist down on Jacobs's desk.

"Oh," Kelly cried. Her body shook.

"Today is my last day working for Platinum." Mike let out a huge sigh. "No, I get paid tomorrow, then I'll quit, after I cash the check."

Kelly slumped in her chair.

Mike felt a rush of relief, so he said it again. "I quit."

"They've ruined our lives. They've ruined our lives." Kelly's weak voice barely squeaked the words and her hand trembled when she reached for a Kleenex.

"Those monsters will pay." Mike shouted.

"We'll appeal the case," Jacobs said. "It may take several months before we can get on the docket, and you can bet Platinum is going to fight us all the way. But we're going to win."

"We have to fight them." Mike continued to pace in front of Jacobs's desk.

Kelly could only hang her head and cry.

************ *********

Fury seized Harley Crane when he read the *Minneapolis Star Tribune* in his office the next day. "Damn those losers. Richter's a vegetable and every drop of money since the beginning of time can't change that."

He hated the part where the newspaper quoted Kelly: "My sister is a racehorse. She is a survivor. If we would have had money when we needed it, she might have recovered." *What did she know about being a racehorse?* He tore the paper down the center.

The entire thing had gone out of control, and now that the press was involved, Platinum looked bad. His boss would be furious. Harley rationalized. He had read the charts, knew Platinum had paid for more than enough time in the coma therapy. And Platinum had offered a full settlement, even though it was a late offer.

But that damn greedy lawyer wanted punitive damages. "Greed." Harley grimaced through bared teeth. *If they paid Richter a hundred trillion dollars, she'd still drool on herself.*

He knew Platinum had made a mistake when the liability claim went unpaid for this long. Some overzealous claims rep had dropped the ball in the attempt to be aggressive in their claims handling. The whole thing left Platinum exposed to huge punitive damages.

At that point, Harley had no choice but to act. His ploy had been brilliant. He would explain it to Roger, who would certainly understand. A simple method to delay payment, and to set up a whole new legal hurdle for that greedy law firm. They'd see the light and realize what kind of fight they were in. Then they'd settle for Platinum's original offer.

They'd settle or Harley would drag this thing out till the sun collapsed into a black hole.

Chapter 20

Mike watched as gloom and utter despondency overwhelmed Kelly. After the meeting with Jacobs, she crawled into their king-sized bed and curled into a fetal position. The drawn shades made the room dark. Although it was a comfortable 70 degrees, Kelly became increasingly hot and sweaty.

She cried.

No words.

Only crying.

She cried until she collapsed into sleep. When Mike came into the bedroom, he found her lying in her underwear curled up tightly against herself, with her thumb in her mouth. Though she shivered, her skin felt damp with sweat. She looked small and helpless in the big bed.

When she woke, the tears came again. Cry and sleep. Sleep and cry. The cycle continued for days.

A week passed before Kelly allowed Mike to take her to the clinic. The doctor said she was mentally and physically exhausted, put her on a schedule of medications, and told her to rest in bed.

Kelly wanted to be in a coma.

Alex still "lived" in a persistent vegetative state.

And Mike had all but lost his mind.

************ *********

After two weeks, Mike finally forced himself to go to the nursing home to look after Alex. As he walked down the hall, he could hear her choking. He raced into her room and an unbearable stench besieged him. Yellow stained sheets covered Alex. Her eyes were rolled back. Spittle formed a long line of drool that fell past her chest and pooled onto her lap.

The machine inhaled the saliva in a torrent as Mike put the suction tube in her mouth. He patted her on the back, praying as he tried to get oxygen back into her fluid-filled lungs.

Mike ripped off the soiled sheets and threw them into the hallway. He turned back to Alex and saw her diaper puddled with urine and feces. Alex looked at him with a death-like gaze. Her eyes had lost all sparkle. Contorted more than ever before, her face communicated pain.

He bellowed down the hall in a roar of outrage. "I need some help, and I need it now!" No one came. He ran to the front desk. "I need to see the head nurse."

"I'm sorry, but she's out for the day."

"Give me the phone." Mike strafed his arms across the desk as he threw everything to the floor. "I mean *now*." He called 911. "I'll be in Alex Richter's room, and I want to see the person in charge."

Mike raced down the hall into Alex's room. He held Alex's face while she coughed deep in her lungs. "I'm so sorry, Alex. Kelly's been sick at home, and I've been with her the last two weeks. I'm sorry." Somehow, he sensed Alex understood his words. Certainly, she recognized touch.

He gently lifted her off the bed and set her naked body down on the visitor's chair, then pulled off his shirt and wrapped it around her to keep her warm. Alex's skin was raw and blistered from bedsores. Mike shuddered with the pain of the voiceless person. How could someone possibly ignore such helplessness? Alex looked sick, beyond the sickness of the persistent vegetative state. She was pale, with blotches of bright red skin. Her hand squeezed into a tighter fist, and her left eye had almost closed.

Alex continued to choke. Mike leaned her over his shoulder and massaged her.

*********** *********

Two hours later, the doctors at the hospital were able to stop Alex's choking and restore normal breathing. They estimated Alex had been choking for the last three or four hours of the night and thought she was lucky to be alive.

But she wasn't safe yet. Raw patches of skin turned dark red from an infection that was several days old. She had open sores and her temperature rose to a hundred and five. The infection spread throughout her body.

Alex's eyes bulged out of her shrunken eye sockets. Her skin still felt cold and clammy, and she shivered so violently that they had to strap her to her bed. Her mouth gaped open, and her fist clenched totally shut.

Despite her wretched appearance, Mike could only love her. He held her hand in his and gently whispered her name. Her eyes told him a thousand words about the pain.

And there, faced with the prospect of her death, Mike knew in the depths of his heart that Alex was still alive and had potential. Suddenly the living will didn't matter anymore. All the discussions of life and death were irrelevant as he looked into the hurting eyes of this person his wife loved so much.

Now he understood, more than ever before, how Kelly felt. Alex was indeed alive, and her eyes told him she knew what was going on.

An overwhelming sense of love, and a terrible new responsibility flooded into his heart. Poor, wonderful, defenseless soul. Sitting next to Alex on her bed, he held her hand, touched her face, and whispered her name over and over again.

"Al, please hang on." Tears formed in his eyes, as she turned and stared at him. "Kelly and I need you so much. Please–" His hands and voice trembled. "Please know we both love you. I know that none of this is your fault. I'll never be impatient with you again."

Alex's eyes continued to watch Mike, then moved to see his lips form the words.

"Al, my precious friend." Mike wiped his tears with the back of his sleeve. "Did I ever tell you the story about my awesome friend who climbed one of the most glorious climbs in the whole world . . ."

As he told the story, he smiled at her with all the love his heart could show. And somehow, through the depths of her eyes, he knew she understood. Then, in the same way that Kelly made her lifelong vow, Mike brought his head close to Alex's and promised he would be with her forever.

As the doctors and nurses scurried throughout the emergency room, Mike continued to sit with Alex. He continued to touch her face, and whisper how much he and Kelly loved her.

When she took her last breath, Mike felt her squeeze his hand as if to say good-bye.

Chapter 21

"My name is Eleanor, and I hope I can help you today." The white haired woman smiled like a grandma, and motioned for Mike and Kelly to sit on a giant pillow of a couch.

"We're here because we're struggling to cope with the death of Kelly's sister," Mike started. "You're the third psychologist we've seen in the last three years since her death."

"Yes, I read your long letter very carefully." Eleanor looked intently at both of them. "I find it interesting that you both changed careers so abruptly after Alex's death. Tell me, Mike, why did you decide to become a window washer?"

"Because I need to work alone, where I make the rules, and I'm the boss."

"I see." Eleanor knowingly smiled while Mike fidgeted on the couch. "And you, Kelly?"

"I work as a social worker helping women in need."

"It seems to be very similar to the line of work that Alex did as a lawyer."

"Do you think something's wrong with that?" Mike blurted.

"No." Eleanor continued to smile. "But I would like to ask you why you never sued the insurance company?"

Mike clenched his fist and looked at the ceiling. "Because Kelly didn't have the stomach to fight them."

"We would have had to relive Al's tragedy for years." Kelly implored. "Besides, winning would be pointless."

"It would have taught Platinum a lesson." Mike roared.

"But it wouldn't bring Al back." Kelly's voice rose to match Mike's.

Mike covered his face with both hands. "Okay."

"Yeah." Kelly looked the other way.

The counselor watched the exchange expressionlessly. Neither Mike nor Kelly looked at Eleanor. Tension mounted over the next minute of silence. "Why don't each of you tell me the story in your own words. We'll start with you, Mike. If we run out of time, we'll devote our next session to listening to Kelly."

For the next fifty-five minutes, Mike recounted everything for the psychologist as she listened and took notes, never making a single comment, never asking a question. Told through bursts of anger and tears, Mike finally finished, "In the last hours of Al's life, everything in my life was shattered. I felt like I'd been betrayed by Platinum, but the love in Al's eyes made me feel like I betrayed her as well."

"Didn't you tell me that Alex couldn't visually communicate?" Eleanor sat back in her chair.

"Yes, but I *felt* her eyes talking to me."

"Really?" Eleanor smiled.

"It's true," Kelly blurted. "It's the same way I felt ever since the accident–"

Eleanor interrupted. "Projecting."

"What?" Mike spat.

"Projecting is when you think you know how the other person feels. So people have a way of making themselves believe it as truth."

"But I –" Mike started.

The older woman held up her hand to signal time-out. "Listen, right now, you're probably *projecting* that I haven't heard your pain. You may think I'm even cold-hearted. But I do understand." She paused to absorb their stares. "Unfortunately, we're out of time. I want to ask you to concentrate on one word between now and our second session."

"Projecting." Mike's sarcasm projected through the air, swirled around and filled the room.

"That's right." The woman smiled. "Think about it, and what it means in relationship to you and Alex. We'll start from there next week."

When Kelly and Mike got inside their van, Mike kicked the driver's door outward until it whipped back on its hinges. As the door recoiled, he yanked it for extra measure. The door slammed so hard that the driver's side window shattered. The tempered glass exploded as tiny chunks of jigsaw puzzled pieces showered both of them.

Even so, the couple sat transfixed. Neither Kelly nor Mike moved. No one swore. No one said anything. They simply stared at nothing but the parking lot ahead of them.

After several minutes of silence, Mike put the car in drive and started off.

"Do you think we should clean the glass off us?" Kelly asked in a steady voice.

Without answering, Mike stopped the van. "You go ahead." He picked up a piece of glass and squeezed it. "Maybe I'll get lucky and cut myself."

"Mike, I think we should at least give Eleanor one more try."

"This counseling is bullshit."

"Maybe she'll see things from a different perspective, and be able to help you with your anger."

"I'm not angry." Mike slammed his open palm into the steering wheel.

"Mike."

"I'm entitled." He rolled his eyes.

"You're mad."

"No. I'm not mad at you, or Al, or life itself." Mike stared at his throbbing red hand.

"Then who, besides Platinum, are you mad at?"

"Myself."

"Why?"

"Because I was afraid of losing my job. I didn't fight Platinum hard enough or soon enough on Al's behalf. And look what *my fear*, my inaction, cost her and us."

"You can't say that."

"I screwed up by accident, and Platinum deliberately screwed all of us."

"You did your best."

"I think about Platinum every day. Every day. Sometimes when I'm washing windows, I become unconscious in my thoughts. I finish a whole house without being aware of starting it. I think about Platinum and what I should have done for hours on end."

"No matter how terribly and unethically Platinum treated Al," she shook his arm, "you got to let it go."

"I can't."

"Why not?"

"Because you told me you hated them with all your heart. They destroyed our lives, they took away my business, and they killed Al."

"What can you do now?"

"I don't know." Mike stared ahead. "But you don't say words like that without doing something about it. Sometimes I lie in bed until three in the morning just thinking."

"You're the one who told me that Al wouldn't want to be confined to a wheel chair. Yet, you've become a prisoner of woe. Please, for my sake, and the memory of Al, please try to let it go."

Mike's shoulders started to shake, and his head collapsed forward onto the steering wheel. "Projecting." The words garbled inside his tears, his voice barely audible while his body jerked amid the broken glass.

Chapter 22

April 12, 2004 was a windy day on Museum Drive in Highland Park, Illinois. Harley strolled across his stone cut concrete sidewalk knowing that his 2003 income tax return waited in his mailbox. His accountant had already called with the news that Harley owed the IRS an additional $40,288.

"Big freaking deal." Harley stared at the envelope. "A guy works his guts out to make a million bucks and the government wants him to take a loan to pay taxes on it."

Mixed in the assortment of junk mail, a hand-addressed, heavily scribbled letter caught Harley's eye. He instantly recognized the handwriting. There was no return address, but the streaked postmark indicated a Miami post office. Despite his shaking hands, he ripped the envelope open.

Crane,

I'm watching you. Never forget me.

The letter wasn't signed.

Every April for the past five years, Harley had received the same exact note from someone in Miami. Although Harley had plenty of enemies, he knew it had to be Thorson. It didn't matter that the bald-headed freak lived somewhere in northern Minnesota. The payoff money undoubtedly transformed Thorson into a local hick who could afford to travel. After getting the first letter, Harley had called the police, but they only made a report of it. They said there was nothing they could do because the letter was too abstract or some bullshit.

The second time, Harley's fraud department performed a handwriting analysis to confirm a match with Chad Thorson. Even then, the police only offered to bring it to a judge who *might* put a restraining order on Thorson. As if that would help.

Harley noticed his trembling hands, so he flung them in the air. Anything to free himself. Then he took the note, ripped it into shreds, and left the paper trail scattered like bird-crumbs at the end of his driveway.

"Screw 'em, " he muttered, then turned back toward his big house and smiled at his 2003 Jaguar XK8 Convertible. *Shake it off. Shake it off.* Life was simply too busy to give guys like Thorson any extra effort.

Yes, Harley's life was busy. Vacations had ceased to exist, and he wasn't the kind of guy to spend time reflecting anyway. His wheel spun faster and faster. Deadlines. Meetings. Legalities. From 6 AM until 10 PM there was always more to do.

Until one day a month later, no different than the rest. Harley received an urgent call. "This is United Hospital in St. Paul, Minnesota."

"Yes."

"Mr. Crane, I'm sorry to tell you, but your father has suffered a heart attack."

"A heart attack?"

"I'm sorry."

"How is he?"

"It doesn't look good. We've got him stabilized now, but the doctors are concerned."

Harley used the corporate Learjet 35 to land at Fleming Field in St. Paul. He walked into the third floor coronary care unit less than two hours after leaving Chicago.

The first thing Harley noticed when he entered his dad's room was the incessant beep . . . beep . . . beep of the EKG monitor next to the bed. Harley approached the frail man, but his eyes fixed on the green line that moved slowly and irregularly with each pulse.

The older Crane's face looked shrunken. His eyes were closed, and a nasal cannula fed oxygen into his nose. The monitor displayed a wavy white line that followed his breathing, and the blood pressure indicated 70/30 in glowing red numbers. A bottle of nitroglycerin hung on a pole with the tube feeding into his dad's arm.

"Hey, Dad," Harley's voice shook.

"Harley," the old man could barely whisper.

"Are you all right?" Harley leaned over the bed and touched

his dad's face.

"Yeah," he wheezed.

"Dad." Harley's lips trembled.

"Son . . . I'm proud of you."

"I don't know what to say."

"Sit with me . . . and hold my hand."

"Dad."

"It's okay." There was a long pause as he tried to catch his breath. The IVAC hummed quietly next to the bed. "Signed a . . . a do not resuscitate order." The old man gasped. "I expect you to honor it."

Harley said nothing for the next ten seconds while he gently touched his dad's thin, venous arm. "Dad, do you remember how we used to go to the horse races?"

John Crane nodded.

"You were my best friend when I was a boy." Harley wished he had the courage not to lie.

"Mine, too."

Tears formed in the corners of Harley's eyes.

"You know what I say" – he coughed – "about men who cry." The dying man squeezed his son's hand as he spoke. Even in death, the old bull remained true to character. Harley used the back of his sleeve to wipe the tears.

So the son held his dad's hand and looked into his eyes. The two men said nothing. The clock ticked in slow motion that long afternoon as Harley continued to hold his dad.

Finally, the white haired man grimaced and turned sideways on the bed. He reached for Harley's arm with both of his hands. "Come closer, Son."

Harley leaned over the bed while the old bony hands slowly rubbed against Harley's muscular forearm. "You used to be such a frail boy."

"I love you, Dad."

"You're doing your best."

Before Harley could respond, the gnarled fingers fell off Harley's arm. The old man struggled for breath. His neck jerked back into the pillow and his eyes penetrated into Harley's. Then, with a slight twitch, the elder Crane stiffened, and finally drifted off.

Harley picked up the limp hand. The irregular white line on the monitor now displayed a straight line to match its constant tone. A nurse entered the room, checked the leads, then found no pulse on John Crane's carotid artery. She turned off the monitor and whispered "I'm sorry" as she left the room.

Harley sat in the little hospital room and gently rubbed his dad's arm for an hour. He wondered what "doing your best" really meant, and stared at his dad's tired, peaceful face as if it might give him a clue.

As much as he wanted to cry, when Harley left the hospital there were no tears in his eyes.

Chapter 23

July 2004

"I'm stronger now. Even stronger than before the accident." Kelly mused. "I can tell Al is with me."

Kelly and Mike continued hiking along the Minnesota River.

"Hmm." Mike had heard a hundred variations of this line.

"Yesterday I had a dream. Al and I were together, climbing the Diamond. She turned and told me we would always be together – and she loved me."

"Mm."

"Mike, listen. I know Al is with me the same way she knew I was with her – even in her coma."

They continued walking in silence. After a while, Kelly noticed the leaves rustling under her feet. The sound echoed against the mute cavern between them. Like ringing in the ears, the silence only perpetuated the noise.

"I've been thinking, Mike." Kelly stopped walking. "Let's start a company called Adventures in Living or AL for short."

"Where'd you come up with that?"

"I've been thinking about it for months. We could take people rock climbing, canoeing, mountain biking, or on any adventure that involved the outdoors."

"Kel, we've hardly been outside in the seven years since the accident. I don't know if I remember how to tie a figure-eight, let alone climb a mountain."

"I know, Mike, but I'm better now. I'm able to move on from the accident. Let's take some time to go climbing again. It'll help you feel better too."

"Mm."

"Mike, think about it," Kelly urged. "AL could focus on kids. It would be a way to carry on the traditions and way of life that inspired us."

"Give me some time to think about it." Mike's mood seemed ghostly.

They came to a giant cottonwood tree, snapped in half by a recent storm. Kelly stopped. She grabbed Mike's arm. "It took a while, but I've discovered that I'm resilient and tougher than I thought. And I'm also smart enough to know when to bend with the wind."

You didn't bend when Alex was sick, or when I wanted to sue Platinum after she died. Mike wanted to say something sarcastic, but before he could open his mouth, he looked into his wife's eyes and saw them sparkle. He bit down on his lip and said nothing. They both studied the tree. It must have been several hundred years old. It had snapped 30 feet up the trunk. Spires of jagged wood spiked into the sky.

"This tree lived through an awful lot of storms but it forgot how to bend. I know exactly what it went through, because it almost happened to me. But I lived through that, and I'm smarter and better now." She paused. "Mike, you've got to let it go. It's been too long."

Mike smiled as best he could.

Kelly reached up, put her arm around his neck, and searched his face. "I'll help you bend, Mike, if you'll let me. You know I love you."

His inner pain didn't allow him to look back at her. Instead, he looked at the jagged spires, and his guts churned inside him.

He wondered how it felt to break.

Chapter 24

October 26, 2004. Boundary Waters Canoe Area, Minnesota–Canadian border

Mike sat alone on the biff in the woods while the others sat around a campfire about a hundred yards away, on the other side of a hill. Darkness penetrated the forest. He held his hand directly in front of his face, then moved it out till his arm was fully extended. His eyes squinted as his hand disappeared within a few inches of his eye.

Mike heard a creaking sound and clicked on his flashlight like a noise-seeking missile. The beam zeroed in on the food packs suspended fifteen feet in the air between two trees. The wind moved the packs and they rubbed together.

He clicked off the light and darkness devoured the world in front of him. He sat on the cold fiberglass stool with his wool pants hanging from his knees, lost in black, brooding thought.

"Hey, Montane." Dillon Johnson's deep voice boomed across the darkness. Dillon and Mike had been friends since college. "Did you fall in?"

Mike turned his head and shouted toward the camp. "I'll be there in a few minutes."

It took another ten minutes for Mike to decide to be social. He stuffed the flashlight in his pants pocket and carefully felt his way, inch by inch through the dark forest. Anything to distract his mind from the task before him.

Half an hour later, Mike sat ten yards from camp in his black wool layered clothes, invisible among the dark shadows of the trees. He watched the others as they sat around the campfire exchanging small talk. The fire crackled as water whistled and sizzled from the wet wood. The red embers breathed in and out as their glow ebbed and flowed.

Grant Strong jumped when Mike snapped a branch behind him, emerging from the woods. "You scared me." Grant was a high school buddy who had canoed the Boundary Waters a half dozen times with Mike. The red-bearded man currently worked as a realtor in the Chicago suburb of Glenview. Today he wore layers of dark blue polypropylene and fleece that had seen better days.

"Man, are you constipated or what?" Dillon's quick tongue had helped him develop a successful law practice in Detroit. He sat on a big log, his bare hands extended toward the fire. A purple neck gator covered his ears, and the top flopped on his head like a dunce cap. Mike was certain that Dillon purposefully dressed like a moron, and that alone made it an art.

Kelly said, "I was almost ready to come and get you, honey."

"You walked through those dark woods without a flashlight?" The rookie camper, Allison Maki advertised inexperience with her uneasy voice.

"Hey, guys." Mike said in a flat voice. "Sorry I was gone so long." He sat on the end of the log farthest from the fire. It whispered hypnotically and no one said a word until Grant added another log.

"Nice job with the fire." Mike mumbled.

"Thanks. Glad you like it."

"Grant, have you told Allison?" Mike desperately tried to smile. "About the bears?"

"We voted on that earlier today, and the group decided all the bears have hibernated by now." Grant replied. "I mean, everyone knows you couldn't have picked a colder weekend to come up here."

"So tell us again, Mike, 'cause I don't remember." Dillon paused. His eyebrows looked up at the black sky, and he put his hand under his chin as if he were struggling to come up with what to say next. "Maybe you can clarify it for me, oh Mike, Master Trip Planner. We came up here to canoe at the end of October because no one else would be around. And that's true."

"That's right," Mike interrupted.

Dillon smiled at everyone. "So after getting up here moments before winter sets in, we canoe all day long. Not part of a day, mind you. No. We canoe all day long to get into the backcountry. And why?"

"So we can be alone." The whole group answered as one.

"Yes, class." Dillon paused to smile. "Now let's get this right. When we got in our canoes today, not another human existed within twenty miles of our departure point. But now, after killing ourselves . . . there are no humans anywhere within forty miles of us."

Kelly joined in the parade against Mike. "So we canoed our rears off to get twenty miles farther away from nobody." Everyone but Mike laughed. Kelly felt his unease, so she broke the train of thought, "Look, I see a star."

"There are two more," Allison pointed.

"The clouds must be breaking," Dillon said.

"No clouds means a cold night," Grant added.

"Hey, everyone," Mike said, "I'm sorry to leave you, but I'm too tired to be any fun tonight. I'm going to hop in the tent."

Dillon stood and said, "I can't believe you're going to bed, champ."

"Is something wrong, honey?" asked Kelly.

"Nope. Just tired."

"You're going to miss a great fire," Grant said.

"And the best stories," Dillon added.

"I'm dead. I'll see all of you in the morning." Mike kissed Kelly, then went to his tent.

While the others sat around the fire swapping stories until well past midnight, Mike lay down on his sleeping bag and closed his eyes. His heart ached, and he wished he could be with his friends, but he couldn't do it anymore. He had no choice but to retreat.

Now the time had come. He had planned this trip, this day, for a long time. His wife and old friends were going to be unknowing soldiers in a war he would wage against Platinum. Kelly's hand would be forced to fight. He'd show Platinum. He'd get the blood money they owed, and hopefully he'd still have Kelly too.

As the shadows from the fire danced on the ceiling of the tent, darker shadows pounded into his mind.

Had he forgotten anything?

No going back.

What about Kelly?

No going back.

Kelly?

No.

No going back.

Tomorrow he would play his trump card.

Chapter 25

Mike woke and reached for the tent's side pocket to find his watch. The tiny LED display said 6AM. The sun would not be up for two hours.

Dressed in wool clothes over his polypropylene long underwear and wearing a thick wool hat, Mike lay perfectly still on top of his sleeping bag. He had always hated the constricting feeling of a sleeping bag, and now his body shivered in payment. The cold night air had penetrated the tent and found a home deep inside his bones.

He was freezing. Ice cold. He smiled grimly. It was all a part of the plan.

Mike cupped his flashlight and looked over at Kelly. She lay perfectly still, breathing shallow, sound asleep. Bundled in her bag, only her lips, nose, and eyes were exposed to the cold.

The tent zipper showered little shards of ice as Mike unzipped it quickly, making the sound as loud as possible. The tent groaned with the sound of thin ice cracking.

As Mike left the tent, he intentionally bumped Kelly hard enough to wake her. She didn't function very well when she didn't get enough sleep. He counted on it. Needed it. She had to turn into a basket case.

He left the tent and ran to the edge of the water. He shined his flashlight onto the lake. Good. The lake was perfectly still. A shimmering, ultra thin layer of ice covered it. Winter was on the way.

Surveying the camp with his flashlight, Mike found the largest pot in the cook-kit. He went back to the lake, tapped through the thin ice, and collected water for breakfast and dishes. Walking back to camp, he intentionally banged an empty pan against the side of a canoe. The sound echoed in the stillness of morning, almost certain to wake his friends.

For extra measure, he dropped an empty pan against the rocks on a small hill so it clanged repeatedly in its fall to the edge of the lake. At the same time, he let out a loud "umpf" as if he had slipped.

Mike heard Grant moving inside his tent. In the next tent, Dillon whispered to Allison, "It's only Mike. Go back to sleep."

Then Kelly asked, "What's going on?"

Mike spoke loud. "I just slipped, but I'm up making breakfast. It'll be ready soon."

Dillon moaned, "Go back to bed. It's still dark and we're not getting up until eight, so knock it off."

Mike ignored Dillon and started the Coleman lantern, then hung it on a thin nylon rope stretched between two trees, and turned it up as bright as it would go. Less than thirty minutes later, Mike repeatedly banged a metal pot against the side of a canoe. "Wake up," he yelled. "We have a long way to go today, and breakfast is getting cold."

By the time the others crawled out of their tents and finished breakfast, the morning sun had peeked over the horizon. The group moved in slow motion.

"Come on, you guys. Let's move," Mike urged while disassembling Dillon's tent.

"Hey, buddy. Why don't you leave my stuff alone."

"Come on, Dillon." Mike never looked up.

"I can take care of my things myself."

"But the days are short, and I want to get an early start."

"Back off, and ease up." Dillon laughed.

"Don't tell me to back off." Mike stood with his fists raised.

"Okay, man." Dillon stepped away.

"Mike!" Kelly intervened. "You're way out of line."

"Don't start with me." Mike stared at everyone in the group. "I've already told you that we have a long way to go today, and the days are short."

"Ya, but–" Grant started.

"Listen," Mike growled. "I got up before dawn so we could make an early start, and I've been fighting all of you to get your rear ends moving."

"But we're on vacation," Grant blurted, "and no one likes being pushed."

"Okay then." Mike closed his eyes as if trying to think. "I'm sorry," he yelled. "But please pick up the pace."

Half an hour later, Mike heaved the last Duluth Pack into Kelly and Dillon's Alumacraft canoe. Sweat boiled off Mike's forehead, but at last, they were finally ready to go.

The others shoved off, and as Mike put his foot into the Kevlar, he paused, then stood back out on the shore. In a non-apologetic tone he said, "I better go and check out the latrine one more time before we leave."

Everyone moaned.

"Hey. Remind me not to give a shit when you're waiting for me," Dillon said.

"Yeah. Right." Mike ran from the edge of the lake, past camp, and into the woods in the general direction of the outdoor stool. He had hidden an eighth-inch black wetsuit in the woods the night before while the others gathered firewood. He quickly stripped out of his wool clothes and slipped into the wetsuit. Above the wetsuit, he strapped a zipper belt around his waist. The belt contained four bags of four-pound shot weight to give him neutral buoyancy in the water. Then he put his wool clothes back on, hiding the wetsuit and the soft weight.

Chapter 26

"Mike, what's the name of this lake?" Dillon didn't really care about the name of the lake. He wanted to embarrass Mike for accidentally leaving everyone else's map in the van.

"We're on Hungry Ben Lake," Mike said. Mike's map lay folded on the floor of his canoe, right in front of his feet. As they headed in a northwestern direction, the map lay tilted slightly to the right, so the islands in front of Mike's canoe also appeared directly ahead of him on the map.

"Show me where we are now," Grant said. Grant and Allison pulled their canoe next to Mike's, then Dillon and Kelly joined them in a three-way canoe hug.

"While you guys are talking maps, I'm going to strap the canoes together and pull out some gorp," Kelly said.

"What's gorp? Allison asked.

"A mixture of raisins, nuts, and candy to give you an energy boost."

"Oh." Allison smiled. Then, almost as if she were trying to out-do herself she continued. "Some of these lakes have such weird names. Why do they call it Hungry Ben?"

Dillon quickly answered. "It comes from an old story about a logger named Ben who went fishing for a couple of days and got lost. After being four days overdue, they presumed he had died or got lost in the woods. At the end of the fifth day, while all the loggers were sitting around camp, someone looked up and saw Ben way off in the distance canoeing toward camp. When he came within range, one of the men hollered out, 'Are you hungry, Ben?' and the name stuck ever since. And if you believe that, I got some other real estate you may be interested in," Dillon laughed at his own cleverness.

Now Grant and Mike were looking at the map. "Look where we've come from, Grant." Mike pointed at the route hoping Grant would subconsciously burn the return route into his mind. "This route is so straight-forward that maybe you could bring your nephew up for a trip."

"I like that idea." Grant smiled as he continued to study the map.

"Take a look at this narrow opening about a hundred yards ahead." Mike pointed.

"I see. That's where Hungry Ben ends and the Three Forks River begins." Grant's finger drew on the map.

"I thought we were canoeing on lakes, not rivers." Allison's face twisted.

"The Three Forks River is actually a series of lakes and rivers that join together on the U.S.–Canadian border for about 60 miles," Dillon piped in. "Once in a while it gets narrow with fast water, but it's mostly lakes and–"

"You don't need to worry, Allison." Mike blurted as if to shut Dillon up.

"What's your problem?" Dillon stared at Mike.

"Nothing." Mike snapped back. "We need to keep moving. I guess I didn't get enough sleep."

"No way," quipped Dillon.

"I'm going to canoe ahead and cool off a little." Mike began to paddle. After about ten minutes, he settled into a steady rhythm, barely within sight of the others. Around the bend, all of his plans flashed before his eyes. There – just ahead – the river curved to the right, and the water quickened into a narrow gorge. "I can do this." His jaw hardened.

What about Kelly? "I can't let Platinum kill me." He yelled against the wind so no one could hear him.

What about Kelly? Mike raised his head toward the gray misting sky, then shouted toward the woods, "I can't just lie down and die!"

Now the river narrowed. The water moved fast and deep down the middle, with swirling eddies along both shores.

I can't do this to Kelly. The canoe moved into the choppy current. *I've got no choice.* He heaved the canoe sideways in the current, then stood and thrust his paddle upward.

"Now!"

His hand gripped white knuckled around the shaft. His legs spread out and his arms exalted his spear into the sky, daring heaven to fight him.

Though tears streamed down his face, he looked across the misty water toward the woman he loved. She took a stroke with her paddle – smooth, powerful, delicate. He could recognize Kelly's stroke from a mile away. Then she stopped, and held her paddle across her lap as the others paused with her.

"Look at Mike, everyone." Allison wondered why they had stopped. "He's standing in his canoe pointing at something."

"I wonder what he sees?" Dillon asked, trying to shelter the mist from his eyes. "He must see a moose or a bear on the shoreline, but I don't see it."

"I don't see anything, do you?" Grant asked Kelly.

"I don't see anything either."

"Maybe he sees something swimming?" Allison suggested.

"He fell in!" Kelly screamed. "Dig!"

Dillon and Kelly accelerated. Frantic mode. They pushed toward the overturned canoe. Grant and Allison struggled to stay even. Spray flew from the paddles.

Dillon and Kelly surged ahead. A wake foamed behind them. "Mike!" Kelly screamed. Fear bolted through her. "Mike!" she hollered as loud as she could.

No one paced. They dug their paddles. Then dug for more.

Around the bend. "Right draw," Dillon screamed.

"He's not there!" Kelly cried. She dove into the water to search for Mike under the overturned canoe. Within a few seconds, she came up gasping for air. Cold burned her skin. Adrenaline surged. She dove under the canoe again.

When Kelly came up for air the second time, she knew she had to get out of the water. "He's not there!" Kelly gasped. "Hold steady so I can get back in."

"Look again!" Dillon spit the words at Kelly.

"We gotta look downstream."

"Look again." Dillon waved his paddle in the air. He scanned the waters in a frenzied search.

A look of panic swept across Kelly's face. The cold water wanted to kill her. It would undoubtedly kill Mike within minutes. The canoes moved together with the current. Each second brought them farther from shore. "I said he's not there!" She screamed through the pain of the crushing ice water. "I gotta get out!"

At that moment, Grant and Allison swooped in sideways next to Dillon's canoe, and grabbed the sides to steady it. As Kelly struggled to heave herself into the canoe, she hollered, "Mike." Her voice pitched with fever. "Mike . . . Mike!!" Out of her mind with fear, "Mike . . . Mike!!!" Kelly's panic echoed through the woods. "Mike!" "Mike!" "MIKE!"

The moment Kelly landed safely into the back of her canoe, Grant and Allison rolled over the capsized canoe to see if Kelly had missed Mike underneath. When they found nothing, Kelly commanded them to paddle on ahead to see if they could see him under the water. Grant and Allison pushed off and quickly moved down the river.

"We'll find him downstream," Kelly yelled. "Spread out. Push!" She shrieked at Dillon and gasped for breath. "You guys take the Minnesota shore. We'll stay on the Canadian side," Kelly commanded, "Get as close to shore as you can, but don't get hung up on any branches."

Allison's body shuddered from exertion and shock as she paddled as fast as she could. She strained looking desperately for a sign, any sign of Mike. "Oh, God. Please help Mike," she prayed aloud.

The two canoes slithered like snakes on opposite shores. They weaved and bobbed in the current, darting near the rocky shores, avoiding the fallen trees. The rescuers searched the dark water to see if a snag held Mike's body.

The fast-flowing water was deep. There would be no use in diving to the bottom to try to find him. By now, it had been over ten minutes since they had seen him fall. The water was too cold, and they couldn't pinpoint the spot where the canoe had actually capsized.

Now they were a half-mile downstream from the bend in the river. "There's no way Mike would be this far," Kelly screamed at Dillon, "We've got to go back. We missed him."

"Turn around." Dillon waved his paddle in the air, then swung his canoe toward Grant and Allison. "We're going back. Keep looking."

Grant and Allison struggled to point their canoe upstream against the tug of current, while Dillon and Kelly inched their way upriver. "Push, Allison," Grant cried.

Kelly continued to call Mike's name as she dug her paddle hard and deep into the ice-cold water. "Mike," stroke, "Mike," stroke, "Mike," stroke. The rhythm of anguish continued.

It took an hour for Dillon and Kelly to make it back to the overturned canoe. Fifty yards downstream from Mike's fall, an eddy held Mike's empty canoe in a swirl of water. Dillon strapped a rope to the gunnel and they towed it to the rocky beach near the area where Mike had fallen overboard.

Grant and Allison continued their struggle up the river, roughly a hundred yards behind Dillon and Kelly. Every stroke pulled against the rushing water as they laboriously crawled upstream. The water slammed into the canoe, shooting ice-cold spray into their faces. Allison stopped looking for Mike, for the pain in her muscles overpowered every sensation but fear.

Dillon flung the strapped down gear out of Mike's Kevlar canoe. Kelly sat on a giant boulder hugging her knees in an upright fetal position. She rocked back and forth, back and forth as in a trauma. Water dripped from her wet clothes. Her lips mumbled incomprehensibly, "Both . . . both?" Her eyes looked out onto the river. Glazed, they saw nothing.

"Kelly," Dillon said. "Kelly!" He hollered to get her attention. "Help me get this gear unstrapped. We can move faster without it, and maybe we can still find Mike farther downstream."

Kelly, numb, sat in a trance.

"Kelly, come on." Dillon grabbed her arm. He knew she was in trouble, but didn't know what to do.

"Dead," she moaned. "Been too long. Too cold." Tears

dropped onto her rigid cheeks.

Dillon flung open his Duluth pack, pulled out his sleeping bag, then unfurled Allison's bag next to it. "Kelly, you need to lie down, and get warm." He gently pulled her up to the bag, and supported her as she collapsed on top of it. "You stay here. Stay warm. Rest. Allison will stay with you. Don't worry, Grant and I will find Mike."

The empty Kevlar canoe allowed the two men to fly with the current. When they were a mile downstream, Dillon stopped paddling.

"Grant, we have to turn around. I'm worried about us getting back."

"We've got to keep looking."

"Grant, there's no way his body floated this far."

"I think he might be farther downstream and we've got to go and look."

"No. We can't."

"That's bull, Dillon. We're going to find him."

"No."

"Why not, damn it?"

"Because I'm worried about Kelly. She's wet. She's cold. And she may be losing it. We need to get her back to civilization. And I'm worried we don't have a map, and I don't want to get lost out here with winter closing fast."

"But we got to find Mike."

"He's dead, Grant."

Grant refused to look at Dillon. "We still got to find him." He put his hands over his eyes to protect them from the misty rain and continued to scan the water near shore.

"Grant, can you please listen to me for a moment?"

"We're wasting time, Dillon. Keep looking."

"I'll keep paddling and looking if you promise to listen."

"Dillon, you always think you're right. We've got to find Mike."

"Okay. Okay." Dillon swore under his breath, then paddled. "Grant, this water is barely above freezing. People can only survive for three or four minutes in ice water, and it's been an hour since we saw Mike fall out of the canoe."

Dillon's death logic overwhelmed Grant. Though he paddled and looked for Mike his body shuddered against his emotions.

"Grant, you need to understand that all the wishful thinking in the world isn't going to bring Mike back. He's dead, and I'm not ready to join him." Dillon's voice raised near fever pitch. "Are you listening? He's dead! Dead!" Dillon stopped paddling.

"Okay." Grant turned in the front of the canoe. Resigned, he looked back at Dillon. "Okay." Lips turned down, shoulders hung, Grant felt his guts wrench inside him.

"I'm sorry, Grant. I'm scared. It doesn't matter if we find Mike's body or not." Dillon calmed his voice. "How are we going to get out of here with no map?"

"What'll we tell Kelly?"

"We'll tell her the truth." Dillon spoke each word with harsh precision. "Mike is dead. Period."

Chapter 27

"I'm so sorry, Kelly," Grant whispered and touched her rigid arm.

For the first time in years, Dillon didn't know what to say.

Allison tried to wrap her arm around Kelly. No one knew how to act. Words felt impossibly shallow.

And everyone was afraid.

Grant and Dillon crouched next to Kelly and tried to hug her. The seconds dragged into uncomfortable, eternally long minutes.

Finally Dillon stood. "We need to make some decisions."

Kelly's eyes remained glued to the ground. She looked like a zombie, a paper cutout that the wind could blow away. No tears showed. Not a muscle twitched. Her eyes never even blinked in her android trance.

Allison glared at Dillon for his lack of sensitivity. Grant shook his head.

"We need to pull out all the gear to see if we can find a map." Dillon continued.

"I saw Mike stuff the map in his shirt after lunch," Grant said.

"Once the water freezes, it's going to make canoe travel impossible." Dillon scratched his stubble beard. "Without a map and compass, there's no way we can possibly walk through the forest without getting lost. Even if we could walk in a straight line due south, we'd run into lake after lake. They'd all be partially frozen with thin ice."

"But we have enough food to stretch for four or five days." Grant interrupted.

"What are we going to do after that?" asked Dillon.

"I don't know."

"No one even knows where we are. We never got a permit because no one else is here this time of year. Allison and I were planning to take an extra week to visit Minneapolis after we got back from the canoe trip. So no one is expecting to see either of us for another ten days."

"Same goes for me." Grant said. "I told a couple of friends we were canoeing the Boundary Waters, but I never gave them details. I planned on hanging out with Mike and Kelly after the trip. The last words I said were, 'See you in a couple weeks.'"

"My God." Allison blurted. A gust of wind turned the drizzle into a spattering of cold rain. Kelly's eyes remained open, staring, comatose. The rain pelted her face. She sat stiffly. Not a muscle moved.

The others slowly moved away. They began to unload the canoes, slowly, quietly at first – almost afraid to disturb Kelly. Within minutes, fears of making it home overwhelmed them. They *had* to find a map.

They began dumping all the gear out across the rocky beach. Dillon lifted a Duluth Pack upside down. Its contents spilled everywhere. The rain continued. Kelly remained immobile. Allison unzipped and re-zipped every pocket in every pack. No map. Grant dug through Kelly and Mike's pack. Piles of clothes and gear lay across the ground. All the while the rain continued, soaking through everything.

"We got to find a map, somewhere." Dillon's voice raised.

Allison's wet hair fell into her face. With her cold, red hands, she wiped her face. Then she slipped on a wet rock. She landed on her side and her clothes and hands stained brown with the wet, gritty dirt. She couldn't take it anymore. She began to cry.

Then a gust of wind blew a sheet of hard rain.

Kelly remained a statue.

Allison didn't know what to do next. She started to re-pack her wet sleeping bag into the wet Duluth Pack.

No one said anything.

They found nothing.

Finally Dillon asked the others to sit down. "We're all exhausted and freezing. We know we're about a day and a half back away from help, unless we get lucky and find someone with a motor boat on Hungry Ben Lake."

Dillon paused to be sure everyone listened. He touched Kelly gently on the shoulder, then continued to speak softly. "We don't have a map. It must have been on Mike. I want everyone to think hard about the direction we've taken. I think it's too risky to go forward without a map. So we need to backtrack to find our way out."

"Why not stay right here and wait for help?" Allison's voice trembled. "I've read that if you're lost in the woods, you should stay put. Someone will come and find you."

"You're right. But we only have two or three days of food, and no one is expecting any of us home for another week. Even if someone missed us then, no one would probably call the police for a couple days after that."

Everyone stared ahead. The rain kept falling. Kelly remained frozen. Allison started to blubber into an open sobbing, then shifted over to Kelly for mutual support. Kelly never flinched.

Dillon finally continued, "If the Park Service searched for us, the odds of them finding us are extremely remote. This wilderness is over a million square miles."

"We could light a big fire." Grant lifted his head.

"Maybe, but I think the best course of action is to first try to paddle out of here. We'll cut back on our food rations. And if we can't find our way out in the next two days, we'll light up the sky with a big fire."

Grant interrupted. "I spent a lot of time looking at the map with Mike this morning. We're on the Three Forks River now, and I think we should talk about where we are and how we got here. Maybe if I talk it through, the three of you can help me fill in any blanks. Is everyone okay with that?"

Dillon nodded approval. Allison stared ahead, her face turning a milky white color. Kelly remained immobile. Grant had no choice but to continue. "All right, we know we need to head back southeast on the Three Forks. I think we should hug the right-hand shoreline, which is the Minnesota side. In an hour or so, we'll find a small opening into Hungry Ben Lake where we camped last night. We should be able to find our camp. Does everyone agree?"

Dillon nodded yes again. Allison covered her face with her

hands. The rain continued. Kelly stared, blankly.

"I think we hugged the left shoreline yesterday afternoon before we got to camp, so we should hug the right shoreline on our way out." Despite the cold rain, Grant was drenched in sweat. "Then, I think we came through a narrow passage from the next lake."

"I remember a tiny lake after that, and then we'll get to the first lake where we started." Dillon spoke rapid fire.

Allison started to gag. She turned away from the others. Her shoulders heaved up and down. She ran forward, then stumbled and threw up.

The men ignored her. Kelly mumbled something incomprehensible. Dillon continued, "That first lake had a lot of inlets and islands, but it never got too wide. We should be able to find our way through it."

Grant carefully drew a map to Dillon's satisfaction. He made three sketches, then loaded up the canoes with the necessities needed for a safe journey in cold weather. They practically carried Kelly to the front of Dillon's canoe. Once there, she bent over with her head buried in her hands like a robot on shutdown. Unable to think, react, or feel.

Allison continued to vomit and was too sick to paddle.

They left Mike's gear behind, along with all the luxury camping items. Slowly, the two men pushed the canoes through the water.

So began the long trek back toward the camp where they had stayed the previous night. The canoes bobbed like toys in an ocean. They crawled ahead, little by little, burdened with the extra weight of grief. Cold waves slapped the tiny crafts. The rain continued.

Grant never dared to look at Dillon.

Chapter 28

Mike took a final check of his wetsuit and stepped back into the frigid water. He needed to stay out of the current of the narrow channel, so he walked upstream a few feet from the Canadian shoreline until the tug of the water disappeared. Then, where the river became wider, almost like a lake, he swam across.

It took a half-hour of hard swimming before he approached the Minnesota side. Once there, he continued upstream for another hour in the ice water. Mike assumed the insurance and police investigators would never consider looking upstream from the place where he had tipped. Bodies float downstream. If they suspected insurance fraud, it only made sense that he would swim with the current, away from his wife and friends who would be searching for him.

Near exhaustion, Mike finally came to his predetermined exit point from the river. Without making any mark or overturning a stone, he stepped ashore on the rocky Minnesota beach. Pulling his map from beneath his wetsuit, he hiked toward the trail that would eventually lead him out of the woods.

When Mike walked about a hundred yards from the Three Forks River, he took off all his clothes and wrung them out. He had less than an hour of daylight left, and he needed to get to the spot where he had supplies stashed.

As the woods grew steadily darker, Mike quickened his pace. He felt like eyes were everywhere. Watching him. Seeing him commit this crime. He turned around to see if someone followed. No one. "Kelly," he called into the empty woods. "I'm sorry."

Then he snapped back to his task. Sweat poured, like tears all over his face. He continued to turn to look behind him, as if being chased by a ghost. A second surge of adrenaline made his legs move faster. He tried to concentrate, to remember why he had made this choice. The anger toward Platinum pushed him.

By the time he finally got to the main trail, darkness had turned the world beyond the little flashlight into an empty black void. Trees, rocks, earth, and sky blended without distinction and everything became an eerie oneness. The air itself embodied darkness; an impenetrable shield swallowed the beam of light just beyond Mike's next step.

He knew he should have left his hiding spot earlier, but the risks of being caught were simply too great. Now the dark would make him move slowly through the woods on a trail no better than a deer path.

A small branch jabbed into his cheek, a half inch below his left eye. Twisting, he stumbled on a tree root. Unable to see, not knowing where he would fall, Mike's hands shot out to his side. The flashlight flew. He hit the ground hard. And at the same moment, the world turned black as the light went out.

Mike closed his eyes to try to acclimate to the darkness. But no light penetrated the black shield. He crawled and felt his way toward the flashlight. His hands brushed the earth in a giant sweeping motion finding twigs, rocks, branches, and trees. No flashlight.

A little further. He snaked deliberately, painstakingly forward making wider and wider sweeps with his hand. More twigs. No flashlight. A can of instant-cold-sweat poured itself across his face. Now the grass and weeds turned to rock and grit. *How dark can dark be?*

His hands probed farther. They found the light. Relief spilled across his face, but it was still to dark to see. The light wouldn't go on. He shook it. Nothing. He unscrewed the cap, and repositioned the batteries. Still nothing.

Eyes closed, he considered his limited options. Spend the night in wet clothes. Build a fire. Make a torch of some kind to light his path. All choices were bad.

Spending a wet night in the cold woods would probably kill him. Making a fire would give any search team evidence that someone had been there. Platinum would re-double their search efforts if they found even a shred of evidence.

The phrase, *all criminals make at least one mistake* stabbed through his mind. He couldn't believe that he hadn't brought a spare flashlight or compass.

How many thousands of times had he rehearsed this? What kinds of mistakes still loomed in front of him? The act of disappearing had taken all his courage, and the thought of capture was more than he could bear. What would he possibly say to Kelly?

Platinum would try to prosecute him. Evil would win.

Brooding thoughts chased him faster and harder. His breath became labored. Air hissed out of his mouth. Suddenly he was trapped, unable to move – unable to escape the nightmare surrounding him. He remembered Alex's dream, and his arms felt paralyzed beside him. Monsters loomed over him. Ready to plunge their fingers into his mind. Until he died, paralyzed in fear.

Caught in trap, a monster raised its hand for the final blow. Mike jerked and swung his head up and his eyes snapped open.

The nightmare ended. He stood up, and moved his arms up into the dark sky and smiled. There, in front of him, he discovered an unexpectedly wonderful thing. Luck.

Off in the distance a dull orange glow snuck its way through the shadows of the forest. In the splendor of an everyday miracle, a full moon began to slowly rise over the trees. Mike stood and watched as the reflection of light in the southeastern sky lit the trail before him. Soon the shadows of a million trees would fall across the forest floor, providing a directional compass.

Mike began walking again. This time slowly. Eventually the trail wound its way to a huge clearing. There, in the center of the clearing, stood a giant Norway pine. It loomed as a monument to the moonlight. He walked to the Norway, turned directly west, then walked about a hundred yards to the edge of the clearing. Hidden among a grove of pine trees, he found his mountain bike, tent, several protein/energy bars, and some warm clothes he had stashed a week earlier.

He stripped out of his wet clothes and put on his dry polys. Within minutes he had set up the tent and crammed two energy bars into his mouth. Like water in a desert, the rock-hard mixture of proteins and carbohydrates coursed through his weary veins with every chew.

When he crawled into the tent, the adrenaline immediately left him, and his body shook. His numb mind pushed his exhausted body into the depths of the sleeping bag, and within seconds, he fell asleep.

************ *********

The weary foursome paddled into the dark. They used an outlined ridge of trees against the disappearing horizon as their guide over the grueling last hour.

When they finally got back to the campsite on Hungry Ben Lake, an eerie darkness filled the woods, and they felt lucky to have found the camp.

So weary they could hardly stand, they pitched their tents but left everything else lying in the canoes. There would be no campfire.

None of them slept.

Chapter 29

Kelly, Allison, Grant, and Dillon woke to the sound of their tents flapping violently in the wind. The tents groaned and sucked air in and out, heaving like paper bags in a child's hands. The wind rushed unchallenged across the big lake and howled in protest as it slammed into the little island campsite.

During the night, the temperature had dropped into the single digits. The taunting northwest wind had turned the sky a heavy gray and whipped the waves into whitecaps. Light snow hurled sideways through the air.

The group put on their cold weather gear, then gathered around the fire in a futile attempt to keep warm.

"We've got to go back and look for Mike." Kelly looked intently at the others.

"Kelly." Grant gently tried to put his arm around her, but she backed away.

"I'm going back with or without you." Kelly insisted.

"No you're not, Kel." Dillon stood in front of her. "We searched that river for hours."

"But–"

"We looked on the sides of both shores." Dillon continued.

"And the water was freezing." Grant added.

"There's no way he's alive." Dillon said.

"Maybe he climbed out of the river and passed out on shore, out of our sight," Kelly implored. "Maybe he's alone in the canoe we left behind, struggling to make it back here." Now she yelled, "Maybe he's hurt!"

"No!" Dillon commanded.

"We all saw him fall out, Kelly." Allison tried to intervene. "We got to his canoe within a minute, and he'd already drowned. Or else. Or else we would have seen him."

"Grant. Please go back with me."

"I'm sorry." Grant hung his head. "We all care about you and

Mike, but it's no use."

"We've got to get back to civilization," Dillon demanded. "Then we'll get some help to look for Mike's body."

"Mike!" Kelly howled. The vision of Mike's drowning had played itself over and over all through the night. The fall . . . The cold . . . The knowing he was going to die. A hundred variations of the same nightmare haunted her mind.

Dillon put his arm around her. She turned and buried her face in the shoulder of his big jacket. Allison and Grant moved in and wrapped their arms around Kelly while her shoulders heaved and jerked in defeat. With all the might of a child ready to wail in pain, Kelly sobbed.

Even with her friends around her, she was alone.

So terribly alone.

************ *********

Mike woke at seven. He felt toasty inside his sleeping bag, though he could hear the wind outside. The well chosen, sheltered tent site had allowed him to sleep oblivious to the brewing storm.

He reached out and shook the sides of the tent. The ice under the rain tarp crackled for the second day in a row. Winter had begun. Soon all the lakes would freeze over, severely hampering any search for his body.

Suddenly his mind shifted. What about Kelly?

Shift again. With no body, how hard would Platinum try to prove he wasn't dead?

What was Kelly thinking right now?

God, he hated Platinum.

Was Kelly scared? His body began to shake.

How long would Platinum fight Kelly?

"Kelly, I'm sorry." He stared at the top of the tent, the words barely whispered. "Kelly, please God. Please be–"

He cut his own sentence in half. His mind reeled with anger as he thought how Platinum had forced him to act. *Required* him to take justice into his own hands. Now Kelly would have to fight alone. "Damn them!"

The alarm on Mike's watch snapped away his daydream. If he hustled, he could leave in five minutes. He needed a little over three hours to make the thirty mile bike ride to Ely where he had a car waiting.

When he crawled out of the tent, a tiny layer of snow blanketed the ground. The flakes blowing in the stiff wind concerned him. Losing the trail due to snow cover could be fatal without a compass. The low ceiling of dark clouds meant that more snow was coming soon.

He put his camouflage wind jacket over his polypropylene long underwear. Then he disguised himself with a long-haired black wig and a brown baseball-style hunting hat with earflaps. Finally, he stuffed his hands into camouflage hunting gloves, palm-lined with stickums for a good grip on the handlebars.

He rolled the wet clothes and wetsuit inside sleeping bag, then strapped it and the tent onto his camouflage painted mountain bike. A careful survey revealed nothing more then matted grass where he had slept. The light snow continued falling. Soon the white powder would cover the ground and any tracks he might make.

Mike punished the bike hard over the rough terrain toward Ely. He knew bikes weren't allowed anywhere in the BWCA, and hoped to make it to the car without being spotted or shot at by some quick-fingered poacher who might mistake him for a deer.

Mike's body moved into high gear. He ducked constantly to avoid branches. His arms heaved and pulled to steer the machine. Turning the handlebars, leaning into curves, Mike forced the tires over logs and stones. Roots, branches, and rocks tried to twist him up, force a fall. Each leg stroke required constant power.

Now the trail opened. Mike gained speed.

A curve. Suddenly, the rear tire warped against a deep snow-filled rut. The bike slammed down. Mike catapulted into a moraine of wet stone. His arms slapped the wet ground. His elbow bashed on a rock. "Deer path!" he yelled as he flailed his elbow into the air, then forced himself back onto the bike.

Push!

Mud holes, and large trunks tried to grab the cloaked unit. Mike dismounted and heaved it to his shoulder at a dead run. Obstacles became invisible. Throwing his leg up and over the seat. Back down. Then back on the bike, churning his legs at full throttle.

He had never used this trail before. When he had stashed his gear a week earlier, he had carried his bike in via canoe, under a tarp, until he reached his drop spot. He had trusted the map that this was indeed a trail, and had cross-referenced to verify his location using a hand-held global positioning system. Then he had returned to his canoe and paddled back to Ely.

After riding for nearly three brutal hours, the trail improved considerably. Mike raced closer to town. Now all he had to do was stay on the bike and drive his legs as hard as they would go. Everything from this point forward depended on pure speed.

Only a couple miles from the trailhead, Mike neared a giant Norway pine that obstructed his view. He zipped around it and rode straight into the barrel of a shotgun. The man behind the gun looked like Yeti. His long black hair and unkempt beard hid a filthy face of dirt.

His green army hat sported earflaps for the cold and a visor for the sun. Rips and tears camouflaged his dirt-colored shirt. Discolored rawhide gloves covered huge hands. Green army-pants tucked into brown pigmented leather boots, at least a size 16, with leather uppers strapped at mid calf.

With all the power within his grip, Mike slammed on the brakes. The tires stopped, but the bike continued forward, skidding on the dirt and loose snow. Mike swung his bike hard to the left. But the giant never gave an inch of trail. Mike slammed face first into the man's chest. Mike sailed off his bike, tumbling headlong into the undergrowth. The bike flipped onto its side. Then it spun from the momentum, spewing all of Mike's gear across the trail.

The grizzled man gawked. His mouth stood open.

Time froze inside a hundred heartbeats.

The impact never fazed the giant man. He said nothing. The shotgun remained in the crook of his left arm. It pointed down and ahead, exactly at Mike.

Somehow, Mike managed to dribble "'scuse me" through frozen vocal cords. Mike's heart pounded. His mouth turned dry. He knew the man and the gun watched his inability to move. He tried to look, but a sudden tunnel vision controlled his eyes.

Blackness changed into something round, but still black.

Black with a round dark hole in the center.

The barrel of the gun.

Everything else blurred.

Run! Run!

Mike wanted to run. His legs refused to move.

Run! Scream!

The barrel of the gun. Seconds and minutes seemed to blend.

Liquid cement poured through his arms and legs. *I've got to focus.*

Paralyzed. *The barrel of the gun.*

Run! Run! Mike's legs turned to dead stumps.

Breathe. *I've got to breathe.* The black round circle faded in and out. Other colors blurred. Head down, eyes closed, chest panting, Mike slid like a snake back toward the trail.

He dared not look at the barrel of the gun.

The giant said nothing. He didn't move.

Mike felt the wetsuit with his hand. He forced one eye open. *Keep breathing.*

The gun.

Mike forced his legs to lock into a crawl. *The gun.* Both eyes opened. He saw the trail. Giant black leather boots stood on the trail. Mike's eyes refused to follow them up. *The barrel of the gun.*

Go the other way. Now Mike crawled unevenly. Jerking. *Breathe. Don't look up. Don't look.* The barrel of the gun would burn out his eyes.

Breathe, breathe. Mike's sweaty wet hands gathered the sleeping bag, and other contents of his pack. *Why don't you say something? Say something!*

The boots moved a step away, then back toward him. They stopped.

Without looking up, Mike managed to strap the pack onto the bike. *Don't look. Don't look.* He lifted his heavy leg over the bar.

The big man only grunted.

Still unable to look, Mike slowly forced his numb legs to move. The bike teetered. His arms leaned heavy on the handles. *Don't look.* Hell, he couldn't look without falling over. A sixth sense told him the gun remained at his back as he rode away.

The bike continued to wobble. The image of the shotgun bore into him. His hands trembled. His muscles ached. Sweat bled from his skin. He finally turned to make sure the man and the shotgun were out of sight.

New demons raced into his mind. *What had he seen? What if he tells someone?*

Mike had no strength left. Just balancing was suddenly hard. *Breathe.*

Ten eternal minutes later, Mike saw the waiting Oldsmobile. Two inches of loose powdered snow was piled on it. "Thank you, God." *I've made it! I made it!* "Thank you."

He whipped off his hunting garb, but kept on the hat and wig. He threw his bike and everything else into the trunk. A full tank would take him 486 miles. All the way to Minot, North Dakota.

With a little luck and some decent weather, he'd make his final destination in a day and a half. Only a few stops for gas along old US Hwy 2 and he'd be at his secretly rented home in Tacoma, Washington.

************ *********

As the unkempt woodsman watched Mike ride off, his scowl deepened. If that wasn't the damnedest sight he had witnessed in a long, long time. It upset the grizzled man to see some weirdo on a mountain bike in the middle of *his* woods, near his home, where all the locals knew they weren't welcome.

His keen eye caught the flicker of something shiny lying in the snow. He bent down where Mike's gear had fallen and picked up a red jack-knife inscribed with *Platinum Insurance.* "Exactly what I need," the man's deep voice sounded hostile, "a souvenir." He put the knife in his trouser pocket and set off through the woods toward his cabin.

When he came within sight of the log cabin, he stopped and stared at his personal retreat. Nestled among towering pines, the small house with the native stone fireplace blended with the earth to become a part of the landscape. A tiny wisp of smoke filtered up against the light snow with the green pine backdrop.

He dug his gloved hand into his pocket and pulled out his new treasure. He ogled it for a short time in total silence. His eyes penetrated beyond the red casing of the knife, and he studied it as if it contained all the mysteries of the universe.

A snowflake landed on the casing of the knife. He wiped the white away and his eyes began to stare. *Platinum Insurance.* The snow continued to fall silently.

Snow piled onto the big shoulders, but the man did not move. His breath rose in warm plumes of vapor against the cold whiteness.

And he continued to stare.

As the snowflakes bunched together and came down faster and harder, the man felt rage begin to grow inside him. *Platinum Insurance.*

He held the knife high above his head and with one mighty thrust, buried it deep into the side of a white birch. He leaned heavily against the casing until it bent sideways, almost perpendicular to the blade.

"You're going to rust there till this tree dies." A snowflake landed on the red casing as he turned and walked away.

Chapter 30

Dillon broke from the group hug. "It took a whole day to get to this island, so we have a full day of canoeing ahead of us. We need to hurry because today we'll be canoeing against high winds in rough water. Let's get these tents down, grab an apple or an energy bar and be on the water in ten minutes."

Soon everyone stood on the rocky beach next to the loaded canoes. "Look at the whitecaps on those waves." Allison's face tensed.

No one else commented.

The waves crashed on the shore. The empty canoes rocked, slapped in the violent cradle. The wind grabbed at the trees in a steady drone. Snow flew sideways. A hundred thoughts swirled silently in the cold air. Miserable. Wet. Dead. Drowning. Fear.

Drowning.

"Kelly and I will go first," Dillon said. "When we paddle out, Kelly's going to do a right draw. It's the only way we'll be able to turn into the waves."

"What do you want us to do?" Grant asked.

"Watch us, and explain what's happening to Allison. Allison, you're going to do exactly as Kelly does, no matter how big the waves are." Dillon the drill-sergeant pushed Kelly and the nose of the canoe into the lake and jumped in.

The canoe heaved and rolled in the waves as Kelly and Dillon paddled perpendicular to the wind. When they had built enough forward momentum, Dillon hollered, "right draw." Kelly leaned out the right side of the canoe and reached with her paddle as far as she could. The waves slapped hard into the nose of the canoe and the cold spray shot into Kelly's face. She welcomed the physical battle as grief continued to sear through her mind. Her paddle dug hard and deep as she continued to draw the front of the canoe to the right. Meanwhile Dillon made sweeping arches, like a capital C, from the back left side.

When the canoe settled nose into the wind they slowed their pace, and paddled in place against the waves.

"We're going to come around and act as a wave breaker for you," Kelly screamed against the wind. "Allison, even if the waves hit you in the face, keep paddling. Don't stop no matter what!"

Before Allison had a chance to object, Grant pushed the nose of their canoe into the big waves. Allison paddled forward with all her might, as Dillon and Kelly maneuvered up wind to break the waves as much as possible.

"Right draw," Kelly commanded. "Push." She too, tried to push the lonely sorrow out of her mind.

It took every ounce of Allison's nerve to lean into the crashing waves. Her arms reached out to pull the canoe to the right as Kelly and Dillon fought to hold position next to them.

"Push, Allison." The force in Kelly's voice compelled a response.

"I am." Allison gasped.

Ever so slowly, the two canoes turned into the wind and began the long trek home. Only by watching the slowly moving shoreline could they recognize any progress.

They fell into a rhythm of long deep strokes. Dillon called it "digging water." Tediously and resolutely, they made headway against the bitter cold wind. No one said anything except "switch," commanding a simultaneous change of paddling sides in an effort to preserve strength.

Despite splashing waves, no one dared say anything as Kelly labored to keep everyone moving, concentrating on the task at hand. With each stroke, she leaned ahead with her body and reached the paddle far in front of the canoe, then pulled with her bottom hand and pushed with her top hand. Her body language, the fight in each stroke, told the others that they had better keep up.

After two ceaseless hours of struggle, similar to walking up a never-ending flight of stairs, they made it to the next lake. They remembered a little channel of fast water and felt great relief to be on course.

As morning turned to afternoon, the snow came down harder.

Sometimes the big flakes fell so heavy they obscured the shoreline only twenty feet away. The temperature stayed well below freezing the entire day.

The wind-driven snow blistered their faces into a bright, raw red. Their hands and wrists froze from exposure. Gloves would have been uselessly wet, and Allison found it hard to believe how the icy water actually felt warm. After a while, she dipped her frozen hands into the lake with each stroke in an attempt to warm them.

Miserable.

Cold.

Exhausted.

No one dared to stop paddling for fear of Kelly's stare, plus the dread of having to start again. They fought in mute misery against the storm, pausing only to gulp water, or swallow some of their limited ration of gorp.

By late afternoon they slowly paddled past a sign on the shore that said *Superior Natural Forest*, each one felt a silent, ghostly relief. The sign told them they were still on the right path, because Mike had carved the word *Natural* on top of the word *National* on their first day. Only about a mile to the public landing where their van waited for them.

The last hour of hard paddling stretched into a black hole, mentally and physically wearing Kelly to the point of collapse. As her body unconsciously stroked the paddle, hard and deep with every thrust, thoughts of the Boundary Waters she once loved tormented her.

Her psyche skipped back and forth between love for Mike and anger at the world. From nothingness, to love, and back to despair, until anger and despair numbed her mind, then nothingness took over. Her anger wasn't bitter, but rather a resigned resentment for all she had been through. Anguished at the prospect of facing the world alone, she silently shuddered. *How could Mike have left me now?*

The negative thoughts, the worries, and the terrible deep loneliness had all but destroyed Kelly. *Why did he stand in the canoe?* The repetition of the question stuck in her mind like a bad song that plays over and over again.

Drained by the emotional tug of war, she collapsed on the snow-covered beach. No one waited for her. No one, save her three friends, knew of the tragedy that had left her so alone.

The wind blew and pulled at the tips of the big Norway pines. A crow sitting in a leafless birch tree witnessed the foursome stagger onto shore. Their snow-covered van stood alone at the public landing.

Dillon heaved a Duluth pack out of the canoe and carried it to the van. It would only take a few minutes to strap the canoes on top and throw the gear inside. As he walked toward the van, a sudden sinking feeling overcame him. "Who has the keys?" Everyone stared at Dillon as the question registered. "Does anyone remember who had them last?"

"Mike went back to the van when we were about to shove off," Grant said. "After we got started on the first day, remember how he chastised himself for leaving the extra maps in the van? I think he had the keys with him."

"We searched through his pack when we looked for a map. Does anyone remember finding the keys?" Dillon's voice edged on panic.

Kelly picked herself up and stumbled to the van. She dug away the snow around the front of the van until she could get down and slide under it, like a mechanic lying on her back. Mike always left a spare key hidden under the front of the van, usually behind the front license plate somewhere. The key had to be there. "Give me a flashlight," Kelly growled.

"I can't believe it. We *always* have a spare key under the van, but there's nothing here." Kelly's voice screeched like fingernails on a blackboard. "Someone else look for it."

Dillon took the flashlight from Kelly and slid under the front of the van. Then he cleared away the snow at the back of the van and looked under there too. But there was no spare.

"At least we know where we are." Dillon tried to get a grip on himself. "We can pitch camp in the parking lot tonight. And when the blizzard ends, the county will bring a snowplow down the Fernberg Trail."

"I doubt it." Grant growled at Dillon.

"Why not?" Allison cried.

"Because we're twenty-something miles east of Ely and no one," Grant shook his head sideways in disgust, "lives down here in the winter."

"You better cool it, Grant." Dillon glared. "There's plenty of resorts between us and Ely and we'll find help."

"I bet." Grant collapsed on the ground, too exhausted to fight.

Dillon stared.

Allison whimpered – all alone in her own private misery.

Kelly trudged back to the canoes. She picked up a paddle and dragged it limply across the snow toward the van. Everyone watched in silence as Kelly took the paddle in both hands. She raised it over her head like an ax and screamed some incomprehensible growl as she slammed the paddle into the rear window of the van. Glass exploded through the silent falling snow.

"We can cover the window with our tarp," Kelly's red face looked raw and hard. She dropped the paddle to the ground to register her defeat. "At least we will have a warm place to sleep."

Grant crawled through the broken window to open the doors for the others. Beneath the shattered glass he saw all the maps lying on the floor of the van. He wept.

Chapter 31

The wind howled, rocking the van throughout the night. The tarp covering the back window flapped incessantly, making it virtually impossible to sleep. Kelly, Allison, and Dillon lay huddled together in the back of the tin box, buried under the sleeping bags and every piece of spare clothing they had. Grant slept alone on the bench seat.

Morning came slowly. A heatless sun concealed its hiding place behind gray clouds and blowing snow while the four weary soldiers secretly hid themselves behind the veil of sleep. Once awake, the harsh reality of a new day still far from home, without Mike, would substantiate their nightmares.

Now the white powder measured as high as their knees and it still came down. The wind whispered a taunting jeer as it raced through the pine boughs that bent under the weight of the ice and snow. "Worst night of my life," Grant grumbled and wiped the snowflakes from his face.

Kelly scowled. *How could anyone complain now, in the face of Mike's death?*

"We have two choices," Dillon offered. "We can all try to walk through this blizzard until we come to a cabin on the way back to Ely, or we can split up. If we split up, I suggest Allison and Grant stay here at the van with enough food to last for a few days, while Kelly and I walk toward Ely."

"We have another choice too, snowplow man." Grant stared at Dillon.

"What's your problem," Dillon shot back.

"Yesterday, you said the plows would come down the Fernberg Trail. It's practically a whiteout and you want to go on a boy-scout hike."

"I said, what's your problem."

"I don't want to go anywhere, and I don't like splitting up under these conditions. I see no reason why we can't wait for the blizzard to end, so we can get a ride into town in the plow." Grant augered his body into the snow.

Dillon walked slowly toward Grant, and both men grimaced in preparation for a fight.

"Hey!" Kelly shouted and jumped between them. "I don't give a damn what either of you hotheads want. I'm leaving. If I need to walk twenty-two miles to Ely by myself, I'm going to do it. I'm not waiting for a maybe somebody to save me." Kelly kept the truth to herself. *I've got to get help to search for Mike. He might still be alive.*

"I agree with the split-up idea," Allison said. "I'm so sore and exhausted from yesterday, I can hardly move."

"I'm staying right here." Grant said.

"It's settled then," Dillon declared. "Kelly and I will carry all the energy bars, along with a tent and two sleeping bags. That will be enough to last for three days. With any luck, we'll find a cabin where someone will be home. You guys keep the stove and the freeze dried foods."

Dillon had no gloves, so he wore a pair of thick polypropylene socks on his hands with plastic bags on top. He and Kelly each wore their poly and wool clothes under rain jackets, to keep the snow from sticking to them. They wrapped a pair of long underwear bottoms around their faces for protection against the stinging snow.

Swirling, wind-driven snow cut visibility to twenty feet as they waded through the deep powder at a crawl pace. At least they could follow the Fernberg trail to Ely, as it was the only paved road within a hundred square miles.

Poor visibility made it impossible to see any cabins from the road. Kelly's despair deepened as the chances of finding help for Mike blurred into white nothingness. She decided to tie a ten-foot rope between herself and Dillon to prevent separating in the storm. As long as they stayed together, she figured they could endure any weather. They carried extra warm clothes, and if the conditions turned to whiteout, they could always make camp on the side of the road and wait for the weather to improve.

They trudged along what they hoped was the right hand shoulder of the road. Blowing wind now reduced visibility to about five feet, forcing them to grope. They agreed if they found what appeared to be a driveway, they would search the area for a mailbox, or some other sign indicating a cabin. If they couldn't find a sign, they couldn't risk going down a fire service road and getting lost.

One plodding step followed another through the deep howling snow. Each tread pushed a hole into the snow up past the knees. After three terrible hours, Kelly finally spotted what appeared to be a driveway. She had to yank on the line to get Dillon to stop, or he would have missed it entirely. "Looks like a road goes in here," Kelly screamed and pointed.

They stumbled around the intersection with their arms in front of them. Everything was white, indistinguishable, a wild nothingness, and a windy sameness.

As Dillon fumbled his way toward "the driveway," he stepped into the ditch, and the step down caught him by surprise. He fell face forward, down into the belly of the ditch, jerking Kelly off her feet. She landed on top of him as they tumbled into a furrow of loose powder. The snow pushed up, then settled back down on top of them. It found holes in their armor of clothing, crawled down their backs, and into their pants, past their protective raingear. Layers of flakes mashed onto their faces, the heat of their skin acting as a magnet for the cold white dust.

Kelly heaved herself off Dillon, and yanked hard on the rope in a command to make him stand. "Keep looking for a sign," she hollered.

It took twenty minutes before they finally found a sign reading *North Country Retreat*. Kelly remembered visiting there alone with Mike on one of their first canoeing dates.

They continued, careful not to follow any cross-country ski paths that might lead them into the woods. Now, as they changed directions, the wind pushed at their backs. Finally, after plodding for another miserable half-hour, they saw a cabin directly in front of them. The lights were on. They pounded heavily on the huge door, all four fists banging away.

As the door opened, Kelly staggered inside, dragging Dillon with her. The door slammed shut. Cold and wind suddenly stopped. Quiet. It took a moment to adjust. They found themselves in the warmth of a log cabin.

************ *********

The man who opened the door sported a ponytail of long reddish hair. He wore a pair of Steger Mukluk sandals and a thick, soft-looking outfit resembling pajamas. He'd been perusing through his grandson's new picture book, "Thumbuddy You," and just getting ready to cozy up to a little fire when the knocking made him jump.

"Welcome to North Country Retreat." His eyes lit up with curiosity. "My name is Arlen and–"

"I'm exhausted." Kelly's voice broke. She struggled to wipe the tears from her eyes and continued, "I'm Kelly and this is Dillon. We walked all the way up from the public landing. We've been on the road for at least four hours and–"

Arlen interrupted, "Four hours? It must be worse out than I thought. The landing is less than a mile away. I knew it was bad out, but four hours . . . You're lucky you found me." Arlen felt stranded himself. He usually closed his place for the winter by October 9 or 10, but he had stayed on for a couple extra weeks to get a little work done. When the snow started, he regretted his decision to stay, but now his thoughts reversed. "Let me bring you something warm to drink and–"

"But I gotta tell you–" Kelly started. "My husband–" she blurted. "I'm worried about Mike. We have to call the police and get a rescue team to search for him. He still might be alive."

"There's no way he's alive, Kel. We would have seen him or–" Dillon blurted

Arlen started to interrupt, "What's going on–"

Kelly ignored Arlen as her eyes burned into Dillon's face, daring him to disagree with her again. "You're wrong, mister!" she screamed. "If anyone could make it out of there, Mike could. Until they show me his body, I'll never believe he's dead."

"Please tell me –"

"Arlen, we desperately need your help." Kelly's voice shook. Between sobs and hysterics, she told Arlen about Mike and the Three Forks River, and about her friends at the public landing. Arlen got a map so Kelly could show him where everything happened.

"We need to call the Forest Service and tell them what happened," Arlen said. "Use this map to tell them the exact routes you took. If you can't get through to them, call the Lake County Sheriff's office. The sheriff and I have been good friends for fifteen years. Here are the phone numbers. In this weather, I don't know what they can do to help, so all we can do is ask." Arlen put on his boots. "In the meantime, I'm going to get my snowmobiles gassed up and ready to go. We can't go anywhere in this whiteout, but it can't last much longer. When the weather breaks, we'll go to the landing and pick up your friends."

************ *********

Allison's new-found shoulder muscles ached so bad that she dared not move her arms. The exertion and the raw cold had zapped every ounce of courage left in her. She had no appetite and was still too far from safety to harbor any feelings of triumph. Thoughts of a nice hotel, with a hot shower, and a glass of wine filled her void. Her achy hands still felt cold, and she stuffed them under her armpits for warmth, certain they would never be the same.

She struggled to sit up for a look outside the van. More than pain, the fear of being alone forced her to look for Grant every ten or fifteen minutes. "Why doesn't he come inside?" she chanted out-loud, afraid of losing her mind. Grant sat twenty feet from the van on a small stump next to a fire.

The wind whistling through the van made it seem viciously cold. Despite her desperate need to get out to pee and stretch her aching back, Allison knew she would never leave the van unless her bladder forced the issue.

Hour after miserable hour passed. Now it was dark outside. Off in the distance a wolf howled. Then another cry – this time a bit closer. As she hid under the sleeping bags on the floor of the van, she dared an occasional look outside, almost expecting a wolf to stare through the window at her. “Grant,” she whispered, afraid the wolves could hear her.

There was no response.

“Grant,” her voice rose to a hoarse cross between a whisper and a yell.

Nothing.

“Grant,” this time, the hoarseness trembled and trailed off into tears. She lay under the blankets, too afraid to yell, too scared to look. She felt like a coward and a fool, but simply couldn’t help it. Her hand rose over her mouth to muffle her cry, and tears streamed down the sides of her face, then trickled into her ears.

In between gasps, she heard a sound that made her hold her breath. The sweet, very sweet, sound of a motor whispered in the distance. As the whine of the snowmobile engines grew steadily closer, she raced to put on her boots. “Oh!” she exclaimed through her tears, “We’re going to be rescued!”

Chapter 32

When Kelly, Dillon, Grant, Allison and Arlen walked into the Lake County sheriff's office early the next day, Kelly's senses were on full alert. Despite the continuing snowfall and the sheriff's stubborn reluctance during their phone conversation from the day before, she needed to convince the sheriff to help find Mike.

Worse than climbing the Diamond, Kelly felt she could hardly hang on. Emotionally drained, physically exhausted, and very much alone, she needed help. Right now.

She noticed that Sheriff Mason Crow looked like a rugged Native American in his late forties. He had black close-cropped hair, with a hint of gray at the temples. A little taller than most men, his frame looked tightly wired. Kelly was certain he'd be physically able to conduct a search for Mike, no matter how bad the weather.

A commemorative paperweight sat on Mason's paperless desk congratulating him for fifteen years as sheriff. Pictures and trophies strategically installed throughout his office offered the only other signs of life. On the north wall, a twelve-pound walleye twisted in vain against the jig that had captured it. The west wall featured a life-size photo of Mason kneeling next to an enormous bull moose, holding the monster's head up by the antlers, his rifle leaning on the big rack.

Another photo showed him standing with his sled dogs. The lead dog wore a green ribbon around its neck. The caption below congratulated him on placing third in the Beargrease – a grueling 500 mile dogsled race along the north shore of Lake Superior.

A magnificent white wolf stood alone in the far corner of the room. The animal was huge, its paws bigger than a man's hand. The steel cold eyes, growling snarl, and crouched posture froze the wolf into immortal combat readiness.

Arlen had told Kelly how Mason Crow loved his job, except for the occasional wilderness rescue mission to pick up dead bodies.

Mason had kept score and had recently shared the tally with his friend Arlen. "Forty-three dead in fifteen years."

"How'd they die?"

"Usually young people who flirted with rapids, or old men, self imposed heart attack victims of pushing beyond their limits. But last summer their no bear attacks, and only one drowning. I got lucky and spent a lot of time fishing this year."

When Mason first got the call from Kelly, he was pissed. Not that he didn't care if someone had drowned, and it wasn't his intent to hurt Kelly's feelings, but he couldn't believe the absurdity. What kind of moron would canoe the BWCA at the end of October? Why did he stand up in a canoe and jack around in freezing cold water? And why didn't they have a permit?

Now they crowded into his office, expecting him to act. And his friend Arlen encouraged the whole thing.

"To be perfectly candid with you, we are not one hundred percent certain how we should conduct this search," the sheriff said.

"What do you mean?" Kelly asked. "You've had all night to think about it!"

"The lakes have only a half inch of ice on them. We can't snowmobile into the area by lake, and we can't get there by boat or canoe."

"What about the trail running from Ely almost directly to the Three Forks River? We talked about it last night on the phone. It's right here on your map."

"We've already thought of that, but there are too many trees down on that trail. If we try to snowmobile in and go around the trees, our detours would take us into marshy swampland and partially frozen lakes. We could hike in, but it would take a day and a half to walk the thirty miles even without the snow."

"I can't believe you can't take snowmobiles in there. Aren't there any fire roads that can get you close?" Dillon asked.

"I'm afraid not. The closest we can get is five miles away, but from that point, there are no trails into the Three Forks. Kelly, to tell you the truth, I'm very sorry we can't do more for you right now. However, I do have some good news. All of my volunteers from the search and rescue squad are in town and ready to go and we've been promised a helicopter from the State Highway Patrol in two days–"

"Two days!" The bottom of Kelly's stomach fell, and her mouth suddenly tasted like acid.

"I'm sorry, but two days is the best I can do under these circumstances. Probability dictates your husband is already dead. With these facts, I couldn't make the state move any faster."

"Two days?" Kelly said it again under her breath, mostly to herself, but loud enough for the others to hear.

"That helicopter is the most sophisticated piece of search and rescue equipment in the state. It has infrared heat sensors, and if Mike is alive, we'll find him."

"You know, Sheriff Crow," Kelly pleaded with a last desperate hope to influence him, "when I walked into your office, I couldn't help but notice your picture of the Beargrease."

"Yeah, I used to dogsled competitively, but now I do it for fun." Mason had no idea where this line of thinking was taking him.

"Mike used to dogsled."

"Oh, yeah?"

"I think the same year you finished third, Mike came in fourth." Kelly walked over to the picture on the wall and touched it, as if it brought back Mike's old stories from before they had met.

Mason watched as Kelly stroked the edge of the frame.

"Mike mentioned one man in that race who made a big impact on his life. I think you're that man. He said the best part of the whole race was meeting you."

"I didn't realize Mike Montane was the same Mike I met on that race. I never knew his last name."

"He never knew your last name either. He always regretted that he couldn't find you, to call you, to get to know you better afterward. He always talked about this man named Mason."

"My sled was mired down in thick slush a foot deep. One of my dogs pooped on the run. We teach them to do that, and call it 'poop and scoot.' As the runner went over it, the poop caught onto the runner, and froze, slowing us down. Before I could stop the team to scrape it off, we went onto a little pond that was nothing but slop and slush below a tiny layer of snow. The ice built up so quickly that we got stuck. My dogs couldn't move the sled, and as soon as I got one side of the runners cleaned off, the other side froze in the muck." Mason recalled the story as if it had happened yesterday.

"Mike's team ran about a half mile behind me. When he got to the pond, he guided his team around it. He could have kept going, and easily finished ahead of me. But when he got to the other side, he stopped his team. Tied his dogs to a tree to keep them in a taut line, then came back onto the pond and worked with me to get my team out of its mess."

"Why did he stop?" Kelly asked.

"He said he could see I was tired. And I was exhausted. He may have saved my life, because I still needed to mush a half day to get to the next checkpoint."

"And then you went on to beat Mike in the race."

"Yep, by only ten minutes total time. The race was marked by total time between checkpoints, with mandatory checkpoints that required us to stop. Gave us time to sleep, rest the dogs, and regroup."

Kelly's heart raced as the sheriff made the emotional connection. In the steadiest voice she could muster, she added, "Mike told me about the nights around the campfire when you shared stories about you and your people."

"Mike Montane. He never told me his last name. Kelly, if anyone could have survived the cold water and this weather, I believe your man Mike could have. I owe it to him to give him every possible consideration. I'm going to call my rescue teams and get them here right away. We'll chain saw our way through the downed trees and get our snowmobiles out there. It may take all day, but if my crew knows a life may be at stake, they can work fast. We'll get our dog search and rescue team out there too, before the scent grows too old."

"Can I come too?" Dillon's attitude suddenly changed. As he

heard Mason talk about Mike and the Beargrease, it rekindled a small flicker of hope that maybe – maybe – Mike could still be alive.

"Absolutely. It will be essential to have you there to show us the exact place where his canoe tipped over, and to help sort things out at the scene. Make sure you're ready to go inside the hour." As Mason sat down at his desk and made the first call to his search and rescue team, he looked up at Kelly. "Mike Montane is a survivor, and if anyone can find him, we will.

Chapter 33

Mike struggled to keep his eyes open, exerting every drop of strength to stay awake. Only fifty more miles to Tacoma. He rolled down the windows, clapped his hands, and yelled an incomprehensible guttural sound of a man dying for lack of sleep.

His arms felt numb, his head bobbed. It jerked back up. His eyes lied to him, telling him it was okay to keep driving, that he could close one eye at a time.

Then Whap!

The tires rolled at seventy miles an hour onto the shoulder and over the rumble strip. The car jerked wildly. It balanced on two wheels for a split second. Mike's reflexes heaved the car back into its lane.

What little remained of Mike's adrenaline shot through his body, his frayed nerves twitched in rhythm with his pounding headache. His eyes burst through the weight of his eyelids, and in the same instant, his legs and arms turned into a gooey mush.

He drove on.

And on.

The adrenaline drained slowly out of his arteries, like a slow leak in a rear tire, almost imperceptible. Within twenty miles of the rumble strip incident, the glue on his eyelids tried to take another stand. The road pounded in a cadenced trance as the tires sang a lullaby.

Twenty five miles to go.

He pulled to the side of the road. As if his arm was coated in cement, he raised it slowly and uncrossed his eyes long enough to find the hazard lights button, then rolled out of the car.

He stood for no more than a moment, then leaned on the door, managing to raise his arms in a feeble stretch, then limped around the car three times. He got back in and drove away, the whole time his hazard lights flashed a beacon to anyone who cared to look.

Ten more miles to go.

He tried to do the math. Ten miles must be twenty minutes. Too long.

There. A convenience store beckoned and he staggered in for a cup of coffee, despite his distaste for the black magic.

"The coffee machine's broke." The teenaged clerk wore jeans so the waistline rode half-way around his butt.

"I need to stay awake." Mike mumbled while his brain screamed, *Fix it, you teenaged pimple.*

"Try some of these." The clerk pointed to a box of caffeine pills.

Mike extended his hand and the clerk placed the little box inside the palm, as if he were handing out communion.

"Put two of them under your tongue." The clerk offered. "They help me stay awake the night before an exam."

By the time Mike walked up the steps to his temporary new home, the caffeine had penetrated through his body. His hands twitched in a whole new way, almost jerking involuntarily, and an invisible surge of electricity circulated like an aura around him.

It took two hands to stab the house key into the lock. Despite his frayed nerves, he still felt nervous, as though he didn't belong. He paused, turned around, and took in the breathtaking beauty of Mt. Rainier. His red eyes soaked up the rare deep blue sky. Then green seared into his senses. Green grass and velvety moss clung to every part of the earth. Green everywhere.

The lovely descriptions couldn't do justice to the beauty surrounding him. He knew he would feel at home here, and smiled grimly. This would be home for a long, long time. The key turned in the lock, opening the door to a clean, quiet little living room scantily furnished, just as he had expected.

He closed the door, walked into the bedroom, and collapsed on the bed.

The caffeine pills transformed his dreams into nightmares, but despite the thrashing and kicking, Mike slept for the next eighteen hours.

Chapter 34

"Deputy Anderson," the deep voice on the phone sounded blunt.

"Yeah, Andy, it's Crow here. I want you to get your men ready to go to the Three Forks River on the Big Rock Trail."

"You gotta be kidding."

"I mean it."

"We talked about this last night, Mason. The guy's dead. Let's get a chopper in there when the weather clears."

"Listen, Andy. The man we're looking for is a friend of mine."

"I'm sorry, Mason. But if he made it out of the water, why didn't his friends see him on shore? Why didn't he respond when they hollered his name?"

"Maybe he passed out from the cold," the sheriff responded.

"Sheriff, with all due respect, the man's wet clothes and the freezing temperatures would've killed him long ago even if he made it out of the water."

"Andy, I *knew* the guy. If you were out there, I'd look for you, too. Now I want to make this very clear. We are not looking for a dead man. We are looking to save a life. And that's the attitude I want to take to the field."

"Okay, I hear ya."

"I appreciate it, Andy. Now, we've got thirty miles of trail and at least a couple feet of soft snow. We'll need a dozen snowmobiles and gear to cut our way through that old trail."

"I'm your man," Andy answered.

Mason hung up and never gave the logistics a second thought. Deputy Anderson would take care of the men, communications, chain saws, winches, shovels, gas, food, and water. The phone plopped back onto Mason's shoulder as he dialed his close friends, Anica and Jason Dailey.

The Daileys and their dogs Beau and Sprinter belonged to the Northstar Search and Rescue Dog Association (NSRDA). Most counties in Minnesota didn't use search and rescue dogs, and nowhere in the state did rescue dogs require certification. But Mason used them. He had personally witnessed these dogs locate missing children and find hunters who had been lost in the woods.

Mason felt lucky the Daileys spent their summer months living in his county and even luckier they were still in town. By this time of year, they had usually left for California, where dog search and rescue teams were licensed, certified, and an integral part of law enforcement.

"Hey Mason, I didn't expect to hear from you again until the weather cleared. What's up?" Anica asked in her usual warm and friendly voice.

"Jan, when I called last night, I didn't think we had any chance of looking for a live person. This morning things look different." Mason paused. "We think there might be a chance, a very slim one, that a thirty-eight year-old, Mike Montane, might still be alive somewhere near the Three Forks River."

"I see."

"We've decided to go into the Three Forks River via the Big Rock Trail on snowmobiles. Our team is already assembling and they're going to go ahead and cut out the downed trees."

"Mason, I'll need to meet with Kelly Montane and the other people you told me about. We need to find an article of clothing or something that's not contaminated. I can have my dogs ready to go in less than an hour."

"All right. We have a plow going down the Fernberg to the public landing right now. We have a locksmith following him, so they can retrieve the van. I think the van is the best bet for an uncontaminated piece."

"Ask them if Mike drove the van down to the public landing."

"Hang on." Mason put his hand over the receiver. "Hey, Kelly. Who drove the van down to the landing?"

"Mike drove all the way from Minneapolis." Kelly answered.

"It appears Mike drove all the way from Minneapolis." Mason relayed and looked at Kelly simultaneously.

"Mason, make sure no one gets inside that van. Keep it locked.

Tow it back to Ely. Beau and I can meet you at the Big Rock Trailhead in an hour. Make sure everyone involved is with you at the trailhead. I need to ask a few questions. Jason isn't home, but I'll leave a note for him."

"Okay. I'll have a team waiting for Jason and Sprinter when they get there. I'll see you in an hour."

The moment Mason hung up, Kelly had questions. "I understand why we can't fly, given today's poor visibility, but couldn't we use a power boat or a hovercraft?"

"We can't break through the ice with a motor boat. You're lucky you were able to canoe out of there yesterday. In one day's time, the ice is already an inch thick in places. Besides, the water is too rocky and shallow for a motor." Mason didn't enjoy explaining himself, but could see that Kelly would hound him until she felt satisfied. "And we can't use a hovercraft because we don't have any, and I don't think they'll work well over powdered snow."

"But you're not sure? You mean there is not one hovercraft in the state?"

"I'm not sure about that either. I'm going to call the Minnesota Interagency Office next, and I'll ask them. I'll let you know."

"Who are they?"

"They're the folks who connect all the dots from one law enforcement agency to the next so we're all working together. If there's a chance we need a helicopter in there, they'll contact the highway patrol to arrange it. They'll be monitoring our communications to assist with any medical personnel and other needs."

Kelly cut him off. "How are you going to communicate without a cell phone?"

"The Forest Service has 'repeater' stations set up on towers on the biggest hills throughout the Boundary Waters. They receive a broadcast from a hand held radio, then repeat the message to the next site, and the next site after that. You have to trust me. I'm as good as it gets up here, and I'll do everything in my power to find Mike."

*********** *********

As the first group of snowmobilers raced down Big Rock Trail, they moved past a cabin tucked almost invisibly into the thick woods. The Ely locals had several unique names for the owner, but most people called him Goliath.

The man was a true loner who allowed no outsiders to get near his home, with only a few exceptions. The hardware store used a four-wheeler with a special trailer to run supplies and groceries out to his cabin once a month. The delivery person had explicit directions to put everything quietly on the porch, take the handwritten list for the next order, and leave.

The hermit had established a credit line at the hardware store and paid an extra 30% for the conveyance charge. His secluded extravagance created a wealth of rumors. Some locals claimed Goliath was mentally retarded, supported by an inheritance. Others speculated that he had inherited a family trust. But most people figured he was a former NBA player. Probably one of those million dollar failures who got jeered by the fans and chastised by the press until he became a recluse.

Welded sculptures surrounded the remote cabin. Goliath made one-of-a-kind people statues using spare metal parts. One of his figures was a four-foot tall snowshoer. Old radiator parts formed the snowshoes. The snowshoer himself consisted of a thousand parts, ranging from the hubcaps off a tricycle for the face, to hundreds of little ball bearings that made up his beard. Statues of motorcyclists, skydivers, sailboarders, archers, bowlers and countless other sports enthusiasts stood littered across his yard.

In the winter, even more rumors circulated when Goliath locked up his cabin and disappeared until spring. No one ever saw him leave, and only the hardware store owner knew when he arrived home again. As the spring buds came onto the trees, the UPS man made his annual trek to the remote cabin to pick up the strange artwork. Most pieces were shipped to Florida, where Goliath supposedly sold his work at local art fairs.

As the snowmobilers raced past the hermit's cabin and the

snow-covered Platinum knife still buried in the tree, Goliath stood outside in his overalls and tattered jacket. He'd been out chopping wood for the fireplace and had worked up quite a sweat. He stuck his hands in his pockets to warm them as he turned and watched the men and their machines whiz by.

He growled a deep-throated snarl. He never saw the thrill of racing one of those loud machines through the woods. All the smoke, noise, and loud people reminded him of the city. Wherever they were going, they were in a real hurry.

When they were out of sight, he grabbed his splitting mall and turned his attention to his stack of firewood. He brought the heavy mall over his head, and slammed it hard into a knotted section of pine. Despite the knots holding the wood together, the force of the mall ripped the wood in half. "Ought to about do it." Goliath talked aloud to himself out of habit. "That's enough firewood for when I get back next spring. Until then, it's goodbye winter." He smiled at the thought of being able to leave the cold, the shoveling, and the ice behind. Tomorrow his flight left for the warm, sunny beaches of Florida.

"Perfect timing." In his gruff voice, he almost sang the words to himself.

************ *********

The Big Rock Trail parking lot could barely fit a half dozen cars. Seasonal hunters, bird watchers, and occasional day hikers were the only ones who used the trail. After about three miles, it became hard to follow as it dwindled to no more than a deer path.

By the time the tow truck arrived with the van, the advance team reported they were already half way to the Three Forks River. The deep snow made it possible to ride right over most of the smaller trees lying in the trail, and everyone was pleased with their progress.

Anica Dailey had Beau leashed, and the excited German shepherd whined, then pawed the air and arched his back at the prospect of playing "Hide and Seek."

Anica took charge. “Before I open your van, I want all of you to remember the best you can. Did anyone other than Mike sit in the driver’s seat?”

“I did when I unlocked the doors.” Grant looked down. “When we first got back to the van and couldn’t find any keys, Kelly smashed out the back window, and I crawled in. I went right up to the driver’s seat to press the door unlock button, and I’m pretty sure I either sat on or touched the seat.”

“That’s okay. We need to know. We’re looking for an uncontaminated piece of clothing – something that no one else touched but Mike. This piece will have thousands of microscopic skin rifts on it that are unique to Mike, and Beau will use it to find him, if it’s at all possible.”

“When I slept in the back of the van, I was cold, so I piled everything I could find on top of me.” Allison suddenly felt terrible that she had been such a wimp.

“Let me go to the back of the van, and we’ll pull those items, to see if we might find something Mike alone touched or wore.” One by one, Anica tossed out all the tents, sleeping bags, and all the clothes. Then, hidden under the bench seat of the van, they found what they needed.

It was a brown paper bag of Mike’s clothes. They were the clothes he had worn for the drive to Ely – all his cotton clothes, including his cotton underwear. Mike refused to wear any cotton in the outdoors. He had told countless people, “Cotton gets wet, then you get cold.” He always bragged about the high quality of his polypropylene socks, his polar fleece, and even his poly mesh underwear. Mike didn’t care that polypropylene quickly took on the odor of the worst armpit. No sir, Mike Montane absolutely never wore cotton in the outdoors.

“All right!” Kelly shouted. “Now what do we do?”

“I’m going to scent Beau by letting him smell the contents of the bag. After that, I’m going to use a plastic glove to place some of the items in a zip-locked plastic bag to carry with us. The left-over items will stay here, in another zip-locked bag. When Jason and Sprinter get here, he can use it to scent Sprinter, and he can bring the bag with him. I want to make sure both dogs get as fresh a scent as possible." As Anica spoke, she looked around to make sure everyone understood.

"Mason, please instruct your deputies to make sure no one touches the bag. When Jason gets here, he'll use sterile gloves to handle it, and he'll bring it with him to the Three Forks River. We've got to do everything we can to preserve the scent."

"I thought we were going to the Three Forks River to find Mike's body. Not take some mutt for a walk. The river is twenty or thirty miles from here." Dillon looked around for support. He swore under his breath, and shook his head wondering how he had bought into Kelly's ridiculous speculation.

"Shut your mouth, Dillon." Grant glared. "Let them do their job the way they want to do it."

"The first thing I'm going to do is fire Beau." Anica ignored Dillon.

"What do you mean, you're going to fire him?" asked Kelly.

"I'm going to give him a scent. Then I'm going to tell him to go and find."

"But we're thirty miles from the point where Mike tipped his canoe. Can your dog remember the scent that long?" Kelly asked.

"I think he can," said Anica. "And if Beau needs to be scented again, we'll do it when we get up to the Three Forks River."

"You can't be serious." Dillon piped in.

"It can't hurt us to have Beau hot on this particular scent now. If we need to scent him again near the river, it will only reinforce who we are looking for." Anica felt obliged to answer.

"Dillon, the sheriff trusts Anica and her dogs." Kelly tried to keep everyone focused.

Anica ignored Dillon's stare into the sky and called Beau over to her. "Beau, smell. Go and find!" She opened the bag and let Beau smell the contents for all of one second.

Immediately, Beau pulled on the leash, bringing Anica to the very end of the trail nearest the parking lot. When he got to the trailhead where the cars parked, the dog let out a whine. It continued to whimper as it walked around in a tight circle.

"What's going on, Anica?" Mason was startled to see Beau's behavior.

"Beau is telling me that the strongest scent for Mike is right here."

"Are you sure?"

"Yes. Beau's telling me that Mike was here."

"That's impossible," yelled Kelly. "We saw him drown on the Canadian border." She envisioned Mike lying under the canoe they had left at the Three Forks River in a futile attempt to stay warm. Every minute wasted could mean life or death, and she needed everyone to stay focused.

"Maybe Beau smells a cookie." Dillon wisecracked.

"Shut up, Dillon." Kelly said. "This isn't funny."

"Look everyone. I can only tell you what my dog is telling me. He says that this point, right here, is the strongest scent of Mike. He isn't pulling me down the trail, or up the road. He's trained to follow a scent to its strongest point. I don't know how to explain it, but this is it." Anica had to stand by her dog, despite the fact that it made no sense to anyone.

"So what do we do now?" Kelly raised her arms in exasperation.

"I suggest we see what happens when we get to the river." Mason tried to keep everyone moving with the original game plan as he had promised Kelly.

"I don't know what to say, Mason." Obviously disappointed, Anica wished Mason had defended her. "I guess I'll go with the program. But when Jason and Sprinter get here, I want to make sure he fires the dog a couple blocks away. See if Sprinter leads to this same spot. Will you do that for your friend?"

"That's a great idea, Anica. Consider it done."

Kelly was dumbfounded by the whole thing. Impatient, and not wanting to lose the sheriff as her ally, she hollered out, "Let's get moving to the river before it gets dark."

Chapter 35

By the time they got to the Three Forks River, only two hours of daylight remained. The volunteers had done remarkably well preparing the trail. Instead of the time-consuming job of cutting and moving trees off the trail, they were able to pile the deep snow, effectively making a series of ramps over the top of the downed trees.

The river widened into a lake at the trailhead junction. Mason pulled out his binoculars and looked to the other side where the canoe sat. It looked like no one had been there. "Hey Dillon, take a look at the canoe. Is everything the way you remember it? Do you think Mike was there after you left, or took anything with him?"

"Everything looks the way we left it, except there's a lot of snow covering it up. I don't see any tracks either. How about you, Grant?"

"It looks the same to me. I can't be a hundred percent sure, but I don't think anything has moved. And I remember looking back as we paddled away."

"Here's how we're going to proceed: six people are going to cross over to the Canadian side, two at a time. They're going to stay on this wide part of the river, well upstream of the current." Mason pointed across an area wide enough to be considered a lake. "They're going to wear snowshoes and each group will carry an inflatable raft between them. I think the ice here is thick enough to support us, but we're not going to take any chances." Mason barked out directions. "If the ice breaks, fall forward into the raft. Every raft will have a rope tied to it, so we can haul you back to shore. Is that understood?"

Everyone nodded yes and waited for orders.

"Deputy Anderson, you take Dillon with you to the other side. Take some pictures. Then I want you to brush off the snow and take more pictures. Try not to move or disturb anything in the process." He turned to look into Anica's disappointed eyes. "Do you feel comfortable crossing on this thin ice?"

"If the other guys make it across, I guess I can handle it."

"Thanks." Mason smiled. "Once Andy and Dillon are halfway across the lake, Deputy Hillstrom, Anica, and Beau will cross. Then I need two more volunteers to cross."

A couple of the men raised their hands.

"Mike's canoe tipped on the Canadian side of the river. You'll probably find his body downstream from the point where the accident occurred," said Mason.

"You don't think he made it, huh?" asked Anica.

"Now that we are here, I'm afraid not." Mason shook his head and looked down as he spoke. "There's no way he could be alive."

"Why do you think that?"

"Because he was wet. Given the cold water and the freezing air temperatures, he would have frozen to death unless he made it back to the canoe to get dry clothes. It appears no one has touched the gear over there."

"Beau and I will find his body."

"I appreciate your help, Anica." Mason gently patted her back in a gesture of friendship. "All right, the rest of us are going to stay on this side. We're going to push through the forest until we get to the river opening. We're going to scour the shore to look for Mike's body."

While Mason spoke, Kelly sat at the edge of the frozen lake. Unmoving, she stared at the immobile canoe, buried under the snow. The air became bitter cold. Hope turned brittle. Raw. Only a miracle would find him alive, but she didn't believe in them anymore. Her body shook.

"Kelly, I'm sorry." Mason knelt down next to her, and spoke as gently as he could. "I can have one of the boys take you back to town if you'd like."

Kelly gasped. "Mike . . . I had hoped that the canoe would've been gone."

"I'm sorry."

Kelly's red eyes looked at the Sheriff. "I don't want to go back to Ely. I . . . I want to wait till you find his body. I have to see him." As she reached out, Allison came up from behind the sheriff, took Kelly's hand, and sat next to her.

"I'll stay here with you, Kelly."

As Kelly buried her head in Allison's shoulder, the rest of the group fanned out to begin their search. The thin ice held up and now Anica, Dillon, Beau, and the two sheriff's deputies stood near the beached canoe.

"Beau." Anica got the dog's attention to begin the search again. "Beau, smell. Go and find!"

Sheriff Crow watched Beau through his binoculars as the dog snapped his master's line out and began the hunt. First the dog walked over to the canoe, then turned away from it, and headed toward the beach. Beau walked toward the beach and stood for a whole minute at the water's edge as if he were thinking about something. Anica remained behind her dog and watched.

"What does the dog think now?" Dillon asked sarcastically. No way could a dog track in snow.

"Wait a minute and give him a chance," said Anica. "Beau, find. Find!"

Beau stood at the water's edge for several seconds longer before he finally backtracked away from the shoreline. He pulled his master and together they trudged through the deep snow, past some monster boulders and into the woods. It wasn't easy to keep up with the dog, as he pulled harder and harder through the snow.

"Good boy, Beau. Find 'em," Anica encouraged.

From Sheriff Crow's vantage, it appeared to be a game of Follow the Leader. First, the dog plowed through the snow, then came Anica in knee-high steps trying to avoid tripping over anything hidden in the powder. Two feet behind, the two deputies moved like dancers trying to stay in the footprints she had made. And finally came Dillon, his knees lifting the highest of all, probably trying to make sure no more snow inched its way down into his boots.

"Where the hell are we going?" Dillon muttered loud enough for the others to hear. "I said, hey. What are we doing? We're heading into Canada. The water is the other way."

"Would you please be quiet and give us a break, pal." Deputy Anderson snapped at Dillon.

Beau whirled round and round in a tight circle behind a pile of twisted trunks, then put his feet into a small ditch.

"Your man is either here, or was here. My dog is getting a real strong presence."

"Your dog got a strong presence in the parking lot thirty miles away – on the other side of the lake, too," Dillon quipped.

Andy turned and pointed a menacing finger. "I said knock it off."

"Find him, Beau."

Beau whined and pawed into the hollow. Snow flew everywhere. The dog dug his snoot deeper and deeper into the snow. Anica, the two deputies, and Dillon watched the dog work.

As it became increasingly obvious that the dog would find nothing, the smirk on Dillon's face grew exponentially. "Dogs tracking through snow. Give me a break."

*********** *********

When Jason and Sprinter arrived at the Big Rock Trail, an under-dressed deputy honked the horn of the squad car from three blocks away. The deputy paced around the car in an effort to stay warm. "Hey, Jason." The deputy shouted and waved his arms. "It's about time you got here. They have an 'uncontaminated' piece of clothing in the squad for you."

"You look cold, deputy." Jason flashed a disarming smile. He opened the back gate of his Blazer and his yellow lab, Sprinter, jumped out.

Sprinter was a different type of search and rescue dog. She had been trained as an air-scent dog, the kind that runs free to search large areas in a short period. As an air-scent dog, her main purpose was to search for living or recently deceased people. Sprinter didn't track the same way Beau did, following a trail from point A to point B. Instead, Sprinter did more of a zigzag type of search, before ending up at the same point B.

The moment she heard the command, Sprinter came to attention, ready for her momentary sniff. "Sprinter. Smell. Go. Find!" She took off.

The lab ran in an erratic pattern heading in the general direction of the trailhead, like a bird dog trying to scare up pheasants. As she bounded toward the trailhead, Jason and the remaining deputy walked behind her, always giving her plenty of space. When Sprinter got to the parking lot, she slowed and carefully scoured the area. Her nose worked a thousand twitches per minute while her head stayed down and her tail swayed in the sky.

In a flash, Sprinter turned and ran up the trail as if chasing a deer. But as soon as she got about fifty yards from the parking lot, she turned and came back to the same parking area. Then the dog barked incessantly, at absolutely nothing. She turned and ran back to Jason and jumped on him, almost pushing him over. Then she ran back to the parking area nearest the trail and barked at a ghostly scent.

"Deputy, Sprinter tells me your drowning victim was right here – at this trailhead parking lot. I'd bet on it."

"I'll be damned." The deputy looked at Jason. "Your wife said the same thing."

Chapter 36

When they radioed Sheriff Crow with the news, he was dumbfounded. "You'd better get Jason and Sprinter up here to the Three Forks River right now. The other folks are heading back from the Canadian side of the river, and they tell me Beau indicated that Mike had been there too. I don't see how that's possible."

When they brought Sprinter to the Canadian side, the dog led Jason to the same hiding spot that Beau had discovered. Then Sprinter abruptly turned back to the beach, where she whined and barked across the water.

By the time the men and dogs finished looking up and down both sides of the river, everyone could hardly stand from the exhaustion of trudging through the snow. They had searched every nook and cranny, under every overhanging branch, and had even walked in the water immediately next to the shoreline, a full mile downstream from Mike's fall.

As hard as everyone looked, no one found a map, a water bottle, or even a box of waterproof matches. They found no evidence whatsoever that someone had fallen into the river.

Light snow sizzled as it landed on the dozen gas lanterns that encircled the cast of friends and volunteers. The dark woods made any further search virtually impossible.

Allison's body shook and her teeth chattered, but she still sat next to Kelly. Even the shadowy light of the lanterns couldn't hide the puffy worn-out look in Kelly's drooping face.

Despite Allison's company, Kelly's mind circled in lonely dark thoughts. How could the dogs say Mike had been on the Canadian side of the river, and back at the trailhead? Maybe Dillon was right and the dogs were useless. Why did the dogs both go to a place in the woods, out of sight from the water? How did Mike get *there* of all places? If he was there, why didn't he take the canoe, or some of the gear that had been left behind? The dogs must've smelled an animal or food. Nothing made sense. "Nothing." Kelly mouthed the words.

Dillon thumped his cold feet in the snow and mumbled to himself. His face wore a deep scowl. He hated Deputy Anderson for his authoritative attitude, and wanted more than anything to proclaim the dogs a joke.

Grant and the others accepted the whole thing passively. They stood with their hands in their pockets, waiting for Sheriff Crow's next orders.

"All right," Sheriff Crow said, "let's add up what we have–"

"What about the dogs?" Anica interrupted.

"Anica, I don't know what to tell you," Mason said.

"Jason and I have a theory."

"Let's have it."

"Beau tells me that Mike was behind those big rocks that are fifty yards inland from where the canoe tipped." As she spoke to Mason, she turned to look at Dillon who rolled his eyes. "And Sprinter tells Jason that Mike was once at that same spot, then Sprinter led him back to the lake."

"So what?" Dillon asked in the most sarcastic tone he could muster.

"I don't have any idea of how it happened, but we speculate that Mike may have passed out in the rocks. Then he swam over to this very trail, and hiked out to the trailhead, where a car picked him up." Anica hoped to get support from some of the other members of the rescue team.

"That's ridiculous!" Dillon flung his arms up in the air in disbelief. "That beached canoe is a way downstream."

Kelly's eyes darted back and forth between Dillon and Anica, but her mind whipped even faster. How could Anica and Jason even suggest such a thing? The thoughts burned through her mind as if they were playing games with her.

"You might be right Dillon, but then how do you explain both of our dogs telling us that Mike was in the parking lot at the trail head?"

"Because they looked for a Nut Goody, or a female dog in heat, or maybe someone took a big shit at the end of the trial. How do I know?"

"Dillon, zip it." Mason glared at him. "We're all tired and we need to keep our cool. Quite frankly, Anica, I don't know what to think about your idea. I mean, how could Mike have walked thirty miles over rough terrain, in a blizzard, after swimming across a river with a strong current in ice water that would kill you in three minutes or less?"

"That's right." Dillon couldn't help himself. "You know, we saw the man drown." His voice got progressively louder.

Kelly sat in the darkness. Now nothing mattered. The voices became a shrill drone inside the empty void in her mind.

"We've thought of all that." Jason piped in.

"I don't mean any disrespect to you or your dogs," the sheriff said, "but I think your theories are too big a stretch. It's pretty clear to me that Mike is dead. Given the ice-cold water and the long line of improbabilities suggested here, he's probably at the bottom of the river. We've got a drag line stretched across the river about a mile downstream. That line has treble hooks placed a foot apart and will act as a net to snag anything that passes through there. Chances are that Mike's body will get pushed downstream, and we'll pick him up in our line." Mason paused to get the right words. "Tomorrow we're going to bring in a couple of divers to search the area where his canoe tipped."

"Look, sheriff," Anica said, "maybe we've been looking in the wrong places when we searched down river. Beau and Sprinter found nothing down there. What if we give the dogs one more chance, and initiate a search from thirty yards down the trail toward Ely. What can it hurt?"

"Oh, man." Dillon couldn't believe it.

Mason turned and looked at Dillon. "You know, Dillon, I used to think the same thing you're thinking right now. I mean, why does the earth spin, and how can these dogs tell us where a man has been?"

"That's my point. Think about it. It's been windy and snowing. We've got between two and three feet of snow on the ground, and the only place for the dogs to run is down the hard packed snowmobile trail. Of course, they're going to run down the trail. Those dogs would probably bring us right to the Ely Bake Shop if we let them."

"Dillon, you never let me finish my sentence."

"Oh, okay, Sheriff. As if you need my permission." Dillon whirled away from the others and raised his arms to the sky.

Ignoring him, Mason turned to Jason and Anica, "We've seen your dogs do some miraculous things in the past. I can't figure it out, but let's give 'em one more chance." Mason had personally witnessed the dogs find a dead man under a foot of ice on a four-mile-around lake, more than a month after his disappearance. Authorities had used divers and had given up on the search before Mason and his friends brought in their dogs.

But today he couldn't help but silently side with Dillon.

************ *********

When the whole group had moved about fifty yards down the trail, Jason tied a small flashlight to Sprinter's collar. Then he gave Sprinter the scent again. The dog took off down the trail and the flashlight bobbed and weaved in the darkness. Jason and one of the deputies followed behind in a snowmobile, always giving Sprinter plenty of room to do her thing. If the dog ran all the way to the trailhead parking lot, they were prepared to follow.

The rest of the group waited fifteen minutes to give them a good head start. They didn't want to scent Beau, only to have him running up the exhaust end of a snowmobile.

When Anica fired Beau, the whole group followed behind as the big German shepherd walked Anica down the trail. Mason gave her a quarter-mile cushion of space before the caravan of snowmobiles started to inch their way back toward town.

"At the speed we're going, we'll be home at 4 AM if were lucky," Dillon complained to Allison as she clung to his back. She never heard a word he said, convinced that the cold had stopped her brain from functioning.

As Anica and Beau plodded down the trail, her flashlight

bobbing up and down with every step, the line of snowmobiles puttered behind them.

Just when Anica was ready to call it quits, Beau stopped. Maybe Beau had forgotten about the scent, and was simply "taking her for a walk." Dog search and rescue wasn't a perfect science, and no one, including Anica, really knew the outer limits of the dog's capabilities. What Dillon had said, and the way he said it . . . His harsh words made her angry, but more importantly, gave her cause to doubt as well.

Beau stopped in a huge clearing where one lone, giant evergreen tree towered above them. The tree reached into the darkness. "Find 'em, Beau." Anica hoped her dog hadn't stopped to smell an animal that had crossed the path.

With a little encouragement from his master, Beau left the trail and walked through the deep snow toward the western edge of the clearing. Anica signaled with her flashlight to Sheriff Crow and the team of snowmobilers.

Mason stopped his sled and told everyone to turn off the machines. He wanted to make sure no exhaust would hamper the scent. Then he and two of the deputies hurried toward the giant Norway, with Dillon and Grant in pursuit.

Anica stopped her dog when she saw the rectangular imprint. She had to save it for Sheriff Crow, the deputies, and especially for that creepy Dillon to see.

As she motioned with her arm and flashlight to the others to hurry up, she patted Beau on the back and praised her dog. He was the best of the best. How could she have ever doubted her main man, Beau?

When Mason and the others arrived at the area sheltered by a dozen pines, they formed a semicircle of onlookers. Half a dozen flashlights pointed at the imprint. It was unmistakable. A tent had been there.

"Look at that impression. All the surrounding area has long grass and weeds sticking up through the snow. No vegetation is showing where the imprint is. Clearly someone camped here in the last day or so." Mason's voice rose.

"It appears that a tent was here all right. But a tent could have knocked down the grasses three weeks ago. The impression of a tent would still show." Dillon paused in exasperation. "This has nothing to do with Mike." Dillon couldn't believe they were still out there. It was near midnight and his girlfriend was close to hypothermic. "Some hunter might have camped here. But Mike's tent was left with his canoe. He didn't have an extra tent with him, and there's no way he could have crossed that river to get over here. This is ridiculous." Dillon's face and body contorted with skeptic disgust.

Kelly looked silently at the imprint. Now her body shook from the cold and her mind immobilized into a frozen nothingness. Though her eyes saw and ears heard, her mind had shut down long ago, unable to cope with the grief and loss that consumed her.

"You might be right Dillon, but–" began Mason.

"I'm tired of this bullshit. I'm leaving now, and I'm taking Allison home with me. I don't give a rat's ass about any scent." Dillon ran toward the snowmobile where Allison waited.

Allison curled up next to the seat trying to retain the only warmth she could find. Dillon almost knocked her off as he slammed the machine into high speed and tore down the trail.

"Anica, I think you and Beau did a fine job today." Mason smiled at his friend. "Don't let him bother you."

"Mason, I'm beat." Anica normally had the spunk and energy of a kid, but her face drooped in exhaustion. Mason could see she had nothing left to give.

"All right. Let's call it a day. Let's go home, and meet back at my office tomorrow at nine to continue our search. We have a mystery."

Chapter 37

When the dogs went back out to the tent imprint area the next day, they found absolutely nothing new.

The weather cleared, and at Kelly's insistence, the state patrol brought in their big helicopters to complete an infrared search of the entire area. They, too, found nothing.

The drag-line placed at the end of the river didn't even catch a fish.

They brought in scuba divers who searched the area where the canoe had dumped, expecting to find something, anything. Instead, after two days of searching in the ice-cold water, the only thing the divers caught was a cold.

The sheriff and his deputies were perplexed, and privately questioned Kelly's story. They individually interviewed everyone in the group to ask them details of the canoe trip, the accident, the search for Mike, and the escape back to their van without a map. Each individual story remained *exactly* the same.

After five weary days, Mason Crow called off the search. He told Kelly and the rest of the group they would keep the dragline in the water. His men would check it once a week. Mason assumed they would find Mike's body in the spring. When the water temperatures warmed, the body would float to the surface.

************ *********

During the long drive back to Minneapolis, no one had much to say. Allison had taken a flight from Duluth back to Michigan, while Grant and Dillon mutually agreed to stick around Minneapolis to help Kelly through the memorial service. They didn't want her to be alone, and privately, they worried about her breaking down. They remembered how Kelly had crumbled after Alex's court case. They recalled Mike's description of Kelly after Alex had died. "It's as if she wants to be in a coma herself. She lies in the bed and stares at the ceiling, unable to move or respond. I feel like she is trying to put herself in Alex's place, to somehow undo all the terrible things that happened."

Kelly lay down in the back of the van for the five-hour ride back to Minneapolis. She rested on her back, her head and body floating in the relative comfort provided by the sleeping bags spread out under her. All through the ride, she gazed up and out the window, watching as the treetops passed by. The hum of the tires had a mesmerizing affect, and she drifted in and out of a fitful sleep.

While she lay awake, she directed all her thoughts toward Mike. She lived and relived his drowning. Drowning in ice-cold water.

Drowning.

Ice-cold water.

What a horrible way to die.

When Kelly fell asleep, her dreams brought her back to that fateful day with Al. The sudden shove. The sound of the impact as the car hit her. The screaming when she saw her sister lying on the pavement. The ambulance ride. The first time she saw Al in the emergency room. The way Al's heart monitor beeped faster despite the heavy drugs. Al knew Kelly was there. She knew.

Alone with her dreams, Kelly cried. Softly, quietly, for herself and the two people she loved the very most.

************ *********

Despite his worries for Kelly and his terrible doubts, Mike's first week in Tacoma was a busy one. Shaving his head and starting a mustache became the first order of business. Then he dyed the mustache black. A new look for a new man.

He went to the library to search through the obituaries of the last year, looking for a picture of a man near his age that had died in the Seattle area. When he found Roy Dobson, he knew he had a good match. Then he visited a local beauty shop and showed the beautician a photocopy of Roy's picture, telling her they were throwing a surprise look-alike party for him. She put together a matching toupee that fit perfectly. With the mustache and a little makeup help from the beautician, Mike Montane became the spitting image of one very dead Roy Dobson.

The new man called the Washington Department of motor vehicles and reported his lost driver's license. It was a simple process to get a replacement, requiring a twenty-five dollar fee, and an eye exam. They asked for his birthday, height, and weight and used their computers to pull up Roy's old license number and photo.

After taking the standard photo, they gave him a written temporary license. He phoned a printer and ordered a set of business cards under the name of his new business, *Roy's All-bright Window Cleaning Services.* For payment, he mailed the printer a money order paid for with cash.

He dumped his wig in a trash barrel near a park in Renton, then drove to his home in Tacoma. He re-dyed the mustache an even deeper shade of black and shaved his head until it shone like a polished stone.

The next day, he drove his car into Oregon, to a remote area in the southeast corner of the state called the "Outback." He drove over a hundred miles on dirt roads to Warner Alley, a deserted place south of Burns Junction. He had read about the area in some geographic magazine. The magazine had described the place perfectly, except for the rain. The article claimed it only rained an inch a year. "Oh, well," Mike was already getting used to talking to himself, "at least the rain will keep the dust down."

When he got to the middle of nowhere, he stopped the car and pulled his mountain bike from the trunk. He had enough food and water to last him for a week, and he figured the long bike ride back to Tacoma would be good for his sagging spirits.

He drenched the car with gasoline and sprayed gas throughout the trunk and all over the interior. Then he made a long gasoline path over the rain-veneered desert, and threw the empty gas containers back into the trunk of the car. The trail of fire fascinated Mike as he watched it race to his car and engulf it in flames.

He wasted no time. His legs worked hard as he peddled away from the burning car. About a half mile later, he heard the explosion from the gas tank. He never turned around to watch, but smiled as his legs pushed him faster and faster over the naked land.

The past was now the past. He was a new man. He had the driver's license, the business cards, the new face, and the new job to prove he was a new man. Roy Dobson. A smile flashed across his face as he rode through the desert.

************ *********

Kelly spent two days at home with Grant and Dillon before she finally drummed up the courage to make the call. She knew this one call would bring back memories that she had chased out of her mind.

The call was to a friend of Mike's who still worked as an agent for Platinum Insurance. After Alex's death, Mike and Kelly had switched their car and homeowners insurance over to National Casualty Insurance, but still had their life insurance with Platinum. Mike had insisted on it, and no matter how much Kelly protested, he refused to change life insurance companies. He claimed that no one would ever give him the amount of insurance he had been able to get as a Platinum agent. After a terrible disagreement over the whole thing, Kelly finally decided not to argue about it. Now she regretted it.

"Platinum Insurance, this is Zach Aabbatt," came the cheery voice on the other end of the line.

"Hi, Zach, it's Kelly Montane. You may not remember me, I'm Mike's wife." Kelly worked to keep her voice steady.

"Of course I remember you, Kelly. What a surprise. I usually talk to Mike, but how can I help you?"

"Zach, I have some terrible news..." Kelly started to lose it fast. Her lips trembled and tears welled up in her eyes. "Mike is dead." As soon as the words left her lips, she burst out crying. Hearing the words come out of her own mouth – it was the final verdict.

Mike had always told Kelly that Zach Aabbatt had a golden tongue. Normally undefeated by anything anyone ever said to him, this time he was taken aback. He felt a lump form in his throat as he waited for Kelly's cries to subside. "I'm sorry, Kelly. I'm very sorry."

Kelly's crying continued as Zach waited patiently. It took several minutes before she could speak again. "I'm sorry for breaking down, Zach. I don't know what to say."

"It's all right. Would you like me to come over?"

"No," Kelly gasped as she spoke between sobs. "I just . . . I just wanted to make sure that you'll help me to file a claim on his life insurance."

Zach already had the policy up on his computer. He had been staring at it as it flashed across his screen.

"Kelly, his policy is in force, and in a paid status. Of course, I'll help you in any way I can. Don't worry about it. I'll take care of you."

"Thanks, Zach. Mike always said he could count on you."

After Kelly told Zach about the drowning and the failed search for Mike's body, Zach told her he would come over to help her fill out the claim forms. As they spoke his eyes absorbed the neon red letters on the computer screen:

POLICY TYPE :	ANNUAL RENEWABLE TERM
FACE VALUE :	$3,500,000
EXTRA BENEFIT:	ACCIDENTAL DEATH

Zach knew if he visited with Kelly before consulting with the company, he would be fired. An accidental death doubled the benefit to seven million. He put his phone on mute and said it out loud: "Seven Million Dollars and NO BODY." He printed the screen and circled the numbers until his pen tore a hole in the paper. He had no choice in the matter.

No body. He couldn't believe it.

The moment he hung up, Aabbat pulled out the Platinum directory.

************ *********

"Slayton." George Slayton's gruff voice answered the phone.

"George, its Zach Aabbatt. I need to talk to you."

"Zach, how is it that when I really need to talk to you, you don't have time for me? But when you want to talk to me, I'm supposed to stop whatever it is that I'm doing to listen to you. Now does that–"

"George, listen. We can talk about that another time–"

"Don't tell me –"

"Mike Montane is dead."

"What?"

"He drowned over a week ago, and they haven't found his body yet. There is a three and a half million dollar life policy on him, and it has accidental death."

"No body. Shit – tell me the rest."

Aabbatt recounted Kelly's story trying to stay as close to the facts as possible. When he finished the story, Slayton took over. "Listen, Aabbatt, I want to make this crystal clear. You're out of this claim as of now. That means you're not going to talk to Kelly Montane or anyone else associated with the claim. Got it?"

"I promised her that I would bring over the death claim form for her to complete." Zach refused to argue, but felt like a traitor to his old friend.

"I'll deliver that death claim form myself. You stay out of it, or I'll make this my final reason to fire your sorry ass. You got that?" Slayton slammed down the receiver. "Double indemnity. Double shit."

Slayton first called the Special Investigative Unit. They immediately patched him through to Harley Crane at the home office.

"You've got to be kidding me." Crane sat with his feet on his desk, looking out his giant window. "We've got a total of seven mil on the line, and there's no body? Who's this guy that he's got seven million?"

When Harley made the connection between Mike Montane and

the Alex Richter case, he flew out of his chair. "Dammit George, it's the circle of life. That son of a bitch is trying to get us for what he figures we should've paid his sister-in-law. It's a fraud, and the wife's in on it. Son of a bitch!" Harley paced the floor as he talked.

On the other end of the line, Slayton also paced the floor. He wished he could say something – anything – but Harley talked too fast and constantly interrupted.

Harley summoned a picture of Slayton to his computer, then looked at his birth date, years of service, and the obvious lack of company credentials. The black-and-white photo hadn't been updated in ten years because Slayton hadn't qualified for any of Platinum's promotions. "All right, Slayton, I'm going to tell you what to do. You're going to become the most concerned, caring and thoughtful human being who ever lived. You're going to visit Kelly Montane in her home, and express your sincere condolences for her loss. Furthermore, you're going to tell her how sorry you are about her sister. You're going to tell her that you used to be an asshole, but now you've been 'born again' and you realize how awful you were in the past. You got all that?"

"Yeah but–"

"Don't ever 'yeah-but' me, Slayton. There are no 'yeah-buts' in my chain of command. I expect that within an hour, you will not only be forgiven, but will become the Widow Montane's friend and confidant. Do I make myself clear?"

"Yes, sir." Slayton gave Harley the invisible finger.

"That's better. I know all about you, Slayton. I'm looking at your face right now. I see the picture of a man who hasn't qualified for jack in the last ten years. We've got a lot of complaints about you. Most people think you're a bad-ass. You have an opportunity to change my opinion of you, but you're only going to get this one chance. If you pull it off, we'll be inclined to overlook your indiscretions."

"What do you mean by that?"

"You know damn well what I mean. Don't play naive with me. I know more about you than your mother does."

Silence penetrated the phone line as Slayton swallowed a

thousand milligrams of his own poison. At least he was smart enough to know when to shut up. He needed only a few more years until retirement and then he'd find a way to get even with Crane for treating him like this.

The silence didn't bother Harley. He took it as an opportunity to study Slayton's file and let his words sink in. Then he read the summary file on former agent Mike Montane. When he finished, he got bored with the game of silence. "I want to know if you're up to the job, or if I need to find someone else."

"I'll do my best." Now he stuck up both of his middle fingers and waved them in the air at the phone.

"That's what I like to hear, Slayton. I want you to arrange a meeting with the Special Investigative Unit in St. Paul. They'll put a hidden video camera and microphone on you for your little visit. By the time you're ready to go, I'll have faxed you a list of questions to ask. Ask her as many of my questions as you can. Try to get her to talk openly before she has a chance to rehearse her answers. And make sure you don't leave her house without a death claim-form signed. Any questions?" Harley had already planned his next move.

"Isn't a video and microphone illegal?"

"You do what I say and let me worry about that. Anything else?"

"I don't think so." Slayton had heard about Harley through the grapevine. Crane had a reputation for being a fast decision-maker, a guy who could be ruthless when called for. The man wouldn't hesitate to fire him. Slayton's face burned when he hung up the phone.

As Harley Crane disconnected, he pulled up a big picture of agent Mike Montane on his computer screen. Then using his split screen command, he did a search for "Richter" and "coma." The article from the *Minneapolis Star Tribune* popped up.

"Damn!" He screamed to the furniture in the big office. "I can't believe it!" He re-read the part where Kelly Montane had called her vegetable sister a racehorse. "This one is all mine. It's going to be me against you, lady."

He hadn't felt this energized in years. Buzzing his secretary, he ordered the corporate jet. "Cancel all my appointments for the next two weeks!" he barked.

As Harley stacked all his papers into a neat pile and put them in his to-do drawer, he continued to talk to himself. "So the racehorse is dead. Now your husband pretends to be dead. What a chicken shit." He rambled on: "He quits because he can't handle the pressure of the big leagues. I offered a fair settlement, and this is what I get in return."

Harley looked out his window over the big span of blue water, then continued his private speech. "Well, the big bad Company is going to come knocking on your little door, and not only are you going to lose, I'm going to make a federal case out of your pathetic attempt to defraud me."

Chapter 38

Kelly buried her face in the pillow of her living room couch, contemplating the brevity of life. First her parents, then Al, now Mike. Time on earth disappeared like a short winter day. Gone. If only she had one more moment with the people she loved.

One more day . . . The doorbell interrupted her thoughts.

When the door swung open, Kelly found George Slayton standing on the other side. She gasped, covered her mouth, and instinctively stepped back. *Slam the door. Slam it.* Her arm twitched, the door moved, and then an invisible hand inside her heart caused it to stop.

"Hello, Kelly." Slayton smiled sincerely.

She quickly locked the handle of the storm door. "George." Kelly choked out.

Slayton held his hand to his chest. He looked down at the ground, then back up to Kelly as he tried to speak with as much humility as he could muster. "Kelly, I'm very sorry to hear about Mike." He looked back down. "And I don't blame you if you hate me, and think I'm the scum of the earth. I know I deserve it."

Kelly said nothing.

"I have wanted to apologize for years about what happened to Alex, and for my part in that. I'm so sorry." Tears welled as he spoke. "I've been too afraid, and so ashamed of what I did, that I couldn't bring myself to face you and Mike . . . and now..." he sniffled and wiped his face with his sleeve. "And now, Mike's gone, and I've missed my chance to express my sorrow to him."

His words caught Kelly off guard. The man who had brought so much pain into her life stood at her door, begging for forgiveness.

"I hoped we could talk . . ." Slayton gambled as he turned his body slightly, as if prepared to go. "But I'll understand if you tell me to leave."

Kelly's mind swirled. The brevity of life. The need of

reconciliation. No time for anger and sorrow. When she saw Slayton's tears and felt the sorrow in his heart, she couldn't bear to be mean. She hesitated, then unlocked the door and let him in.

"What's caused your change of heart?" Kelly second-guessed herself the moment he stepped in the house.

Slayton paused as if mired in deep reflection. "There are so many reasons, so many things to say." He exhaled loudly.

"I'm listening."

"I don't know how religious you are, Kelly, but the biggest thing that's ever occurred in my life happened about two years ago." His feet shifted and his eyes met Kelly's. "I've been born again. I've re-thought all my values and my actions toward others." Slayton spoke softly. His face expressed sincerity as his eyes looked first at Kelly, then back down at the ground.

"I have learned that I am nothing, absolutely nothing but a sinner, and only grace and forgiveness will save me." He stopped and raised his eyebrows as he gauged Kelly's reaction. He personally thought that people who claimed to be born again were true hypocrites. But he'd heard the story, knew the words, and had no problem acting the part.

"Go on." Kelly replied noncommittally.

"I've thought about you and Mike and your sister many times over the past two years. I've been too afraid to face you to tell you how sorry I am."

"Why were you afraid?"

"Because I knew what I had done was wrong. I want to try to make it up to you. I want to help you." Slayton could see from Kelly's body language that he was making headway. She sat forward in her chair and her face had a pleading look to it. This would be an easy sale.

"How can you help me now?"

Slayton delivered a master's smile of sincerity and looked carefully into her eyes. "When you called Zach Aabbatt and told him about Mike's death, he called me. Zach and I both know that Platinum will never pay a death benefit without a body. Pardon the religious expression, but they'll fight you till kingdom come."

"But why?" Kelly looked anxious.

"Because there's no way to prove Mike's dead. They will say he walked away, that he never really drowned."

"But three other people and I saw him drown."

"I know. Zach told me the story. That's why I'm here to help you. The company calls this type of death claim a 'Walkaway.' People fake their deaths to collect life insurance, get out of a bad marriage, or leave a bad job. There were truckloads of people who pretended to die when the New York towers fell in 9-11 and there are a thousand reasons why people try to commit insurance fraud," Slayton's words rolled as he spoke faster and became more compelling with every sentence.

"But Mike didn't walk away from anything," Kelly protested. "We were happy, and he loved his job."

"You may not be aware of this, but he had a death benefit of three and a half million dollars. It pays twice that if he dies in an accident." Slayton stopped to study her face as he told her the news. He wanted to be sure the hidden video got a good shot of her reaction.

"I know. He had over a million dollars when he first started as an agent. You were the one who told him that he should have a million dollars. You convinced him he'd never be able to sell it if he didn't believe in it himself."

"I remember that. Mike was one of the few agents who took my message to heart, and he made a lot of million dollar life sales." After a pause, he continued. "Can you tell me why he had an extra two and a half million?"

"He bought that extra coverage when Al was sick. I have a lot of coverage too. When my folks died, they had virtually no life insurance. We wanted to be certain there was enough money to provide quality care for Al for the rest of her life."

"I see." Slayton's reflective attitude continued. "You know, Kelly, the company is going to fight you over this. They're going to ask you why Mike and you didn't lower your death benefits after Alex died, and they're going to tell you that Mike had seven million reasons to commit fraud against Platinum."

"I hate Platinum." Kelly's worst fears were coming true.

Her response was exactly what he wanted. "Unless we work with them . . . and I'm here to help you as much as I possibly can . . ." He looked passionately in her eyes to make sure she believed him. "They're going to say that Mike faked his drowning in order to get revenge on Platinum for not paying Alex when they should have. I think you would be wise to hire an attorney, but you need someone to keep you informed of the company's position. I'd like to be that someone, to try to undo some of the damage I've done in the past."

"George, I don't really trust you, but I'll accept your apology." Kelly couldn't believe she said it. She wanted so badly to trust him.

"I understand. Kelly, I wouldn't blame you if you never trusted me again for the rest of your life. I'm truly sorry with all my heart." If he had to say he was sorry one more time, he thought he'd puke.

After another long silence, Slayton decided the next person who spoke would lose, so he sat and studied the floor in front of him. The clock ticked in the background, getting louder with each passing moment.

After several minutes, Slayton couldn't fight the clock any longer. He moved to the edge of his chair and stood. "Kelly, thanks for letting me in your home. I'm forever sorry for what I did, and I appreciate your acceptance of my apology."

He turned toward the door and made the ultimate wager. If Kelly didn't stop him now, he would have to face Crane with the news that he had nothing. But every morsel of old–school salesmanship told him he had no choice but to show his willingness to leave. Today he sold sincerity, and now was the time to pull out his signature move.

As he touched the doorknob, Kelly's cautiousness gave way to her emotions. "George, I can't believe I'm saying this. But right now, I'm going to try to trust you. I don't want to fight anyone, and I don't want to fight Platinum. I'll accept your apology, and your help."

Slayton smiled.

************ *********

By the time Harley Crane's plane was half-way to Minneapolis, he'd already interviewed Zach Aabbatt by phone and knew most of the facts. He called the pilot and had him file a new flight plan to make his first stop in Ely, Minnesota. The local authorities needed to be involved.

Harley sniffed the air. If he'd been a cribbage player, he would have thought that he smelled skunk.

Chapter 39

Slayton popped open his briefcase and pulled out a tape recorder and a sheet of paper.

"What are you doing?"

"Kelly, after I heard what happened from Zach Aabbatt, I prepared a list of questions that I figure the company might ask you. I'd hoped you would let me help you, and I want you to prepare for them. If you don't mind, I'll tape record our conversation to make sure we don't miss anything."

Slayton had nothing to lose. He already taped her anyway. Getting her permission at this point would simply be icing on the cake. Moreover, if she declined the recording, she might be more open with him. Either way, he would have his recording and he'd win.

"I don't want to be recorded." Kelly thought about calling Dillon for legal advice and suddenly felt uncomfortable.

"Hey, Kelly, I certainly understand." Slayton practically threw the tape recorder back into his briefcase. "If you'd like I can leave these questions with you, or I can ask them right now and try to help you figure out what follow-up questions the company might have. I think it's probably best if I ask you the questions, and work with you. We don't need to write anything down, and our conversation will be between you and me only."

"I'd like it if we talked things out right now. No notes or recorders."

"All right. If I ask you a question that you're uncomfortable with, let me know."

"Okay."

"Kelly, tell me what happened. Tell me whatever you want – whatever you think is important for me to know."

Kelly spent the next two hours telling Slayton the entire story. She told him every detail of the drowning, the scramble to find Mike, the canoe trip to the van, the blizzard, the help they got from

Arlen, the meeting with Sheriff Crow, and the subsequent dog search and rescue attempts.

Slayton sat and listened quietly to the whole thing. His hidden video camera would allow him to review the entire story at will. It was tough to feign interest for two long hours. He didn't care about canoeing, didn't care about the other people in the group, and certainly didn't appreciate it when Kelly started crying. But he sat forward and tried his hardest to appear sympathetic.

"So that's what happened, George. Now we're here. What do we do next?" Kelly looked exhausted. As she told the story aloud – from beginning to end – she wondered how many times she'd have to repeat it in the days to come.

"I'd like to ask you some rather pointed questions that the company will probably ask. You'll want to be prepared." Slayton, the soldier, followed Harley Crane's directive to gain knowledge in a taped interview. They'd be able to compare future interviews for inconsistencies, and with any luck, they'd catch her lying.

"Go ahead and ask."

"Why were you canoeing up there at the end of October, when it's cold, and the probability of ice existed?"

"Mike and I love the solitude of being alone with our friends. We go when there are no crowds. We do many things when there aren't many people around. We go to the movies on Sunday nights, and we go out to dinner after 9 PM when most people are home. We've gone canoeing in the end of October the last three years in a row."

"Seems reasonable to me." Nothing here sounded reasonable to Slayton. Only young people liked the outdoors, not him. Not ever. "Why didn't you tell the rangers where you were going, and why didn't you get a permit?"

"I don't know. Mike took charge of that. I don't think he ever got a permit because he said the purpose of the permit was to prevent overcrowding."

"Didn't he break the law by not getting a permit? What if a fire got out of control, or what if someone got lost? How would anyone know where you were to come to your aid? Did you ever discuss this?"

"We did, but Mike had a lot of wilderness experience. He was a tremendous outdoorsman. He never got lost, and was always careful with his campfires. He once told me that they probably wouldn't grant a permit that late in the year because of the weather."

"I see," Slayton said. "Why didn't the rest of the people have a map?"

"We don't know why. It seems like everyone forgot their maps in the van. Mike made sure to bring them with him because last year he accidentally left all the maps at home except his own."

"What do you mean?"

"Mike usually teaches people how to read a map and compass. He really enjoys helping others learn about the outdoors. But last October when we went to the Boundary Waters, Mike forgot to pack the extra maps. He left them at home by mistake."

"Oh." Slayton periodically nodded to keep her talking.

"So anyway, this year he remembered to bring the maps with him. One map for each of us. But in the haste of getting our canoes launched, we must've forgotten them, and no one thought twice about it until we were a half hour into our trip."

"So why didn't you go back to get them?"

"We figured they were in someone's pack. And even if they weren't, no one wanted to go back."

"Kelly, I'm sure the company is going to emphasize that Mike was a strong swimmer and canoeist. How'd you answer that?"

"He's very good at both. I guess he must have hit his head when he fell out of the canoe. I don't know, maybe the cold water got him first."

"But why would he stand up in the canoe in the first place?"

"Like I said, he pointed at something, maybe a bear, or a moose."

"And you never saw it?"

"No. None of us saw anything."

Slayton continued his rapid-fire questioning. "If his canoe was turned sideways, and he fell out the back side of the canoe, there's no way he could have hit his head on anything – right?"

"I don't know, maybe his head hit his paddle. Maybe he hit a rock in the lake?"

"In forty feet of water?"

"I don't know." Kelly's voice pitched up.

"I'm not trying to upset you, but I want to be certain I understand the facts, and the irregularities and potential loopholes that Platinum will try to find in your story." Slayton looked concerned. "When I talk to them, I want to erase doubts before they even surface."

"I'm sorry I got excited. It felt like you were interrogating me."

"I'm sorry. Try to relax. I'll only ask you a few more questions today. You know, Kelly, we really should have you sign this death claim before we talk further. I want to make sure we don't forget. Are you all right with that?"

Kelly nodded, and signed the form. The signed death claim form gave Platinum the legal right to pursue an investigation into the case. If Platinum could prove Mike was alive, they could potentially prosecute for attempted fraud.

Slayton continued with his questions. "Why did it take you so long to get to the overturned canoe?"

"Mike was probably a hundred yards ahead of us. Plus the wind and the river pushed his canoe farther downstream. A football field is a long way to canoe as fast and hard as you can." She used her hands as she spoke, to show her left hand getting closer to her right hand while the right hand continued to move farther to the right.

"How were you and Mike getting along?"

"Mike was my best friend. In all our years of marriage, I think these last ones were the best." Kelly smiled.

"In retrospect, do you think Mike had any girlfriends, or outside activities you weren't aware of?"

Her face twisted. "Never!"

"Did he act strange in any way?"

"No."

"Is there any reason to believe Mike may have committed suicide?"

"Absolutely not."

"How about your finances? How were they?"

"We're doing pretty well. We filed bankruptcy after Al's death, but since then we've always paid our bills on time, and we've got some money in the bank again. I don't think we had any money problems."

"You know that suicide isn't covered." Slayton lied in an attempt to trip her up.

"There's no reason to believe he committed suicide, and I don't like the insinuation behind such an insulting question. How could they ever argue a suicide? There's no evidence, and no one has even mentioned this."

"I'm asking questions the company might ask me." Slayton paused when he heard the back door open and someone entered the house. "None of you really witnessed Mike drown, did you?"

"Yes, we did. We all saw him fall out of his canoe." Kelly stood and put her hands on her hips.

"That's what I mean. You saw him fall backward, out of his canoe. When he fell, the canoe shielded him from your line of sight. And by the time you got to the overturned canoe, Mike was gone. So you never did see him drown."

Dillon entered the living room like a bull seeing a red flag. "Hey, who are you?"

Slayton stuck out his arm to shake hands. "George Slayton. I'm from Mike's life insurance company."

"George Slayton, huh?" Dillon pointed at the door. "You can get the hell out of here right now."

"Dillon!" Kelly said.

"Mike told me about this guy. We talked about him a couple months ago when we planned the canoe trip. He told me that Slayton here is the biggest liar and backstabber he ever met in his life."

"George has changed his life. He apologized to me for all the problems he caused and he's here to help me."

"Slayton's not interested in helping you, Kelly. He's a company man."

"And who are you?" Slayton asked in a sarcastic tone, wanting to get Dillon's response on camera.

"It's none of your business, Slayton."

"Are you and Kelly lovers?"

"How can you ask such a thing?" Kelly glared at Slayton. "An hour ago you were telling me how sorry you were. You're way out of line. Good-bye, Mr. Slayton."

"Get out of this house right now, before I call the cops," Dillon yelled.

After Slayton left, Kelly and Dillon returned to the living room. "Dillon, he asked me if Mike committed suicide. You know, I never thought of that. Then he told me that the life policy wouldn't pay if he had. You don't think?" Kelly looked pale.

"Of course not. Mike was happy. You guys were happy. He lied to you anyway. Suicide *is* a covered claim if the policy is over two years old. But if they prove Mike committed suicide, then they wouldn't have to pay any extra accidental death benefits."

"How could they ever prove that?"

"They can't. There's no suicide note or any reason to think it. Slayton tried to scare you."

"I shouldn't have let him in. But he seemed so apologetic, like he really cared about Mike and me."

"Don't worry about him. I'm sure he just snooped around for Platinum."

Slayton's insinuations came back to haunt her. "You know, Dillon, we never did witness Mike drown."

"I know. But all the evidence points to death by drowning. I wouldn't give the life insurance policy a second thought. Platinum will deny coverage because there's no body. They almost have to do that. Next spring, the body will surface, and then they'll pay, and that will be the end of it."

"But what if Mike's body isn't found?"

"Then we'll sue Platinum. Four of us saw him fall out of the canoe into ice water. To assume he didn't drown is ridiculous.

There's no way a jury will ever agree with the insurance company. Four eyewitnesses, three of whom have nothing to gain financially. This time Platinum will pay. I promise."

************ *********

George Slayton drove away a happy man. That son-of-a-bitch Crane would be proud of him. The loopholes were enormous, and any moron could see Kelly lied.

*Standing in the canoe, and falling out. No one saw what Montane pointed at. No one actually saw him drown. No body. No maps. No permit. Scent dogs that led everyone to Montane's escape in a parking lot near Ely.*_ Slayton laughed.

These people were hiding something. They were in cahoots. Mike wasn't dead. Or maybe he did commit suicide because his wife slept with that bastard who threw him out of the house. Maybe they killed Montane together, and used this drowning story as a cover up for murder. Maybe Montane tried to pull a walkaway.

The possibilities excited him. As he drove back to the Special Investigative Office to turn in his catch, he called Harley's office, where they re-routed the call to Harley's cell phone in Ely.

"This is Harley."

"George Slayton here. I got everything you need and then some."

Chapter 40

Harley knew where to find Sheriff Mason Crow in Ely. He and Crow had worked "together" on the Thorson case.

The sheriff had thought Thorson was innocent, while Crane insisted on his guilt. Mason had a gut feeling that Thorson was an honest man who had been railroaded. Yet, when Mason had begun to pursue his own investigation, his boss called him off the job.

"Hi, Mason." Harley stuck out his arm to shake hands.

"If it isn't Mister Guilty-As-Sin." Mason never extended his arm. He'd be a hypocrite to feign happiness at the sight of Crane.

"I can't tell you how sorry I am about the Thorson case. You were right, and I was wrong. I thought about calling to apologize after you called me with the news, but you know how busy life can be." Harley sat down across the desk from the sheriff and watched Mason.

"I'm not the one you should be apologizing to, Crane. You put an innocent man in prison. You destroyed him, and hurt a lot of others in the process." Mason spoke matter-of-factly.

"You're right. I personally met with Thorson to offer my apologies to him." Harley felt the lie was inconsequential. "No one felt worse about that case than I did. When you called me with the news, it devastated me. I made sure that Platinum paid him every dime they owed him, plus interest, plus restitution for wrongfully prosecuting him. I delivered that check myself, with the apologies of the company."

"Mr. Big Man Crane delivered the check himself?"

"That's right."

"What did Thorson have to say?"

"That the money was meaningless." Harley looked straight into Mason's eyes. "He took the money anyway, and implied a threat that he'd never forget me. His last statement was, 'Never.'"

Mason watched Harley speak without a flicker of hesitation. "What brings you here today, Crane?"

"I'm here today to undo an injustice of the past."

"I'm listening."

"I understand you did the search and rescue operation for Mike Montane."

"Ya." Mason couldn't wait to hear what Crane would say next.

"The people at Platinum are worried there is no body. Mike Montane had seven million dollars of life insurance, and his wife has filed a claim which Platinum thinks is fraudulent."

"And you don't?" Mason said it with an air of cynical disgust. "Tell me, why do *they* think it's fraudulent?"

"Mike was a Platinum agent. He left the company on bad terms after the company screwed him and his wife over." Harley explained the story of Alex Richter, how the company had denied her claim and paid off the drunk driver instead.

"I can see why he'd be pissed. But you say that happened over seven years ago?"

Harley waited to make sure Mason had finished. "The whole thing with Alex caused enormous strain on Montane and his wife. They almost divorced and had to file for bankruptcy. He lost his career. Then Alex died from lack of proper care in the nursing home."

"I'm still listening."

"Needless to say, the company never offered an apology. Never paid a dime. They screwed the man as hard as they could."

"So you think he came up here to stage a drowning to collect big." Mason wanted nothing to do with this.

"No."

"No what?"

"No, Mason. I don't think that at all. The company thinks it."

"Then why are you up here?"

"I'm up here because . . ." Harley paused to get the words to come out in the right order. "The company made a lot of mistakes the way they handled the Alex Richter claim." Harley never blinked. "Mike Montane and I got to know each other pretty well. He was an honest and hard-working young man. He did an excellent job for the company and they cheated him."

"I thought you were some big-shot with Platinum. I heard they promoted you after you rotated Thorson. All of a sudden you're done screwing people and you're a Boy Scout?"

"I never liked being a scout. But I know in my heart that Mike Montane was an honest man."

"You're lying." Mason stood behind his desk.

"I don't blame you if you don't trust me, but think about this for one moment. How could anyone have had the patience and the tenacity to plan an act of revenge for seven years?" Harley paused.

"You tell me, Crane."

"They can't, and you know it, Mason." Harley's body, arms, and face spoke with the same passion and conviction that his voice carried. "And I won't stand idly by while the company tries to cheat his widow once again."

"What do you intend to do?" Mason asked.

"I intend to conduct a full-scale investigation, and report my findings to Platinum in a positive light. I want them to do the right thing. I have a lot of influence in the company now, and I intend to use it in a constructive way. For once in my life, I want to make a difference."

Harley envisioned his dad, slapping him on the back with pride for the way he handled Mason. *Harley's body moved to the left, the ball hit a rock and shot hard toward his face. His hands moved to intercept, snagging the ball out of mid air. He snapped the ball out of his glove and rifled it to first base. "Out," the umpire's finger pointed at the bag, the fans cheered, while his dad smiled, "way to stay in front of the ball, son."*

"Hmm," Mason grunted while he watched Harley's face slip into a daydream.

"I need your help so I can help Kelly Montane."

Mason looked into Harley's eyes, and Harley stared right back. There was nothing left to say. Silence crescendoed through the room. Harley could hear his heart beat all the way down in his shoes. His mouth felt dry, and he fought the urge to blink as he watched Mason and let his speech sink in.

"I guess that I'll help you under those circumstances," Mason finally broke the barrier. “But I want you to understand one thing, and let’s make no mistake about it.” Another long pause. “I’m doing this because investigating this thing a little further is probably the right thing to do, and not because I suddenly believe you have a soft heart. The first hint I get that you’re out to thump anyone, I’m out.”

Harley smiled a deep smile of gratitude. “Thanks, Mason. I understand how you feel, and I appreciate your help.”

Chapter 41

It took three hours to show Harley all the details in the Mike Montane file. Mason Crow had impeccable notes. Maps were marked and labeled with dates and times. He left nothing to memory. From the time of the accident, to the search, to the interviews of the four survivors, to the moment he called off the search, Mason chronicled every detail.

Mason's thoroughness impressed Harley. "You've really done a tremendous job here, Mason."

"Thanks. Especially since that episode with Thorson, I'm very careful about doing things right."

"Can I ask a few things to make sure we've covered all the bases?" Harley needed Crow as an ally.

"Go ahead."

"First, it appears that this incident occurred both in and out of your jurisdiction. Did you notify the Ely police and the Canadian authorities?"

"I didn't see any need to. It happened on the U.S.–Canadian border, and it's our problem. There's no need to involve the Canucks," Mason said.

"You're the expert, and you're probably right. But let me play the Devil's Advocate and ask you the hard questions that Platinum might ask me."

"Shoot."

"Let's assume all four of the survivors are lying. I'm not saying they are lying, but what if they are?"

"Okay."

"If they killed Mike, they may have killed him in Canada, which would make this a Canadian crime. They may have killed him before they got in the canoes. It may be a good idea to have the Ely police check the van and the canoes and equipment to see if there is any evidence of foul play."

"I don't think that's a possibility. We videotaped all four

witnesses individually. You can watch the tapes yourself. They tell exactly the same story. We even tried various approaches to see if we could trip them up. There's no way they're lying. My deputies and I are certain they're telling the truth."

"I'd like to see those tapes later on."

"No problem," Mason said.

"Now let's look at three other possibilities. Mike may have committed suicide. If Platinum can prove it, they won't have to pay for the accidental death portion of the claim, and it will save them three-and-a-half million. Next, Mike may have acted on his own to escape from something in his life, or to get revenge against Platinum. In that case, he's still alive. Or Mike and Kelly may have orchestrated this thing together, in which case Mike is still alive."

"Let's explore your possibilities," Mason said. "I doubt he tried to commit suicide, because quite frankly, drowning in ice-cold water is a horrible way to die. Plus, his friends tried to rescue him."

"I'll grant you that, but it doesn't make sense that he stood up in his canoe. He was too experienced for that."

"That puzzles me, too."

"If he wanted his friends to see something, he certainly could have waved his paddle in the air while he remained seated," Harley said.

"So this was highly unusual, and it's a major red flag, but it still doesn't indicate suicide."

"I think a moron would know not to stand in a canoe." Harley had never canoed a day in his life. "And there are a lot of other red flags that Platinum is going to point out. Like the map issue, the key-to-the-van issue. The fact that those sniff dogs–"

"Search and rescue dogs." Mason corrected him.

"Those search and rescue dogs smelled Mike's presence here, here, and at the trailhead." He pointed with his pen on the map to the tent site and Mike's hiding spot.

"I've spent hours thinking about that. The dogs are good but they aren't an exact science." Mason looked at his huge wolf as he spoke. "I saw a show the other day about tracking dogs identifying murderers. The courts have never successfully prosecuted using dog identification as evidence."

"I saw the same show." Harley lied again. Harley had an impeccable memory and a knack for remembering whom he had lied to, and what the lie was about. "But at the same time, search and rescue dogs have been wonderful in finding missing people – at least that's what I've heard."

"You're right, Crane. I have seen those two dogs at work on numerous occasions to find people lost in the woods. I don't know what to think of the Mike Montane case."

"Let's assume that the four eye witnesses are all telling the truth. Let's recreate the scene on the map." Harley walked over to a large-scale wall map of the Boundary Waters. "Now suppose that Montane turns his canoe sideways, then stands up, and points to get everyone's attention. Suppose he does that so that he can have his eyewitnesses. Then he dumps the canoe and uses it as a shield to hide from the others. Are you with me?"

"Yes, although I think in the freezing water he'd be a fool."

"I agree. But I'm hypothesizing now." Harley looked at Mason to be sure they were still working together. "So he uses the canoe to hide, and he swims to the Canadian shore where he runs into the woods and hides where the dogs smelled his scent."

"I'm listening."

"Then after the rest of the group searches for his body and finally leaves, he makes his escape."

"But how and where could he go?" Mason had already thought through all this. "He's surrounded by water. If he goes north into Canada, he's a hundred miles from the nearest road. If he tries to swim across the Three Forks River, he'll drown from the current or the cold water. If he tries to swim to the Big Rock Trail, he would be in the lake for an hour, and die from the ice water in the first ten minutes."

"Why didn't the divers who looked for Mike's body get hypothermia?"

"A wetsuit would explain a lot of things." Mason's mind raced as he thought about the possibilities.

"Yes, it would." Harley was thrilled to see the sheriff coming over to his side. "Did you ask the survivors who did the packing for the trip?"

"Mike did. He has a history of organizing and planning these outings. He buys the food, prepares the menu, and provides the maps and compass–"

"Maybe that explains the map and compass issue," Harley said. "If no one else has a map, no one can see the trail that leads into Ely because no one but Mike knows it's there."

"All right, I'll give your theory some room. But let's consider this. Even if Mike was able to swim across the Three Forks River and make it to Big Rock Trail, he couldn't have gotten there until dark. And if he swam, he'd have no tent, no gear, nothing to protect him from the cold."

"Unless he hid it somewhere up there."

"That's a big jump, Crane."

"What about the tent imprint?"

"Even if we consider this possibility, we have some problems. If he had a tent and warm gear hidden, how could he have made it out of there? It's a thirty mile hike, that under the best conditions would take a full day, and . . ." Mason paused to gather his notes, "and on that day, we got a first-class blizzard that dumped several feet of snow."

"I don't know." Harley's brain moved in overdrive. "What time did it actually start to snow?"

Mason studied his notes. "We had light flurries early in the morning, but no accumulation until about 10 AM that day."

"So it's possible that he could have had a four or five hour head start down that trail before the snow and the wind would have forced him to stop."

"That's right."

"And how far can a man in a hurry walk in four or five hours?"

"If he ran the whole way, there's a remote possibility that he could have covered thirty miles, but it's an awfully rough trail."

"I'm not trying to jump to conclusions, but it appears that we have a possible scenario of a walkaway and maybe insurance fraud."

"I'll give you that, but I still think it's very remote." Mason wished that he had thought of this on his own.

"Does anyone patrol the various trailheads or monitor the vehicles that are parked there?"

"The Ely police do a drive-by every day. They write down vehicle license plates and note the day and time." Mason was excited. This could possibly explain why Beau and Sprinter both acted as if Mike was at the trailhead. Mason stuck his index finger in the air to signal time-out, then speed-dialed the Ely police.

"Yo – Jerry – it's me, Crow. Say, I need some info for the Mike Montane drowning case. I need the parking record for the Big Rock Trailhead."

"Tell him you want the records back to a couple weeks before the drowning." Harley whispered as Mason waited on the phone for an answer.

"Ya, that's the life insurance investigator. Do you remember the name Harley Crane?" Mason looked at Harley with a glare that undid the momentum they had built over the last few hours. "Yep, you're right. He's the jerk who orchestrated the Thorson murder case . . . Yeah, never mind that. Just give me what I need."

Two minutes later Mason hung up. "Crane, here's what we have. There was only one car parked there for longer than two days. He's going to fax me a copy of the rest of his log, but we got one car parked there the weekend before the drowning. It sat there for eight days, and it was gone by 11 AM the day after the drowning. No other cars were parked there the day of the drowning, or the day after."

"So, assuming that car was left for Montane, how could he have hiked out by 11AM the next day?" Harley scratched his head. "Maybe he walked all night?"

"Not if he used the tent site we found. Someone definitely slept there. The weight of a tent matted the grass down. And we think the person who tented there left the tent site after it had already started to snow."

"What makes you think that?"

"There were some faint footprint-like indentations in the snow. Trees sheltered the whole area so the wind never touched it. Whoever camped there picked a pretty good site."

"So if he left after it had already snowed, then how could he get out by 11AM?"

"There's no way."

"We've got to think outside the box, Mason. Tell me more about that trail."

"It hardly qualifies as a deer path near the Three Forks River. It's an old snowmobile trail that's been closed to anything with a motor for many years."

"So no one maintains the trail?"

"Only for the first three miles or so from Ely. A few hunters might use it."

"No motorized vehicles allowed, huh?"

"If he had somehow stashed a dirt-bike back there, we would have heard about it."

"How's that?"

"There's a half dozen people who live near the trail. They would've heard it and complained. I got fifteen years experience on their complaints."

"Mason, stop thinking about Mike Montane. Pretend it was you. How would you get out of there in a short time, without being spotted?"

"I wonder if I'd use a mountain-bike?"

"That's it!"

"It would've been a helluva ride."

"Desperate men have done worse."

"Here's what we need to do to test our theory. We need to track down the owner of that car. Then we need to pull a list of all permits for moose, deer, bear hunters etceteras to see if anyone saw someone on the Big Rock Trail that day. Also, there are a few people, mostly hermit types, who live back in the woods near the trail. We need to interview them to see if they saw anyone." Mason worked at warp speed.

"How about the dogs?"

"No, they've already done their part. Besides, they're in California now, and the scent is too old and has been contaminated by our repeated searches over the last several days."

"I sure appreciate all of your help, Mason." Harley stuck out his hand again.

"Crane, I want to make sure that you still understand. My goal is simply to do the right thing. I'm not your buddy, and I still don't trust you. You're going to have to earn that. But I'm willing to proceed." With that said, he shook hands with Harley, then added: "Frankly, I hope Mike is dead and we find his body."

"Why would you hope that?"

"Because I knew Mike Montane as a friend a long time ago. He helped me out of a jam when he didn't have to. And it cost him . . ." Mason paused. "If he's dead, he will remain a man of integrity and character in my mind forever."

"And if he's alive?"

"Then something more horrible than you or I can ever imagine must have changed him from the man I once knew."

"So I can still count on your help?"

"Like I said, I'll do everything in my power to uncover the truth. The truth is the truth."

"We're both after the same thing. I want to show my company beyond any doubt that Mike is dead so we can pay the claim and treat his widow right. And the only way I can do that is by finding a body or disproving other possibilities."

************ *********

While Mason went to work to find the owner and whereabouts of the car that had been parked at the Big Rock Trailhead, Harley went to the local television station to spread his version of the story.

He remained convinced that Mike Montane still lived. It didn't take a rocket scientist to figure out what happened, and soon enough, Harley would uncover the mistakes Montane had made. Harley smiled when he thought of Mason Crow unwittingly doing the legwork for him. Harley would have his proof, make his case, and find the former agent. *The guy had once threatened him. His wife had called her vegetable sister a racehorse, of all things. Then they had gotten a greedy lawyer to sue for punitive damages. Now this. What some people would do.*

This case belonged to Harley. Montane had made it personal. "It's me versus you, baby." Harley's words hung in the air.

The weather turned ugly as the day ended. Harley and his pilot checked into a Grand Ely Lodge on Lake Shagawa on the edge of Ely. The huge timbers framed a building of giant windows. Harley stood next to one of the great panes of glass that separated him from the woods and the raging storm. The snow came down in heavy matted flakes. The lights on the outside of the building reflected the white flurries as they passed through the black sky. Inside, where the fire crackled in the warmth, Harley decided to "camp out" for as long as it took to get the job done.

Later that night in Ely and the surrounding area, people hunkered down in front of their television sets, trying to stay warm as the storm raged. The lead story on the ten o'clock news featured a local story about a "missing person." The segment showed a picture of Mike, followed by a detailed map of the drowning site and the Big Rock Trail. It ended by offering a $30,000 reward for anyone who could help authorities find Montane – dead or alive.

Harley smiled as he watched the report. Every Tom and Dick in Ely had a snowmobile or two parked in his garage. Tomorrow, the real manhunt would begin.

Chapter 42

Harley and four of his Special Investigation Unit (SIU) men watched and compared the video-taped testimony of all the campers. Then they watched Slayton's hidden video recording of Kelly. They played them side by side, point by point, and the story repeated itself every time.

No group of people could lie that consistently. Harley decided they told the truth – at least regarding the events on the canoe trip. Therefore, he ruled out the possibility of murder.

It left only two options: Montane did drown, or he and Kelly were trying to pull down a big life insurance fraud.

If he drowned, they should have found a body. The sheriff's body search had been thorough. And why did the dogs find his scent at the trailhead? No, Montane didn't drown. The maps, the lost van keys, the dog scent, the standing in the canoe, the pointing his paddle at nothing, the tent imprint. No way. Harley's nose could out-smell a search and rescue dog. The stench of something foul told him he was right.

Harley's team went back to dissect the fraud theory. "Let's go through it one more time." Harley barked the orders. "I want you to convince me that Montane acted on his own. Give me a reason to say he did."

"He wanted out of his marriage." A thin middle aged man with a flattop offered.

"Not a chance. Everyone, and I mean everyone says Montane and his wife were happy together. You can't hide stuff like that." Harley shot back.

"He hated his job and wanted a new life." This time a heavy-set older man with a mustache spoke.

"Nah. Montane made good coin and a lot of it in cash. He had no boss, no rules, and a lot of repeat business."

"He wanted to get revenge on Platinum, and his wife didn't." A young, blond haired, good looker whose arms bulged from weightlifting raised his hand as he spoke, as if he needed permission.

"I doubt it!" Harley roared. "Kelly's sister's the one who died. If anyone wants revenge, it's her." Harley gave little room to disagree with him. "I want a list of convincing reasons why they're in cahoots."

"Kelly is the only life insurance beneficiary." The flattop man spoke. "And they would have to get together, sooner or later, if he wants to share in the proceeds."

"Who could be dumb enough to pull a walkaway without getting money for it?" Harley piped in.

"Absolutely everyone we've interviewed says they were happily married. And happily married couples usually share the same plans and dreams." The SIU psychologist, a guy whose bald head made him look like Captain Picard, spoke for the first time.

"If you were happily married, and perceived that Platinum was somehow responsible for your sister's death, wouldn't it be reasonable to assume you'd work together to pull this fraud?" Harley asked.

"Absolutely." The psychologist paused. "If Montane acted on his own, think of the potential downsides. Think how devastated Kelly Montane must be, if she really thinks her husband is dead. What kind of a guy would purposefully do that to his wife if he loved her?"

"If Montane is still alive, and his wife thinks he's dead, what makes him think she won't fall in love with someone else? She's got a lot of cash potential with this life insurance, and she's a looker." The heavy-set man whistled.

Harley paced the floor. "Logistics make it impossible for him to work alone. After all, how would he get the money if he's doing this on his own? If he's alive, he's got to be scared. He wouldn't dare contact Kelly for fear that we'd catch him. How would he even know when she got the life insurance money?"

When everyone had paused for a moment, the young body builder commented, "If Montane finally figures out that she's been paid, we'd catch them when they got together. She'd probably hate him by then, especially after deceiving her."

Harley snapped on the VCR and re-wound Slayton's stealth interview of Kelly. The sound and picture from the camera hidden inside Slayton's briefcase were surprisingly good. The men huddled in front of the television to watch Kelly's reactions. Harley played the part where Slayton had asked Kelly: "I'm sure the company is going to emphasize that Mike was a strong swimmer and canoeist. How would you answer that?"

Kelly had responded with: "He's very good at both. I guess he must have hit his head when he fell out of the canoe–"

"What's going on here?" Harley asked.

"She's obviously talking about her husband in the present tense, as if he were still alive." The psychologist Picard spoke in a matter of fact tone.

Both of Harley's arms shot over his head like exclamation points. "So she's in on it. She knows he's not dead."

Picard spoke slowly and evenly as he tried to slow Harley's pace. "I think we should explore all of our options before coming to any conclusions."

"What options?" Harley spun and glared at the group of men.

"A lot of times after a death, people talk about the deceased as if he or she were still alive. It's a natural way of coping with their loss."

"Well, today I'm not buying it."

The flattop guy piped in. "Or it may have simply been a slip of the tongue."

"That's bullshit." Harley was sweating now. "Watch the tape again. She talks about Mike in the present tense several times."

Picard spoke even slower. "The way that Kelly speaks may merely mean that, in her mind, Mike possessed and will always possess these character traits. It may be the way she remembers him and will always choose to remember him. Instead of present tense being the focus, Kelly's words simply give ownership of a trait to Mike."

"All right, I've heard your argument." Harley whirled around. "But I still don't believe it. I think everything we've discussed says that Kelly is involved and knows Mike is alive. This is no slip of the tongue, or placing ownership of a trait, or method of coping."

"We can't use this tape as evidence in a trial, because you made it without her permission." Picard added.

"I didn't ask you to comment on the legalities of the tape." Harley snapped at the psychologist. "I've followed my gut all my life, and my gut tells me that she's in on it. They're both in on it."

************ *********

Mason Crow spent the next two days answering wannabe bounty hunter's questions. The $30,000 reward and the fresh snow brought all kinds of geeks to Ely. Suddenly the woods near the Big Rock Trail became a giant checkerboard as hundreds of snowmobilers crisscrossed the area, which had previously been closed to snowmobiles, in search of the prize.

Even people from a scuba diving club showed up at the sheriff's office. Twenty people did an under the ice arm-in-arm drag search. They combed every inch of the lake and river where Montane's canoe had dumped. They found nothing. No body, no tennis shoes, no sunken cook-kit, no map lying on the bottom of the lake. Nothing.

Meanwhile, Mason found the registered owner of the Oldsmobile that had been parked at the trailhead. Mason interviewed the older man by phone.

"I used to own an Olds."

"When did you sell it?"

"About six months ago."

"Who did you sell the car to?"

"I knew it! I smelled a rat when I sold that car."

"What do you mean by that?"

"The guy who bought the car bought it sight unseen. He called and asked if the car was reliable and safe. Then he asked more questions about me than the car."

"What kind of questions?"

"How old I was. What did I do for work, stuff like that."

"Why did he ask you that?"

"I don't know. I guess he wanted to know how well I maintained the car. He said I sounded like an honest man."

"Then what happened?"

"He told me he would mail me a cashier's check for the full asking price."

"What other things did he ask?"

"Why was I selling the car. Did I hire someone else to maintain the car, or do it myself. Things like that."

"Did you answer his questions?" Mason asked.

"Sure. I wanted to sell the car."

"Okay."

"He made me promise that I would leave the key under the driver's floor mat, with the doors unlocked, after I got his money."

"So you never met the man who bought your car?" Mason reiterated the question.

"No."

"Did you know that he never transferred the title into his own name?"

"No, but I made a photocopy of the cashier's check." The old man sounded proud of himself.

"Why did you do that?"

"In case the guy would get a hundred parking tickets, never pay the fines, and the police would think I still own the car."

"I'll have an officer stop to pick up that copy."

The cashier's check came from a small bank in the western Minnesota town of Willmar. Mason noted the issuance date on the check. Maybe they would get lucky and find that Mike had purchased gasoline or something else on his credit card that day in Willmar. If they could tie him to the cashier's check, it would help piece the puzzle together.

Mason put out a national search for the missing car. The search included the license plate number and vehicle identification number. Sooner or later, someone would find the car and lead him to the new owner.

************ *********

Meanwhile, Harley sent his SIU men to interview all the people who lived anywhere near the Big Rock Trail. They were able to track down almost everyone who lived within two miles of the trail, but they came up empty. No one had seen anything or anyone.

Harley sent his men to interview every gas station attendant between Minneapolis and Ely. If Mike had made his escape from the Big Rock Trailhead in the mystery Oldsmobile, he had to drive it to Ely sometime earlier, when he planted his tent and other gear. If Mike had stopped for gas or food, someone might remember him. They had a picture of Mike, the license plate numbers of the Montane van, and the license plate number of the mystery Oldsmobile. They placed $30,000 reward posters in most stations.

They might even have him and his car on videotape. Most stations kept a video log of their gas pumps to aid police in catching the pump and go, non-paying customers. If they could find Mike on a tape, it would give them definitive proof that he owned the Oldsmobile and had used it to make his escape.

Harley's wheels turned at full speed. With every passing day, his conviction grew. And with every obstacle, he became more and more obsessed with winning. *I'm going to take Montane and his "racehorse" wife down.* He made his vow.

Chapter 43

Hundreds of people attended Mike's memorial service in Minneapolis, including George Slayton and Harley Crane. Together, the two men meandered through the church community room where throngs of people crowded around three handmade billboards, each as big as a sheet of plywood, all loaded with pictures of Mike Montane.

"Jeez, the guy did it all." Slayton commented. "Looks like he flew, rock-climbed, dog-sledded, scuba dived. Even parachuted. I never knew he did all that."

That's because you're a horse-shit manager, Slayton. Harley couldn't stand being with such a loser.

"Looks like he had a lot of friends." Slayton said.

Harley's loud voice grated through the air. "People look at these pictures to see if they can see themselves."

"Look at that stinking mountain!" Slayton whispered in awe as he studied a picture of Mike climbing the Diamond.

"Shut your mouth, Slayton. I'll meet you in the church. Make sure you sit in the back." Harley had called a press conference the day before the service, and wanted to see if any reporters might show up. He did it despite the fact that his boss, Roger Phillips, specifically asked him to keep a low profile. Roger felt there were too many potentially embarrassing issues tied to the Alex Richter story and the fact that Montane had quit the company despite his award-winning status. In addition, Roger felt Harley's revenge theory had too many holes in it. The seven year span between Alex's death and Mike's disappearance was simply too long.

But Harley couldn't help himself. People held grudges a lot longer than seven years. His confidence in the "Walkaway" theory was so powerful that he bet the Vice-President of Auto Operations a thousand dollars on the case. Harley had researched his computer files and studied the almost-forgotten information about Alex Richter. He printed the newspaper article about Richter and enlarged the part where Kelly Montane called her sister a racehorse. He pulled up a computer photo of a wretched woman lying in a bed, with her arms twisted near her chest, and her hands grossly clawed into a fist. One eye stared out, while the other eye opened halfway, and her mouth hung open in a warped, perverse manner.

Then he looked at the picture of Alex Richter swinging off a mountain. Yes, Harley privately admitted, Richter might have been some type of racehorse in her prime. But the accident certainly wasn't his fault. *There was no way a gazillion dollars would ever have brought her back.* It would have been a huge waste of money.

Now, at this so-called memorial service, Harley found himself daydreaming about Mike Montane, the man who had threatened him when they tried to release Richter from the hospital.

It all came back so vividly. He remembered how Roger rarely reviewed individual client files, but Montane had sent a personal letter direct to Roger's house. Then Roger and Harley had met to discuss the case.

Harley explained his position. "Agent Montane was in close contact with Platinum's health claims division throughout Alex Richter's hospitalization. Furthermore, agent Montane sold a lot of health insurance for Platinum, including the policy Richter owned. He clearly knew the policy limitations, yet Platinum went far beyond the call of duty, and paid for Richter's hospital stay for seven months after the accident, despite no improvement."

"So you're telling me that we've been fair in this case?" Roger asked.

"More than fair, sir."

"What's the prognosis for Miss Richter?"

"No one knows. Our medical people have been watching this file and most of them believe that Richter will remain comatose or in a vegetative state for life. On the other hand, she has made some limited recovery, and our examiners caution that she is young, strong, and could possibly have a complete recovery."

"Then why haven't we paid the policy liability limits?"

"Because, we're not sure of the outcome yet. And because we're still covering her medical bills. I've checked with our legal department and they think in this case it might be prudent to delay a settlement offer." Harley knew this was a slight step beyond the truth. *But who really cared, and for what end? So an unaware vegetable could "live" for another year or two?*

Harley left the church pew and wormed his way through the crowded church lobby. He couldn't help but stare at the poster-sized picture of Mike Montane hanging off some cliff by his fingernails. *How could such a tough guy be so cowardly as to quit his job? Why didn't he have the courage to sue? I'll bet that loser was ecstatic when his vegetable sister-in-law died.*

Harley finally walked into the church and sat next to Slayton without looking at him. As the people shuffled in, Harley studied them, trying to get a glimpse of Kelly. A group of teary eyed women clung to each other as they walked up the aisle. *At least Montane could get on with his life after Alex died. Harley had done him a favor. How could such a puke hide behind a skirt?*

The daydream snapped as a smiling, not crying, "Widow Montane" walked arm in arm with Dillon Johnson toward the altar. *How could anyone possibly question my walkaway theory?* He saw a sparkle in Kelly's eyes. A sparkle! Where was the sadness? Everything became very transparent . . . the method and motive *sparkled* into crystal-clear view. He'd play along with this memorial shenanigans, but in the end, Harley would prove to the world, on live television, that he had his man. The press conference and this memorial would only make his victory that much greater.

************ *********

Dillon sat Kelly down in the front row, then proceeded alone to a heavy wooden door and walked up a dimly lit stairs to the church balcony. He wanted to be alone to go over his eulogy one last time, but as he reached the top stair, he noticed two men whispering to each other behind a large camera on a tripod.

"Who are you?" Dillon asked.

"We're with Channel 7 news."

"Why are you here?"

"Don't let us bother you. We'll keep a low profile."

"If you tell me what's going on, I might be able to help you." Dillon unleashed his short list of credentials. "I'm a close friend of the Montane family, and I'm giving the eulogy."

The reporter studied Dillon as he spoke. "You might be able to help. We got an anonymous tip that Mike Montane isn't really dead."

"What?" Dillon's face dropped.

"That's right. He's not dead. He's in hiding, trying to collect money from the life insurance company."

"Who told you that?"

"Like I said, it was anonymous."

"I was there when he drowned. I witnessed the whole thing, and searched for his body myself after he fell into the icy river. Believe me, Mike Montane is quite dead." Dillon looked at the reporter as he held out his tape recorder. "So why would someone say he's alive?"

"Our source tells us that Montane's got seven million dollars of life insurance with Platinum. They tell us he was a disgruntled agent."

"So what?"

"We followed up in our computer database and discovered that Montane had come to us about seven years ago with a story about how Platinum had allegedly cheated him and his family on a claim with his sister-in-law."

"She was in a coma and died because of a lack of care."

"Apparently, Montane felt Platinum should have paid her some big money. Now your friend is taking justice into his own hands."

"I can't believe it."

"That's what we got."

"I can't believe it." Dillon repeated as he walked away from the reporter. How could Platinum make a public statement that Mike committed life insurance fraud without advising Kelly?

Dillon walked to the men's room. He needed to be alone. His mind raced back to the drowning and he envisioned Mike standing in the canoe. Pointing at something. Dillon remembered the struggle for balance. The fall. By now, after re-living the scene a thousand times, Dillon could practically see the horror on Mike's face. Had he somehow imagined or dreamt about it?

Dillon remembered Kelly's dive under the canoe. His skin prickled as if he could still feel the cold misty-rain. He saw Kelly's face when she surfaced and screamed, "He's not here!" And how could he ever forget the utter powerless feeling that seized him when Grant and Allison rolled Mike's vacant canoe upright?

He shook at the thought of it all. Several cold minutes later, when the shaking finally stopped, he sat in the bathroom stall and wept for his lost friend.

************ *********

Dillon spoke deliberately as he delivered the eulogy, allowing the opportunity for every single word to sink in. Sometimes with laughter, sometimes with tears, but always with passion, Dillon shared the life of his friend. "Mike Montane was the kind of man who truly lived . . ."

The eulogy lasted twenty minutes, but his speech continued for the sake of the camera in the balcony. He looked down on his notes and read, "Mike once told me that he and Kelly had married each other for better or worse. Let me tell you the definition of 'for worse.' Despite impossible odds, they cared for Alex Richter twenty-four hours a day, seven days a week for three sleepless years. Although Mike worked hard as a Platinum agent, they purposely delayed payment for a legitimate liability claim to pay for Alex's care. Then, Mike and Kelly had to endure betrayal when Platinum paid off the drunk driver who hit Alex. Finally, when it seemed that nothing worse could happen, Alex died from lack of care at the nursing home."

Dillon paused and looked out over the people in the church. His eyes focused on the cameras as he said, "I have to ask you if that sounds like a bad deal?

"I think most men would have quit a lot sooner. They would have walked away from that marriage and out of that hopeless situation. Do you know what Mike Montane told me?

"He told me that he loved his wife, and things would get better. He was my friend. A man who always saw the good in things, who always gave his very best in everything he did."

Harley could barely contain himself. What devil in hell gave this man permission to slam Platinum in the middle of a eulogy, with the press recording every word?

"I was with Mike and Kelly and two other friends the day he drowned. It was a beautiful day, and we enjoyed life and our friendship together canoeing in the outdoors that Mike cherished. Mike died doing what he loved to do. He lived and died, fully alive to the last day."

************ *********

The next day the vultures swarmed around Kelly's front yard. When Kelly stepped out, the questions came from all directions amid a throng of microphones and cameras. "Did Mike talk about revenge against Platinum for what they did to you and your sister?"

"Are you aware that Platinum has evidence to suggest Mike is still alive?"

Kelly stopped in her tracks. She had expected Platinum to deny the claim until they found Mike's body. She even assumed they would consider life insurance fraud, especially given the circumstances. These steps would be prudent in the claim settlement process of any insurance company.

Surely, they should have waited until next summer to give the body a chance to surface. To accuse Mike or her of fraud now – with his body somewhere under the ice in that river – it was unthinkable. "What evidence?" Kelly looked at the reporter.

"They theorize that Mike hid in the woods after dumping his canoe, then swam across the river in a wetsuit, and walked out of the woods to a waiting car in Ely." The reporter pushed his microphone back in Kelly's face as soon as he had given her the bare facts.

"You say they have a theory. What evidence do they have to

support it?" Kelly glared at the reporter with red-rimmed eyes. "I saw Mike die."

"The dog scenting, a tent imprint in the snow, and the fact that there is no body despite exhaustive searches."

"That's not evidence. That is pure conjecture, and you know it. Platinum hasn't even had the courtesy to tell me they are denying the life insurance claim. Yet four of us witnessed Mike drown in freezing cold water. They never found the bodies of the Edmund Fitzgerald victims either. Don't you remember the man who died in Lake Nokomis? Minneapolis police used professional divers, but didn't find his body until it floated to the surface two years after his disappearance. Bodies rarely float in ice water." With that Kelly put her hand in front of her face and pushed her way through the crowd.

The reporters wanted more. "Have they told you about the Oldsmobile parked at the trailhead up until the day after Mike disappeared?"

"I don't know what you're talking about." Kelly continued to push.

The reporter persisted. "Did you or Mike ever own an Olds Cutlass?"

"No, we didn't, and I have nothing more to say."

Chapter 44

Later that night, a fragile Kelly found herself alone. It had been a long and brutal day. Closing the door, she turned and stumbled back into the empty house. She put her hands over her eyes in an effort to shake the vision of the reporters. *"Platinum has evidence to suggest Mike is alive."*

"I saw him drown." Kelly answered into the empty room.

"Platinum has evidence to suggest Mike is alive."

"Mike," Kelly whispered.

"Mike is alive." The reporter's words echoed.

No. She had seen Mike drown. Or maybe . . . she only saw him fall out of the canoe? Her brain worked back and forth from image to image.

She went to the fridge and grabbed a beer without knowing why. She hadn't had a drop of alcohol since Al's accident, but suddenly found herself looking for something, anything, to cope with the visions that raged. She snapped on the TV to distract her thoughts. The news came on.

As she reached for the remote to change channels, the TV flashed a picture of Mike. In the serious voice of gloom and doom, the news anchorman reported, "Today's top story is about former Platinum Insurance agent, Mike Montane, who disappeared, perhaps drowned, in the Boundary Waters Canoe Area ten days ago."

Kelly shot out of her chair as the station broke into a commercial. She frantically threw open the cabinet door that held the VCR then shoved a tape into the machine and hit "Record." The phone rang.

"Look at the news on Channel 6. They've got a story about Mike." Grant spoke so fast the words ran together.

"Tape it for me, Grant. I'm watching channel 7 and they've got a report on, too." Kelly hung up as the news began.

"Today's top story–" The newsman delivered his monologue

with detachment. His face looked solemn, the words rote, almost a repeat of the news from the night before, and the night before that. The TV showed a map of the Boundary Waters, then highlighted the Big Rock Trail as if it were a four lane highway.

Kelly held her breath as she watched the story. Her mouth hung open as she watched in disbelief. The words became a blur as the TV flashed two pictures side by side: Al climbing the Diamond and Al in her coma. They must have saved the pictures from Mike's previously vain efforts to get the media to air a story about Al when she was in her coma. Then came a short clip of Dillon's eulogy.

Kelly turned the TV off. A thousand trillion thoughts raced simultaneously through her mind. She remembered Mike sitting in the pile of broken glass. The giant tree snapped in half during the storm. The way he wept when Al died. The rainy mist in the Boundary Waters. All the pictures blurred together.

Past conversations chaotically replayed themselves. "If it's the last thing I do. I'll get the money." "I promise those bastards will pay." "I want to get them." "You don't say words like that without doing something about it." "Sometimes I lay in bed until three in the morning just thinking."

Then the impact of ice water hit her. It caused her body to shake. She was cold, alone, without hope. But she wasn't without life.

Those bastards from Platinum would never, never ever, be allowed to screw her a second time. If Mike was dead, they were going to pay whether they found his body or not.

And if he was alive? They'd pay anyway.

She was done crying.

*********** *********

Harley, too, watched the news in disbelief. At the end of the show, the newscaster reported on the air that thirty-seven people had called the station to announce their plans to cancel Platinum Insurance.

Before Harley went to sleep, he got a phone call in his posh room at the Minneapolis Hyatt.

"What the shit happened?" Roger Phillips, who rarely swore, never waited for Harley to say hello.

"Roger, I –"

"I don't want to hear it, Harley. You defied my orders and leaked this case to the press."

"Roger, I –"

"You listen to me. That eulogy will be repeated a thousand times across the nation. Our competitors are happy, the Commerce Departments will have us under a magnifying glass, and you have unnecessarily re-exposed Platinum to a mistake that we made seven years ago. You have single handedly shown the whole world our ass. Mr. Crane, let me remind you that you acted specifically against my wishes."

"I–"

"The higher the monkey goes into the tree, the more people can see its ass. Do you understand that, Crane?"

Silence vibrated through the line. Harley didn't dare speak, but couldn't put the receiver down.

"Are you listening to me, Crane?" Roger's voice boomed across the dead air.

"Yes, sir."

"You had better find a way to win this case. And you'd better figure out a way to put a positive spin on it or you're fired!"

The line went dead. Harley threw the phone across the room. The cord stretched tight, and the phone recoiled back. Harley roiled into rage. The veins in his forehead pulsed, ready to detonate. He picked up the chair and waved it over his head toward the picture window that looked over downtown Minneapolis.

Then he set the chair softly on the carpeted floor. He walked to the bathroom sink and stuck his head under the cold water, slapping his face with the cooling liquid. The battle may have been lost, but the war was far from over.

*********** *********

By now, Mike had a start of a good-looking mustache to go with his bald head. He had a decent day as Roy Dobson, doing business as Roy's All-bright Window Cleaning Service. His first advertisements in the local newspaper netted a dozen jobs, and it felt good to be back in business. Today he had worked from 7AM until dark and had $300 cash to show for it. *Not too bad for a day's work.*

When it was time for the ten o'clock Tacoma news, he settled onto his couch, wearing nothing but boxer shorts and a Seattle Mariner's tee shirt. With a Killian's Red in hand, he looked forward to a relaxing time to unwind.

About half way into the news, the TV flashed a picture of him. In a disaffected voice, the news anchor rambled through his report. "We have some news from Minnesota tonight about a former Platinum Insurance agent, Mike Montane, who reportedly drowned ten days ago. Investigators believe he may have faked his death in an effort to defraud his former employer with a seven million dollar life insurance policy."

The news showed a picture of Minnesota, then zoomed into the Boundary Waters, then zoomed again to show the same aerial shot of the lakes that Kelly had seen on TV.

They went on to discuss the entire story. It laid the whole thing out perfectly. First, the tragic story about Al. Then the drowning followed by an exhaustive search and no body. Finally, a map of the Boundary Waters showing the theory behind his escape and attempted fraud.

By the time the piece ended, Mike's ears burned bright-red. His chest pounded the blood into his skull. Not a drop of sweat came off the rest of his body. He suddenly felt cold and weak. His mouth fell open in disbelief. The beer fell from his hands and spread across the floor. His legs quivered, unable to move. He remembered falling and breaking his flashlight . . . the shot-gun . . . the barrel of the gun. A nauseous feeling swept over him. The man in the woods. How did they know? What did they *really* know? What *other* mistakes had he made? Mike raced to the bathroom and vomited.

Chapter 45

Harley decided his best approach would be to try to make temporary peace with Kelly. Obviously, she had plenty of reasons to worry, but he needed her cooperation until he had more evidence. The media became the enemy – at least for the time being.

When Kelly answered the door dressed in her black spandex workout clothes, Harley couldn't help but notice her body. *Nice face, tight buns, perfect sized breasts. Montane was a fool to leave such a good looker.* "Mrs. Montane, my name is Harley Crane, and I'm from Platinum Insurance. I am terribly sorry for all the rumors in the news about your husband's death."

"I know who you are." Kelly glared at him. "You're a Nazi. You're responsible for my sister's death."

Harley never expected her to know his name, let alone know anything about him. "I'm sorry about your sister."

"I've heard that line before. One of your little goons named Slayton told me he was sorry, too. It must be another company line."

"But Mrs. Montane, I am truly, truly sorry." Harley replied in his most sincere tone.

"So what do you want, Oh Sorry One?"

"I'd like to talk to you for a few minutes."

"Why? So you can tell me that you are denying Mike's death claim until a body is found. So you can proclaim the depth of *your* sorrow. So you can pretend you feel bad for me while you accuse me and my drowned husband of insurance fraud."

"Please, let me talk with you for a few minutes." Harley pleaded.

"Send what you have to say in the mail!" Kelly slammed the door in his face.

************ *********

The US Mail delivered the letter the next day. It was short and to the point:

> Dear Mrs. Montane,
> I am writing to express my sincere sympathy for you in this difficult time. We at Platinum Insurance are all truly sorry about your situation.
>
> I regret to inform you by mail that your life insurance claim on the life of Mike Montane has been denied at this time. The reason for the claim denial is that there is no proof of death.
>
> However, we will continue to keep your claim open and will pay all death benefits due under the policy plus interest at 5.25% from the time of death, once official proof of death has been received.
>
> Sincerely,
> Harley Crane

The letter meant nothing to Kelly. She had anticipated it, and crushed the paper into a ball and threw it across the room. Now she was ready to sue.

************ *********

I've been waiting for years for you to stop by, Kelly." Attorney John Jacobs looked as fit as ever.

"I know. I didn't have it in me to fight Platinum after Al's death."

"And now?"

"I'm ready."

"I understand. I've read the whole story ten times in a half dozen newspapers, plus I took the liberty of calling the Lake County Sheriff's Office and talked at length with Sheriff Crow to get all the inside details. You know, Kelly, the easiest course of action is to wait until the spring thaw. They'll find Mike's body and Platinum will have to pay you, and you won't owe us anything."

"What if we sue them now?"

"I don't think it's a good idea. First, the judge will probably agree with their motion to wait until spring – maybe even make you wait a couple years to see if someone finds the body. You'll still have to wait, and if you hire me and my firm to sue now, you would need to pay us thirty percent of the death benefits at the time of settlement."

"So what should I do?"

"Not much. I'll write a formal letter of protest to Platinum, and threaten to sue them for not settling in good faith. After they respond to me with the same information they've already sent you, we'll file a protest, then wait."

"But what if Mike's body isn't found?"

"Are you sure he didn't walk away?" Jacobs asked.

"Mike wouldn't do that. He loved me and I loved him. I know he still felt a lot of pain and anger toward Platinum, but he would never do anything to hurt me."

"All right then. I understand that you and three other people witnessed him fall out of the canoe. Even though you never witnessed him in the actual act of drowning, a jury would never find on the side of Platinum unless they had hard evidence."

"I can't imagine"

"What?"

"Do you–" Kelly stammered. "Do you think they have any hard evidence? I mean, what about all this stuff on the news about Mike using a wetsuit?"

"Kelly, I–"

"What about the dog search?"

"All they have is a theory supported by wild guesses. The dog search means next to nothing in the courts. Dogs have taken their masters for a walk since the beginning of time."

"And the tent?"

"Anyone could have tented where they found that tent site in the snow."

"Do you think they might be right?"

"No. Even the sheriff thinks the walkaway theory is a long shot. He's certain they'll find Mike's body in the spring thaw."

"What about the car that had been parked there for a week before our trip and was gone the day after Mike drowned? They're trying to say that Mike planted the car there to use as his escape vehicle." Kelly wanted someone to help her understand all this. She needed someone on her side who would still listen objectively to the whole story.

"They said the car was an Oldsmobile. Did you or Mike own one in the last six months?"

"No."

"Sheriff Crow told me the car was purchased six months ago with a cashier's check from a bank in Willmar, Minnesota. The sheriff is going to show a picture of Mike to all the bank employees to see if any of them recognizes him."

"I'm not worried. I don't even know where Willmar is."

"All right, Kelly. The sheriff told me they want to know where Mike was the week before you guys went canoeing."

"Why do they want to know that?"

"Because they want to know if Mike had time to go to the Boundary Waters to hide his gear."

"Let me think about it for a minute. Oh yeah, Mike took a trip to Sioux City, Iowa to do some duck hunting."

"When did he do that?"

"The weekend before our canoe trip."

"Are you sure that's where he went?"

"Yes. I pay the bills in our house, and I remember from the Visa receipts that he bought gas in Albert Lea, Minnesota on his way to and from Sioux City. Plus he paid for a hotel room in Sioux City that weekend on his Visa."

"Sioux City is the opposite direction from the Boundary Waters. How long was he gone?"

"Just for a three day weekend. There's simply no way he could've gone to Sioux City, then to Ely, back to Sioux City, and then home in one weekend."

"How about the week before your canoe trip?"

"Oh, Mike had all kinds of window washing jobs. People try to get ready for winter at the last minute. I have all those receipts and names of the clients he worked for."

"Did he get any ducks?"

"Yes, he got six and we ate four of them. I still have the two other ducks in the freezer, and one of them had a leg tag on it."

"Did any of the birds have birdshot in them?"

"I think they all did."

"All right. Don't eat the last two. We may need the ducks to testify for us, the same way Platinum might try to use the dogs. The leg tag might even give proof that the duck resided in Sioux City." Jacobs laughed. "It seems that all the evidence that Platinum has is purely guesswork. It won't hold up in court, and they know it."

"So why aren't they paying?"

"Because they don't have to pay yet. Unless the authorities rule that Mike is dead, the courts will allow the insurance company to sit on all payments until the statute of limitations runs out six years from now. They can treat him as a missing person. But after the six years, the courts would probably force Platinum to pay given your eyewitness testimony."

"Six years," Kelly sounded defeated.

"I'm afraid so, unless you sue them. However, you need to understand that if you sue, you'll open yourself up to a huge investigation. Platinum will use special investigators to check all your financial records, taxes, and phone calls. They'll interview you and your friends, and you'll have no choice but to comply with their requests as part of their legal right to defend themselves."

"I have nothing to hide."

"I'm sure you don't, Kelly, but they'll make your life hell. They'll try to convict you of trying to pull a fraud in the civil courts due to a preponderance of the evidence. In other words, if the jury thinks that you are committing a fraud, you will be fined, and then,"

Jacobs paused, "and then they will try to come back at you for a criminal offense."

"What's the difference?"

"In a civil trial, all they need to do is prove that it was likely that you committed a crime. In the criminal case, they would need to prove their case beyond a reasonable doubt, and for that you would probably go to prison."

"So none of this can happen if I don't sue them?"

"That's right. But if you don't sue, you won't get paid anything without a body until perhaps six years from now."

"And if I do sue, I open myself up to their investigation and a probable counter-suit of fraud."

"Yep. You see, right now as a beneficiary, you don't even have to talk to them. You don't need to provide any records either. But they simply won't pay you. You'll have a cold war on your hands."

"I guess my choices are limited then. I'd like you to write Platinum threatening a suit for unfair claims practices. And I'll send you copies of all my receipts, phone call records, and anything else you can think of from the last two months that will help establish Mike's whereabouts. Then, we'll wait till next summer. By September 1st, if there's no body, we'll sue Platinum."

"This time, Kelly, I promise you're going to win."

************ *********

Later that week, the mail brought Kelly a pleasant surprise. Her grocery store had awarded her two free tickets to the Vikings game. She had never won anything in her life, and had never been to a Vikings game, so she called Julie Jewel, and invited her along.

While Kelly was at the game, Harley and two of his closest men used a garage door encoder to drive their van into Kelly's garage. They closed the door and went through her house to photograph as many receipts and documents as they could. They downloaded her Quicken financial disks and every file in their home computer. They put a tracking device on her internet server to allow remote access to view wherever she went. They bugged all the phones and hid a couple of cameras in the house.

Harley didn't care if his actions were illegal. His job was on the line. He even sold his Jaguar XK8 Convertible so he'd have a little extra cash for the job. Of course, his men each earned a nice little cash gift for their quiet loyalty.

They ransacked the place thoroughly, and took the TV, the VCR, and some of her jewelry to make it look like a juvenile vandalism and theft.

Harley figured the poor boy would get lonesome and try to contact Kelly. It would take a while to go through all the data they collected, but Harley knew he had a lot of time. The fact that they hadn't been sued meant everyone planned to wait to see if a body appeared.

************ *********

One of Sheriff Crow's deputies drove to Willmar to interview the people at the bank. They showed a half dozen pictures of Mike to see if anyone recognized him, but had no luck.

Harley put two men on Kelly round the clock in an effort to learn every intimate detail about her. They needed to listen to her every conversation at home or work for the smallest of clues.

He wanted a list of every person she talked to including names, dates, and phone numbers. Using a mere three thousand dollar bribe, one of his FBI contacts "persuaded" a post office employee to allow Harley's men a daily check of Kelly's mail. Even so, Harley's men sorted through the garbage cans inside her garage, by using their garage door decoder. Anything to find clues.

They got several bad leads from some gas station personnel, and they spent hours studying surveillance videos until each of the phony leads dead-ended.

Meanwhile, Harley's team in Ely finished calling every person who had a hunting permit for the BWCA during the time of the drowning. All of them wanted the $30,000 reward, but no one had seen Mike.

They interviewed the people who lived within five miles of the end of the Fernberg Trail, near Arlen's North Country Retreat Center.

They also questioned every man, woman, and child who lived within five miles of Big Rock Trail. That is, everyone except the person who lived at the cabin that sat tucked in the woods, closest to the trail. The locals said a man called Goliath lived there, but he wintered somewhere in Florida every year. None of the others offered any new clues.

Legalities or illegalities never bothered Harley in his quest to win. He spared no expense with Platinum's checkbook as he covered every possible angle. His job, his reputation, and his very identity within himself hinged on being right.

Harley would stand in front of the ball, and knock it down with his teeth if he had to. *It's one thing to make it to the majors, and another to stay there.*

************ *********

After three months of clueless searching and dead end chasing, Harley brainstormed on a unique ploy to end it all. He called *Inquiring Minds Magazine*, and made them promise in writing that they would not publish anything about the case until he solved it. In exchange, they got exclusive first-interview rights as long as they would help him play one more round with Kelly.

For their part, they only needed to match his bribe. Platinum would throw in $250,000 if *Inquiring Minds* would add another quarter million. The inexpensive cost would give them incredible returns on breaking this national story if Harley's strategy worked.

The *Inquiring Minds* crew knocked on Kelly's door in the middle of a cloudy Saturday afternoon. The reporter was blunt and to the point: "Mrs. Montane, I'm here to offer you a half million dollars cash for the exclusive story of what happened to you, your husband, and your sister. We want to know your side of the story so we can show the public what horrible devastation you faced when your sister died. We want to give the public reasons to support your husband's attempted insurance fraud."

"What?" she hollered.

"A half million dollars and a written promise from the insurance company not to prosecute you if you come clean and tell us what really happened to your husband."

"There is only one true story and I've already told it," Kelly screamed as she slammed the door in his face.

She hoped the door broke his nose.

Chapter 46

When the ice melted in May, Sheriff Crow and his team spent several days dragging the Three Forks River area for Mike's body. Harley increased the reward to $100,000 because he was certain no body would be found, and he wanted to get all the locals who owned as much as a snorkel to join in the search.

The Big Rock Trail became a major avenue for hikers, naturalists, and other bounty hunters. When Goliath saw the flood of people walking past his cabin day after day, he resented it. He cherished, even *needed*, the solitude of the woods, especially after spending the winter at the noisy Florida art fairs.

By mid summer, Goliath posted signs all around his property warning people to stay away. Who were these boisterous people who suddenly clambered around his woods? The invasion of privacy infuriated him.

A couple of audacious people even came to his cabin in the middle of a rainstorm. They pounded on his door and asked him if they could come inside. That they were cold and wet had nothing to do with life or death. They were poorly dressed city people who had no business being there, so the only "hospitality" he showed them came disguised as the nose of his Remington.

The big man didn't care what anyone thought of him. Solitude was all he sought.

************ *********

Harley had spent the last six months learning everything he possibly could about the Montanes. He knew when Kelly woke up in the morning, and when she went to bed. She never even took a shower without Crane's men listening.

With each passing day, Harley's intrigue increased over the Montane's resolve to *not* contact the other. Their tenacity was tougher than he ever thought possible, and the mental gymnastics made Harley ever more determined to win.

"Hey, boss." One of Harley's men walked into the Platinum's Minneapolis Claims center. Harley never bothered to look up.

"What's up?"

"It's a . . . It's been such a long time with no results. All the men are exhausted and bored. It seems obvious that she's not going to contact him–"

"You sound like a whiner," Harley's eyes remained on his work as he spoke. "If the work was easy, we could have anyone do it. But it's hard work, and someday it'll pay off."

"But, Harley. I've got to give the men a reason. A deadline of some type. Why haven't they contacted each other yet? How long can we keep this going?"

"I'll tell you why they haven't contacted each other. It's because of you. You and your men have them scared shitless. They know that we know. You tell your men that we're winning. The Montanes are going to break, and your men will have their reward."

"Boss, I'll do what I can."

"Tell your men that the game is much more exciting when everyone plays."

After the investigator left, Harley hung his head. First the pressure from his conservative boss. Now pressure from below. Harley's contempt toward Roger Phillips grew. His gutless boss was no doubt trying to turn Harley's own men against him.

Hell could turn into a ski resort before Roger Philips would've put his cry baby face in front of a baseball. Harley couldn't believe how, just a few short years ago, he had worked so hard to win such a loser's approval.

One truth remained. Harley certainly didn't need a boss he couldn't respect. Once Harley had won this case, he'd find a way to take the man with the pocket pencil-holder out of the picture. Then he would have no more bosses.

Harley knew what it took to run the company.

Chapter 47

A week later, the Oregon Department of Natural Resources called Harley. "We identified your missing Oldsmobile from the secondary engine identification number. The car's been torched."

"What about the VIN plate?" Harley asked.

"We couldn't find it. Most thieves are smart enough to tear it out of the car, but the secondary engine VIN was traced, and this is unmistakably your car."

"When was the fire?"

"Our arson people say it happened sometime last November."

"Do you have any witnesses?" Harley knew the answer would be no.

"Nah. The car burned in a desert. There's no question someone tried to lose it. You're lucky we found it."

"How about fingerprints?" wished Harley.

"Not a chance."

"Give me something more. Anything." Harley pleaded into the phone.

"I don't know how this helps you, but there are some unmistakable mountain bike tracks that led away from the burned up wreckage."

"It's been six months. How do you know that?"

"We figure it must've rained the day of the fire. This is high desert country, and it hasn't rained up here for about six months. The scars on this type of earth take a long time to heal. Some of the ruts from the wagons of the first settlers from two hundred years ago are still here."

"Thanks a lot." Harley finally got his first break. His men would be ecstatic to hear the news. "A bike. I was right. The son-of-a-bitch used a bike!" Harley shouted for anyone who cared to listen.

He decided to launch a search within a three-hundred-mile radius of the burned car. Harley figured that Montane needed to stay in a cash business, something that didn't require his social security number, and knew that Montane made good money washing windows in Minneapolis. There was no reason to think he would give it up.

Harley focused his search in the larger metropolitan areas first: Seattle, Spokane, Portland, Salem, Boise, Salt Lake City, even San Francisco. Mike had already established an advertising pattern that made him successful in the Twin Cities by sending fliers to all wealthy area homes as an insert in the local papers. He would probably repeat the same routine in his new hometown.

Harley's men searched backwards, beginning in October, as they scoured the window cleaning advertisements. A bulls-eye would be finding a new ad for a start-up company.

They found one. Roy's All-Bright Window Cleaning Services located in Tacoma. They called the local telephone company to get a billing address.

With a little help from Mason Crow, Harley got the local police to get a warrant. As he parked his rented Lexus behind the police car in front of Mike's condo, Harley's heart raced. Every breath was fast. "I got your ass." Harley's lips smeared the words across his smiling face.

One policeman walked to the back door to prevent escape. Harley stood behind the cop at the front. When the doorbell rang, a million thoughts ran through his mind. *He'd be the man, once again. He'd show that chicken-shit, Roger.*

No one answered the door. Harley wavered. Now the cop banged his fist on the door. Harley's pulse pounded with the rhythm. Still no answer.

"Knock the door down." Harley bleated.

"That would cause too much damage," the cop replied, then without pause, tapped his nightstick through the wing window next to the door. "Glass is a lot cheaper. Easier on the body, too." The cop reached through the broken glass and unlocked the door.

Harley started to follow the cop into the condo.

"You need to stay here." The cop motioned with his hand.

The wind in Harley's sail collapsed. He turned and paced back toward the car, then watched the cop disappear, announcing "police" as he went.

Harley couldn't stand it. Not knowing was worse than torture. Less than a minute later, Harley crept silently though the condo. The place was empty. Spotless. It reeked of cleanser residue mixed with stale air.

Tiptoeing in total silence, Harley peeked into the naked kitchen.

"Police!" the cop's voice boomed, and swung around with his pistol. Harley fell to the ground.

"I told you to stay outside!" The cop stood over Harley and kept the gun pointed in his face.

************ *********

A day later, Harley was informed of the results of the fingerprint search of the condo. "What do you mean there were no fingerprints?"

"That's right. Whoever rented that condo cleaned it so well that we couldn't lift one print out of the place."

"How about a stray hair?"

"Nothing." The cop answered.

"Did you check the light bulbs?"

"I said there was nothing."

The office buzzed as Harley barked out questions that demanded answers. "Why had Dobson paid the landlord for a year's rent in advance? Why was the phone service disconnected shortly after Montane's funeral was aired on national television? Why had Dobson moved without leaving a forwarding address? Why weren't there any prints?"

Harley took out a full-page advertisement in the Tacoma Times newspaper, showing a sample of the flyer that Roy's All-Bright Window Cleaning Services had used. He offered a $30,000 reward for information that would lead him to find Roy Dobson.

One All-Bright customer saw the ad and called. Within fifteen minutes, Harley and three men were at the customer's house.

"What did the window washer look like?" Harley demanded.

"What about the reward."

"If you help us, I'll pay you the reward."

"How do I know if this is legit?"

"Here's my card." Harley smiled like a cat. "If you'd like to call my office in Chicago, you'll find that I'm exactly who the card says I am. Furthermore, here are the details of the reward, already spelled out in black and white."

"A vice-president, huh?"

"That's right."

"He was bald with a big dark mustache."

"Could he possibly have been this man?" Harley showed several pictures of Mike.

"Not a chance."

"Do you mind if we fingerprint your windows?"

"I don't know."

"Here's $500 for your trouble, up front."

"It won't do you any good."

"Why not?"

"Cause the window washer wore gloves the whole time."

Then the man who made Roy's business cards saw the ad and called. He said he never met Roy – that they had done all their business by phone. However, he did say that Roy ordered 2,000 business cards. Surely enough cards to stay in business for at least a year.

Harley asked Mason Crow to do a search to find Dobson. Armed with his name and address, the State of Washington Department of Motor Vehicles should have been able to track him down. It took a little bit of work, and in the end they found that the Roy Dobson they were hunting for had died over a year and a half earlier.

Harley asked the State of Washington for a copy of the photo on the driver's license. Then he and his men argued among themselves. Sure the picture looked like Roy Dobson. But Dobson had died a year before the picture was taken. Who was the phony? Why would he go to such great lengths to make himself look like a dead man?

Harley looked out the window of his Platinum office at the Seattle claims headquarters. The lowest branches of a giant Oak tree extended ten feet off the ground, almost parallel with the earth. As a boy, it would have been the perfect tree to climb. Today, Harley's mind envisioned a rope wrapped around the lowest branch. Following the rope off the tree, an open noose extended, ready for a very dead Roy Dobson to cinch around Mike Montane's ugly head.

The noose, indeed, was getting tight.

************ *********

When Mike had left Tacoma the day after the news broadcast, his paranoia increased exponentially. He drove his jeep to Kalispell, Montana where he took it to a detail shop and had it washed and waxed inside and out until every possible trace of himself had been removed. Then he sold it to the kid who did the detail work for a third of its value in cash.

From there he hired a guide to take him by snowmobile to the western edge of Glacier National Park on the U.S. – Canadian Border. Armed with a pair of snowshoes and enough freeze-dried food to last a couple weeks, Mike snow-shoed his way into Waterton Park in British Columbia, and eventually hitchhiked his way to the little resort town of Jasper, Alberta.

He knew from previous mountain hiking vacations that Jasper was a friendly resort/railroad town. Three hours north of Banff and Lake Louise, most tourists never made it that far. The people who frequented the town were true outdoors people, the kind who loved wilderness and solitude.

Mike figured he could wash the local business windows for cash. He would offer a ridiculously low price, and a money-back guarantee if his work was unsatisfactory. There would be no advertising, only word of mouth, and only cash. And he would go by his middle name.

He rented a small bedroom on the second floor of a tiny house from an old lady who told him she liked it quiet. Fine by him. The room was only big enough to hold a bed and a small desk to set up a laptop computer.

Mike spent his days working, sometimes doing odd jobs, always for cash. He kept to himself and worked hard. People weren't sure what to think of the bald man who never said anything. But they respected his hard work, and there was never a shortage of jobs for someone so willing.

Still, Mike was nagged with doubt. Worry ruled. His sagging, dark skin under his eyes contrasted with his ashen colored face. With no sleep and no appetite, the nervous man's face aged by a decade. Suddenly, it seemed like everyone looked at him, maybe because he had become so ugly.

He remembered the great pains he had taken to create an alibi and to cover his tracks. Kelly never knew that he drove their van the five hours from Minneapolis to Sioux City, rented a hotel room, messed up the bed, then left immediately for an eight hour drive to Ely. He had left their van in Sioux City where the Oldsmobile had been in storage for the last six months. He wore his wig on the way to Ely, and used six-gallon jugs of gas in his trunk to refuel the Olds. After hiding his gear, and leaving the Olds parked at the Big Rock Trailhead, he hitchhiked all the way back to Sioux City. Then he checked out of the hotel, bought a half dozen ducks from some local hunters, and drove the van back home to Minneapolis. He made sure that he used his credit card for the gas purchased in Albert Lea on both journeys to and from home.

Now his stomach ached. His mouth felt dry. He remembered how he had dusted every inch of the condo. How he wore gloves and vacuumed the floor, the walls, the couch, the chairs – everything. How two people looked at him when he threw the bed sheets and covers in a trash dumpster on the other side of town. Paranoia didn't allow for any more mistakes.

Then his mind shifted back to Kelly. Day and night he worried about her. About her loneliness. His loneliness. He wanted to reach out and touch her so badly, to tell her that he was still alive and say he loved her.

Mike constantly thought about her suffering. First Al's death and now his. What kind of hell might she be going through to try to collect the life insurance money from Platinum? What were they saying and doing to her? How badly were they treating her? What kind of advice could Jacobs give her? How close was Platinum to solving his crime? When would the trial begin?

Sometimes Mike lay in bed and pondered the shadows on the ceiling for hours as he tried to relax, tried not to think of Kelly. What if they put doubts in her mind about his death? What if she fell in love with someone else? What if Kelly wasn't as strong as he thought she was?

The questions kept coming at him. There were never any answers.

He stayed up often and wrote Kelly sweet love letters. He told her about his day, about where he lived, about the grizzly bear that had roamed into town the other day. He told her about the books he read, and reminded her constantly of how much he missed her. Then he would put the letter in an envelope, write her name on it, and place it under his pillow so that he could sleep next to her.

The next day Mike brought his letter to the fireplace and watched it burn. He hoped the little clouds of smoke would carry their message to Kelly's heart a thousand miles away.

On the nights he couldn't sleep, Mike tried to sit up and read. He read page after page, only to realize that he hadn't read anything, that he still thought of Kelly. Finally, utterly exhausted, he would nod off while sitting in the chair. He'd wake the next morning stiff and sore, but his thoughts remained on his best friend.

He dragged himself to work, and then gave his menial job the effort of any two men. It was his only way of coping. He hoped he could last long enough to see her again.

*********** *********

Kelly made a decision – not to decide anything. Until September first. She knew speculation could only bring anxiety. Being anxious wouldn't do any good, and she had done enough worrying in her lifetime when she worried day and night for her sister.

When Mason Crow called her after the July 4th holiday to tell her they had officially given up the search, all the terrible sad feelings rushed into her. She mumbled “thanks”, then hung up the phone and curled onto the floor.

Crying couldn’t help her. But her body felt drained. Empty. Beyond being alone, she felt lonely. There was no one to talk too. No one to hug. No one to even hold hands with. Nothing to look forward too.

Abandoned.

She spent several days in utter isolation, unable to work, afraid to call someone – anyone – for help. Fear of isolating herself even further; fear of burdening someone else with her problems overwhelmed her. These fears merged with her loneliness, and made her seclusion even worse.

Then came the second-guessing. She began to wonder if Harley Crane was right. What if Mike was alive? Every nerve and fiber of her being, every thought both day and night revolved around the words, “We’ve given up looking for his body.”

She finally called Dillon at his law firm in Michigan while Harley’s men taped the conversation. “Hey, Dillon.”

“You sound like you need a friend, Kelly.” Dillon’s sympathy melted the words.

“They called off the search.”

He paused, and there was a long silence. “Kelly, I wish I could be with you. We knew they were going to do this sooner or later.”

“I know, but why didn’t they find him?”

“The river moves fast. Mike’s body could have floated two miles downstream. We’ve talked about this before.”

“But what if it’s true?”

“What?”

“What if Harley Crane is right?”

“Why would Mike do it?”

“I don’t know. We loved each other.”

“And we know Mike wasn’t motivated by money.”

“But I get these doubts, Dillon. Mike hated Platinum for what they did to Al and us."

"He was a man of principle. The same way he stuck with you and Alex."

"We were happily married on the day he drowned."

"I know."

"I'm sorry I called you, Dillon."

"Kelly, I –"

"I miss Mike so much."

"It's okay."

"I've re-lived the day he drowned a trillion times."

"I know."

"Nothing felt wrong, except the maps, and that wasn't necessarily his fault. Who would possibly know what happened to the spare key for the van? It may have fallen off, or maybe he had used it to unlock the door, and never put it back."

"Kelly, what can I say?"

"Sometimes I walk around the house and talk out loud, as if Mike were standing next to me."

Of course she was unaware that Harley's men listened to every word.

"You've got friends, Kel."

"They're mostly acquaintances. They're busy with their own lives and families."

"You can call me anytime."

"You're busy too, Dillon. It gives me a weird, imposing feeling to call. I mean, how can I suddenly thrust myself into other people's lives?

"Kelly, I'll always have time to be your friend."

"Did you know that I go to the movies alone?" There was a long pause as if she expected an answer. "After everyonc leaves the theatre, I'm the only one there, and most of the time my mind is empty."

"Kel." Dillon acknowledged.

"And eating alone is the worst. I used to love to eat, and now food has become a burden of necessity."

"There are lots of people who'd love to share a meal with you."

"I don't know." Kelly shook her head and began to pace the floor, lost in her own thoughts. "I only eat frozen pizzas and the quick fix sandwiches. I can't eat out because I hate sitting alone. I feel like other people watch me."

"Lot's of people eat out by themselves."

"Dillon, that's a joke. I never see people eating by themselves," Kelly huffed. "I feel like I have to try to look content and normal while others laugh and carry on conversations. I even bring magazines or a book to dinner with me."

"That's a good idea." Dillon tried to be helpful.

"Yeah, but my eyes just gloss the pages."

"Have you thought about getting a dog?"

"What if it runs away?" Kelly paused and the dead air between Minneapolis and Detroit spanned the line. "I must sound awful. But what if the dog died?"

"I don't know what to say."

************ *********

After another week of brooding, Kelly decided that immersing herself in her work would be the best way to cope. It was her only outlet.

Her boss thought she had the best worker on earth as Kelly pounded down twelve-hour days and volunteered for Saturdays almost every week.

Each day represented one small step. Ever so slowly, she thought less and less of the drowning and the upcoming battle with Platinum. "Decide not to decide" was the only way she could cope.

September one she would sue Platinum. That day would come soon enough.

Chapter 48

Junk mail.

Mike's mailbox contained nothing but advertisements and waste paper. No one ever sent a bill because Mike paid cash or money order for everything. The solicitations and form letters always came addressed to "Occupant." The man named Mike Montane had ceased to exist to the outside world.

The fugitive/dead-man spent two hours a day scouring the net for news of home. Using the word "Platinum," and "Richter," Mike ran searches through Google, Yahoo, and MSN trying to garnish any hint of news. Then he scanned two pages of "favorite sites" as he reviewed every available web page of the writers, columnists, and editorialists who had discussed Platinum in the past. Surely, some reporter would be following this case, especially after it had received brief attention in the national media.

Despite his vigilant efforts, he found nothing. Night after lonely night, he sat alone in his tiny room in front of the computer. Maybe they had paid Kelly and closed the case against him. What if Platinum's private police somehow found him? What would he do if Kelly found a new man? More than anything, he wanted to be back with her. What if she married him? What if Platinum found his car? What if they interviewed that monster with the shotgun? What if he told Platinum about the wetsuit that had spilled onto the ground? Did that man even see the wetsuit? Why didn't someone – anyone – write about his case anymore?

Mike felt like a dead man walking. He burned with an overpowering need to tell Kelly he was alive and loved her. He wanted to hold her, touch her face again, and look into her eyes. He needed her warmth and tenderness. He felt so terribly alone.

But more than all of that, he still needed her to believe he was dead. It was the only way she would fight Platinum. The only way he could eventually lose the devils that plagued him. If his plan worked, he'd get Platinum's money, and get Kelly back at the same time.

He tried to shake his doubts and dream about his "next life." He even went so far as to go to the local print shop where he created an elaborate glossy brochure about an adventure company called Adventures in Living or AL for short. His company would take people on trips they would never forget. Rock-climbing, canoeing, kayaking, paragliding. Kelly once shared this dream with him, and he had casually disregarded it.

If only he could go back to that day. The empty dreams, and his inner anger toward Platinum took turns torturing him.

He couldn't risk making friends, or they might ask questions. Easy conversation became impossible. People asked where he was from and wanted to know about his past. Beyond being lonely, he became a loner in every sense of the word. He talked as little as possible, paranoid that even his voice might give him away.

He grew to despise shaving his head every day, and longed for the day when he'd be able to grow out his long blond hair. He especially hated the ugly black mustache. It didn't look good on him, and he had to dye it black every few days. Then he had to smell the dye until the odor disappeared, sometimes a whole day later. The ugly hairs on his face itched, got in his food, got icy in the winter, and he had to be careful when he blew his nose. But the disguise could have fooled his own dead mother, and he was simply too afraid to ever consider shaving it off.

The lonely recluse existed in a tortured state of mind that made him feel even less worthy than his illegal alien status. He became a stranger even to himself, as he continuously doubted his own decisions. Why couldn't he let go of the injustice Platinum had dealt him? Why couldn't he have listened to Kelly's words of wisdom when she told him to move on, when she pointed out their happiness together? He knew now that she had been right.

He longed to tell someone, anyone, his story. Yet he dared not. His sanity wrestled with the insanity of silence. He had to know what was going on back home.

He even drove to Winnipeg, where he rented some time on the internet in a local coffee shop. He wanted to be certain that no one could trace him, or his IP address to his home in Jasper. Even if Platinum somehow tapped into Julie Jewel's computer and traced it to Winnipeg, the thousand-mile distance from Jasper would never bring a search so far.

He chatted on line with Julie Jewel, who had her e-mail address on her business cards. He typed a well-prepared, simple story: "I'm an old girlfriend of Alex Richter's. I was in the same 4H club with her and Kelly when they were in grade school in Kentucky. We rode horses together."

"What's your name so I can tell Kelly who I'm talking with?" came the typed response.

"I'm Cassie Kaleigh, but Kelly probably doesn't remember me because I was mostly friends with Alex. Alex and I used to barrel race against each other." He used the name of a girl pictured in one of Alex's scrapbooks, but someone whom Kelly had never mentioned.

"Nice to meet you. How can I help you?"

"I'm very interested in the case against Platinum Insurance. I think they are a horrible company, they wronged Alex, and their actions ultimately caused her death. I hadn't thought about Alex in a long time until I saw the story about Mike Montanc's drowning on TV. I'd like to know what's happening."

"Why don't you call Kelly and talk to her about it? I'm sure she could use your encouragement and support."

"As I said, I don't know Kelly that well. I haven't talked to her in twenty years, and I feel nervous calling her. But I knew you used to work with Alex, so I thought I'd contact you. And I'm sure Kelly has told her story a thousand times and doesn't want to tell it again."

"So what can I do for you then?"

"I'd like to know what is going on, but I'm tired of reading through the Minneapolis paper to see if there is any more news. I own a hair salon and have two young children, and I don't have time to keep reading through the paper."

"Right now, they're doing nothing, except waiting to see if Mike's body surfaces. Kelly told me she plans to sue in September even if there is no body, and her lawyers have told her that on the strength of the eye witnesses, she'll probably win the case."

Mike raised his arms in joy. She was hanging in there, fighting Platinum. Tears streamed down his cheeks, as he held his one and only picture of Kelly in his hands. Then he quickly typed, "How is Kelly holding up through all of this?"

"Pretty good, I would say."

"I would appreciate it if you could keep me up to date." He wished he could ask more questions, but dared not.

"I'd be glad to e-mail you. What's your address."

"I don't own a computer. I'm using a friend's right now."

"What do you suggest?"

"I have a fax number. It would be great if you would fax me any new information about the case. I know you're busy, and I remember Alex telling me how the two of you used to donate time at the Dorothy Day Center as volunteers together. I want to make a donation."

"You don't have to donate anything." The typed response came back.

"I expected you to say that. But I'd like to anyway. Each time you fax me an update, I will donate a $10 money order payable to the Dorothy Day Center, and I will have the money order sent to your office."

"You don't have to do that."

"Just the same, I would like to thank you for keeping me in the loop, and it's a small donation."

"What's your fax number?"

He typed in the rented number of a fax system called "Never Busy Fax." It held up to a hundred faxes in queue, and the retrieval could be performed at any remote location. It would allow him to get faxes anywhere in the world without being traced.

Mike trembled as he walked out of the coffee shop. Relief overwhelmed him. When he got in his car, the lonely man collapsed on the steering wheel and cried. The sun still shined. Kelly still had strength and was fighting a good fight.

Mike Montane, and hope, still lived.

Chapter 49

The fall day felt cold and crisp at the county courthouse. As Harley and his entourage strode into the courtroom, Kelly sat alone at the front desk. Her friends Dillon, Grant, Allison, and John Jacobs were all on their way – probably trying to find a place to park.

Harley had waited for the moment. He sauntered up the aisle and his stare burned through Kelly's skull. With deliberate callousness he turned and stood directly before her. He never stuck out his arm in any attempt at greeting, but instead gave one of those big fakey smiles. Then he leaned down and brought his face close to hers. "Kelly Montane, I presume. My name is Harley Crane, and I'm the man who came to your door a year ago to chat."

Kelly looked impassively back at him. "I already told you that I know who you are."

Harley kept his big smile going. "Yes, I believe you called me a Nazi, the one who murdered your sister."

"You sound like you're proud of it." Kelly's smiled.

"I'm proud of most things I do. And I want you to know that today, you've played your last card." He paused for effect as their eyes locked in combat. "Today, the judge is going to give me permission to invade your life, to protect Platinum against low-lifes like you. And I'm going to find Mike alive if it's the last thing I do. When I do, we're going to prosecute you to the full extent of the law."

"Mr. Crane, you must be an awfully lonely man. What on earth happened in your life to make you so angry?" Kelly spoke in a way that was not condemning, nor condescending; just quiet and penetrating.

"You're a bitch, Montane. I can smell it like you're in heat. I've got you, and you know it." Just then, the door in the back opened and Kelly's group shuffled in. Harley turned, and as he walked away his voice turned snide, "you'll always remember me."

Finally, the judge came in. He looked tired and his eyes had dark bags under them. His face appeared worn as if he had seen or heard it all, and was bored with his job.

Harley's side got to go first. Over the next two hours, they laid it all out: motive, method, circumstances, the weird things associated with the mysterious Oldsmobile, and the very dead window washer named Roy Dobson who happened to be the same age as Mike. It had been a year since the alleged drowning. Despite an intense search with several hundred volunteers and reward seekers, they had no body.

Harley's team of high-priced lawyers moved for dismissal. Mike Montane had clearly walked away from something in his life, and the revenge motive overshadowed everything.

The judge listened quietly, then gave Kelly's side an opportunity. Jacobs first brought in forensic experts to prove that some bodies simply do not float in cold water.

Then Jacobs called in a seventy-something-year-old widow. "Can you tell us about the circumstances surrounding your husband's death?" Jacobs asked.

"My husband, Fred was last seen alive about three years ago. My son dropped him off to go fishing in our small boat on Lake Nokomis." The widow's thinning white hair and heavily wrinkled skin made her appear ancient, yet she spoke in a commanding, matter-of-fact tone. "When Fred didn't show up for his ride home for dinner, my son called the police. They found Fred's empty boat floating next to the southern shore of the lake, but they never found my husband."

"How big is Lake Nokomis?" Jacob's asked.

"It's a small lake."

"Can you tell us how small?"

"It takes me about an hour to walk around it." She waved her finger in the air and created a circle. "And I don't walk fast."

"What happened then?"

"The police searched for Fred but never found him."

"Can you tell us about that search?"

"Oh yeah." She paused for a sip of water. "They assumed he

had drowned at first. So they searched the shore and even did a drag of the whole lake."

"What did they find?" Jacobs asked.

"Nothing."

"Then what happened?"

"They brought in Scuba divers."

"And?"

"They still couldn't find him."

"Then what happened?"

"Fred's disappearance made it to all the local TV and radio news stations in the Twin Cities. The newspapers and TV even showed a picture of Fred."

"But they still couldn't find him?"

"No."

"What happened with regards to his life insurance?"

"The insurance company denied the claim because there was no body and no hard evidence of death." She waved her gnarled finger in Harley's direction. "I had to sell my home and move in with my son's family."

"When did they find your husband?"

She sat up straight in her chair. "Two months ago his body surfaced, and a jogger found him floating near the southern shore."

"Can you tell us the specifics?"

"He was almost unrecognizable except that he wore the same clothes he always wore when he went fishing."

"How else did they identify him?"

"His wallet and drivers license was still in his back pocket."

"Thank you." Jacobs said.

"Damn insurance companies." The widow muttered as she left her chair.

Jacobs smiled at the stone-faced Harley, while the judge impassively watched the exchange. Then Jacobs admitted into evidence Kelly's financial statements to show they were doing well before the drowning. Then he produced two dozen signed statements from friends of Mike and Kelly's that agreed to testify that they thought the couple had been happy together.

Jacobs showed, in court documented records, where other people had gained false identifications from dead people. "It's a relatively common scam," Jacobs looked again at Harley, "and the insurance company knows it. We're arguing that Platinum's speculations are purely wild guesses."

Jacobs reached over to touch Kelly's arm, then spoke in his most tender voice, "Even though Kelly Montane has suffered from the loss of her husband, she and the other drowning witnesses have agreed to take lie detector tests. They have nothing to hide and want to prove that they have told the truth regarding Mike Montane's drowning." Jacobs pointed at Harley. "Platinum can ask whatever questions they want – no holds barred, and this will be the litmus test to prove what Platinum already knows. They simply don't have a case."

Jacobs paused to let his words sink in, then presented his close. "Every life insurance policy that Platinum sells has a two year contestability clause for suicide. This means if you commit suicide after two years of owning a life policy, you are still covered. Platinum and the rest of the insurance industry uses a two year clause simply because it presumes no one can buy a life policy and have the wherewithal to wait for two long years to commit suicide. Too much life happens in those two years. The question begs itself: How can Platinum possibly argue that Mike Montane carried out a revenge plan for seven years after Alex's death without telling anyone?"

The courtroom turned silent when Jacobs sat down.

The whine of the forced air system even stopped. No one said anything. All eyes looked at the judge.

The judge closed his eyes and breathed in a deep, cleansing type of breath. "I have conflicting thoughts on this case. The strength of the eyewitness testimony makes me believe that Mr. Montane is truly dead. I think Platinum's arguments are speculative and circumstantial, but I appreciate their creativity." He let out a tired smile and looked directly at Harley Crane as he spoke in a matter-of-fact tone. "However, I still believe Platinum should be allowed to conduct a full-scale search for Mike Montane. Anything less would be a violation of their rights. Given the circumstances, I cannot force them to pay a death claim without a body.

"As this is simply a preliminary hearing, I'm going to give Platinum nine months to conduct their investigation. This will give Platinum more than adequate time to conduct a thorough, legal, and binding investigation. We will have a jury trial in June next year, and I do not want this case to be appealed. Furthermore, it gives nature one more season to produce the body."

************ *********

The drive to Edmonton took three and a half long hours. A minimum of a hundred cars passed Mike as he crawled across the snowy tundra at two-kilometers-per-hour below the posted speed limit. If he had an accident, or got pulled over for the most minor infraction, Mike knew the Royal Canadian Mounted Police would throw an unlicensed, uninsured American in jail. There he'd be fingerprinted, identified, and the rest would be history.

The radio had stopped working, so Mike made the long drive with nothing to distract his thoughts. Though it was a sunny day, the wind swept snow streaked horizontally across the road, buffeting the van and making the drive extra difficult.

Mike's thoughts raced faster than his van. September and October had come and gone, and Mike couldn't understand why he hadn't heard from Julie Jewel. Why didn't someone write about the case after Jacobs sued for Kelly? Doubt plagued the fugitive once again. He found his mind spinning out of control with negative thoughts and worries.

By the time Mike drove into the Edmonton Mall parking lot, he could hardly see from exhaustion. More than being physically tired, his body could not compensate for the mental fatigue. He parked his car on the far end of the lot to force a long walk.

Thousands of Christmas shoppers pulsed through the mall. Lights, banners, and Santa stuff filled every square inch of wall space while holiday music played through every store. It seemed everyone walked in pairs. Parents with their kids, young lovers, even grandmas and grandpas held hands as they shopped. Mike felt like a barren island in the middle of an ocean of joy.

By the time he got to the Mail-Boxes-And-More store, his walk became an unconscious trance. Eyes glazed, Mike bumped into an old woman, and almost knocked her down. He forced his hand to find his wallet, then gave the clerk the phone number for his Never-Busy-Fax, and braced himself for more news of nothing.

Five minutes later, the clerk came back with a dozen faxes in her hand. She laid them on the counter.

The top fax was an advertisement from a travel company, but within seconds, Mike saw the fax from Julie Jewel. Her short letter explained the preliminary hearing and the judge's decision. She said the judge thought Platinum's arguments were purely speculative, lacking solid evidence. His eyes read the words again: *No solid evidence.* Kelly and her lawyers were happy and confident of victory.

"Confident of victory!" Mike's voice sang the words. He leaned across the counter and shook hands with the clerk. "Merry Christmas and thanks a lot!"

The suddenly living man skipped through the crowded mall. As "Jingle Bells" played in the background, Mike sang along as a big smile broke across his face. Finally, things were moving forward. The judge had even set a trial date for the end of June. Only nine more months and it would all be over! He could hold his breath for nine months!

Then he'd play his final card. With a little luck, he'd be with Kelly again!

And he'd have Platinum's money.

When he stepped outside, Mike breathed a sigh of relief. He looked up to the sky, and pumped his fist in the air. "Yes!"

Chapter 50

Harley pushed his way past Kelly as he entered her house. Armed with a sheriff and a search warrant, he planned to conduct an "official" search of her premises to find new evidence that would lead them to Mike.

They asked for all receipts for the last two years. Perhaps they could find a mountain bike receipt, or notes about an Oldsmobile. Gasoline and mileage records could verify where the cars had been. Maybe a note, or a phone call could somehow collaborate a financial connection between Mike and Roy Dobson's place in Tacoma.

They called every long distance number listed on the Montane's phone bills from the last two years. Harley wanted to know who Kelly and Mike had called and the purpose of every call.

Harley's suit-and-tie goons hunted through every one of her drawers, her closets, and scrapbooks. They looked between the pages of her books to try to find a clue. They searched the attic and lifted up her mattress to see if anything had been hidden.

They demanded, and received, a list of all Mike's customers for his window washing business, and contacted them to see if they had paid Mike by cash or check. They asked if Mike had ever mentioned Platinum, ever spoke of revenge, or ever discussed Alex Richter's death. They asked if Mike ever talked of another woman or a girlfriend, or if he said anything harsh about Kelly.

Harley wanted to know if Mike had enough cash to pay a year advance rent on the Tacoma condo. Mike's cash income was compared to the income reported on his taxes. Knowledge equaled power. Harley wanted the IRS in his corner. It would make a powerful threat over Kelly's head.

In spite of a small army of Platinum special claims handlers, the investigation still took five long months to complete.

************ *********

Roger Philips paced across the plush floor, staring out the giant windows with his hands in his pockets. Harley and a SIU psychologist, the one whose bald-head made him look like Captain Picard entered the room at the same time.

Roger never turned to face them. “Have a seat.”

Harley and the Picard look-alike sat at the oval conference table, and no one spoke.

“Harley, I’m going to recall your support people and equipment off the Montane case.”

“I need more time,” Harley blurted.

“I used to believe in you. But something has changed you.”

“I’m the same man I’ve always been.”

“No, Harley. In the last year, you’ve only spent a few months in Chicago.”

“Roger, you hired me because of my tenacity to finish a job, no matter how difficult.”

“Yes. And I also hired you because you used to be devoted to higher principles, had sharp ideas and were willing to take a risk.”

“That’s still me, Roger. I’m fighting Montane on principal. He’s out there trying to take seven million dollars from us.” Harley raised his hands and glanced at the bald man sitting next to him.

“No, Harley. You’ve become so emotionally involved in this that you’ve ignored my repeated requests to hand it off to someone else.”

“I’m not emotionally involved!” Harley boomed.

“Listen to yourself, Harley.” Roger paused. “While you’ve played cop and purposefully disobeyed my orders, the entire company has grown in a thousand different directions. You’re out of the loop.”

“Roger, I can never undo the damage of that newscast of Montane’s memorial service, and for that I’ve already expressed my sincere sorrow to you. It was the biggest mistake of my career. But you have to believe me when I tell you that Montane is still alive and–”

“I don’t think so.” Roger impassively looked into Harley’s

eyes.

"You don't think what?"

"For one, I don't have to believe you. For two, everyone thinks Mr. Montane is dead, including your men, the judge, our trial lawyers, and me."

"He's alive, Roger." Harley slapped his notebook shut.

"What concrete evidence do we have?" Roger looked at the SIU psychologist.

"We have nothing, sir." Picard looked at Roger in order to avoid Harley's stare.

"Harley, I'm going to make a choice. I'm going to choose to ignore your emotion surrounding this case. You see, Harley, there is no way that Platinum will ever allow the press to rip into the Alex Richter case again. There's not going to be a trial."

"Roger, with all due respect, I think–"

"The media frenzy will stop before it starts. You have no hard evidence of fraud, so you have no case. Harley, we don't have a snowman's chance on a July day in hell to win this case while fighting a widow and three eyewitnesses who have nothing to gain from Montane's death."

"What do you intend to do?" Harley's legs suddenly felt weak.

"We're going to offer the widow a full settlement on May 30, one month before the scheduled trial. That will give the ice enough time to melt, and allow one more search of the area."

"What will you say to the press?"

"We're going to pay Kelly silently, without fanfare, and without admitting any wrongdoing. If the press does come forward, we'll tell them we conducted a full-scale investigation and determined that Montane had drowned. That will be the end of it."

"But–" Harley began sweating.

"I'll ignore your indiscretions regarding this case if you come back to work and do the job I hired you to do. I'll leave the choice to you. If you go back into the field to pursue the Montane case, I'll fire you on the same day I write that widow a seven million dollar check."

Chapter 51

Harley had no choice but to stay with his gut. "You stinking hypocrites" became his favorite war cry whenever he traveled alone in his car. "I'd rather be fired, then turn and run," his lips mouthed the words in disgust. "I'd *choose* to have the ball break my face before I'd *choose* to quit." His hands flew in disgust.

Now, with only two months left before the big ax fell, Harley had one last opportunity to interview Kelly in a formal deposition. He walked into a small conference room where Kelly, Jacobs and a court reporter waited for him.

The interview was a simple question and answer session that revealed nothing new. After an hour, Harley reached into his briefcase and handed Kelly a set of telephone records. "Take a look at these," his voice growled.

"What about them." Kelly answered impassively.

"Page two. The highlighted area. What do you think?"

"It looks like several calls from my house to Tacoma in the months prior to Mike drowning."

"That's right!" Harley's face turned red.

"No." Kelly answered.

"What do you mean, no?"

Kelly answered with all the calmness of someone who was truly innocent, "Mr. Crane, I think you fabricated these in an attempt to somehow scare me. I have already reviewed the phone logs with my attorney as we prepared our lawsuit against you, and these calls were never made."

"That's bullshit!" Harley thundered.

"I'm certain the phone company can verify all this." Jacobs responded.

"I'll bet he bugged my house and tapped my phones, too." Kelly stared at Harley, not sure if she believed her own words.

"What else have you done, Crane?" Jacobs asked.

Harley sat speechless.

"How's it feel to squirm?" Kelly taunted him.

"I got these records from my men." Harley's gulp seemed to lodge in his throat. "I've always followed the book. When I'm done here, I'll do my own internal audit to see where this came from." He got up and walked around the room in an attempt to regain his composure as Jacobs lectured him on the penalties of perjury.

As the seconds slipped away, Harley battled a growing sense of doom. *"Stay in front of the ball."* His lips mumbled, "stay in front of the ball."

The court reporter interrupted him. "I didn't understand you Mr. Crane."

"I didn't say anything," sighed the weary man. He continued to walk around the room while the others watched. Finally he sat across from Kelly, looked steadily into her eyes, and asked, "If you should win in court, and later on find that Mike is alive, what would you say and do then?"

Jacobs told her that she didn't need to answer the question, but she said she wanted to.

"As a matter of fact, I've thought about it a lot. There is a big part of me that hopes your 'walkaway' theory is right." She smiled as she turned and looked at her lawyer, virtually ignoring Harley. "If I knew Mike was alive, my heart would race with joy. I miss him so much. I loved him and he loved me. He was my best friend and the most loyal, caring husband anyone could ever ask for. I would run up to him, kiss him, hold him, and love him forever. I would never even be angry for what I have been through. I would simply rejoice because my Mike was alive."

"But what about the money?"

"The money?"

"Yes – the money."

"I suppose it would be nice if I had enough money to be comfortable, and it would be nice to have a little extra in case of emergencies. But I sure don't need seven million dollars. I think I'd give most of it away to a charity that helps people who are victims of coma. Yes, I'd keep two million dollars and give the rest away." She smiled as a look of contentment came across her face.

"But what if they find him alive after you've already been paid the money?" Harley pressed her.

Kelly stopped looking at Jacobs and now stared intently at Harley. "If Mike was alive, I would say we've earned every dime after what you've put us through." She paused for a moment then added, "After I win in court, whatever money I don't give to charity will be hidden so well that you'd never find it – or Mike and me again. You could spend your lifetime looking, but you'd never find us."

"I'd find you." Harley snarled.

"Don't bet on it. You'd be fighting an uphill battle, with no more support from your big bad company."

"I'd hunt you down myself."

"The world's a big place to hide when you're a rich woman. You know damn well that you'd never find me."

************ *********

With the deposition ended, Harley found himself stuck in a cheap Minneapolis hotel room, all alone against the world. He poured over his notes, looking for one piece of missed evidence. He had stacks of boxes of detailed records, observations, phone numbers, contacts, commentaries, and explanations. In addition, he still tried to monitor Kelly on his own, using equipment he had "borrowed" from Platinum.

The calendar clock radio read 7:00 AM, May 22. Only one week to go before the company wrote the check that would change Harley's destiny forever. Exhaustion overwhelmed the sleep-deprived man. His face puffed under his eyes from lack of sleep, and his nose steadily dripped a clear fluid that signaled the beginning of a cold.

A drip formed on the end of his nose and he tore his bare hand across it, then wiped his hand on his pants. His hands trembled and his legs ached like he had the flu, but it was only a cancerous rage overriding his body.

He remembered the time the baseball hit a rock and slammed past his outstretched glove, pounding into his face. He was only twelve. The ball ricocheted into the outfield after breaking his nose in four places. Blood spattered everywhere. The pain was so intense that he slithered on the ground, like a worm that had been chopped in half.

As the medic applied the ice-cold towel to his face to reduce the swelling, the coaches and the other players gathered around him to gawk. Then his dad came over and laughed. "You stayed in front of the ball, Harley. Remember, Son, only racehorses stay in front. Your broken nose will give you character."

The clock ticked on as Harley's thoughts drifted back and forth between his boyhood and the present. His eyelids fell but he forced himself awake. He sat in a chair overlooking a parking lot with nothing on the table in front of him, yet he refused to give up. Said no to lying down.

Now the time read 2:00 PM and the dreams continued to push in and pull out of his harsh reality. Then as the ball came up toward his face, his glove snapped out.

He saw it.

How could he have missed it?

No one had interviewed the man named Goliath. The man lived right on the trail. He had been out of town all winter, same as the winter before. He had to be back by now. Just maybe, Harley would find the missing piece.

The image of his dad standing in Harley's Chicago office flashed through his mind. *"It's one thing to make it to the majors, and another to stay there."* Harley's heart raced, and a giant smile spread across his face. Mike Montane was not dead yet, and neither was Harley Crane.

He ran out of the hotel room, down the cheaply carpeted hall, and practically flew into his car. Ely and Goliath were only five hours away.

Chapter 52

Harley never stopped for gas or a bathroom on his way to Ely. He drove 75 to 95 miles an hour – whatever he felt he could get away with, and pulled his Mercedes into the Big Rock Trailhead parking lot less than four hours later. Adrenaline had stomped all exhaustion into complete submission.

Four-wheelers had torn and ripped the heavily worn trail leaving a small strip of muddy grass down its narrow middle. A five-day-old beard, knotted hair, and a wrinkled suit from three days of non-stop wear made Harley look like a hobo as he ran up the trail. When he sank to his ankles in a leaf-covered patch of mud, his thousand dollar wingtips flared out and he almost fell. A sudden flash reminded Harley that he was alone in the woods.

The flat soles of his wingtips skidded along the mucky path forcing Harley to slow his pace. An owl hooted loud enough to cause him to pause, and now his ears listened intently to every unfamiliar noise echoing through the woods. The wind whistled through the springtime forest. A menagerie of birds whistled in the trees everywhere, invisible to Harley. For the first time, it occurred to him that the sun would set soon, and there wouldn't be a lot of time for an interview.

Despite his fears Harley pressed on. *"It's one thing to make it to the majors, and another to stay there."* The familiar words obscured the strange sounds of the forest.

After struggling on the spongy trail for nearly an hour, he slipped and fell into a big mud slick. As he fell, he wrenched his arm and an old baseball shoulder injury seared around his back, up his spinal cord and locked into his brain.

He looked pathetic, covered with mud, in his three-piece hobo suit. He held onto his sore right arm as he continued up the path. Finally he saw the log cabin. A light was on.

Harley smelled the smoke of the fireplace wafting through the trees as he walked up to the cabin as quickly as his slippery wingtips would allow. He knocked on the door, but no one answered. He knocked harder, and hollered out, "Is anyone home?"

Nothing.

"Shit" he screamed. Harley peeked in a front window. The place had one lone rocking chair that sat next to a giant native stone fireplace. He thought he heard a noise.

Nothing.

On the far wall, windows opened the log room directly into the back yard woods. There were no pictures on the wall. Two shotguns hung on a gun rack. Otherwise, the place was spotless.

Harley looked at the weird metal sculptures littering the yard. Freaky. Some of them were red from rust. They seemed like ghosts hiding strategically around the yard.

As he walked toward the back of the house, he noticed a huge pile of split and neatly stacked logs. A heavy splitting mall and several wedges leaned against a tree. Clearly, the logs had been split by hand.

He worried that daylight would end soon, and as he turned to gauge the sun's position in the sky, something familiar caught his eye. The little Platinum jackknife shimmered, still stuck in the tree where Goliath had put it. Part of the tree had grown around the knife in an effort to heal its wound.

Harley's dad suddenly appeared, clapping and whistling for his boy. "Way to go, Son! Nice grab!" The crowd cheered as Harley rifled the ball to first base, and a cloud of smoke plumed out of the first baseman's glove. The umpire screamed, "You're out!" and everyone in the stands knew that Harley Crane had saved the game.

Harley's wide grin could've snared a thousand bugs if he were riding a motorcycle. Platinum employees and agents were the only people who owned such knives. Why was the knife here? Hell, Harley knew why.

Maybe it had Mike's fingerprints on it. Harley would've bet his Mercedes that a forensic lab in Minneapolis could find Mike's DNA all over that knife. He studied the knife, wondering how to extract it from the tree without touching it. Maybe if he used a pliers, or what if he put on gloves.

"What are you doing here, mister?"

Harley jumped and turned toward the hostile voice. The nose of a shotgun barrel stared at him. At the end of the gun a man wore camouflaged army clothing. His wild long hair matched his thick mustache and unkempt beard. The hairy beast was huge. Even bigger than Harley had heard.

The shotgun never moved away. Instead, as the two men looked at each other, the big man's eyes grew wide, and he pushed the gun until it jabbed into Crane's face.

"Hey, what did you do that for?" Harley raised his hands above his head, like he was under arrest.

"I asked you a question, pal."

"Please don't point that at me. I'm an investigator from Platinum Insurance, and I came out here looking for you to ask you some questions." His voice pleaded, but the gun never moved an inch.

"What questions?" Goliath's voice growled.

"If you will please put the gun down, sir. I'm here all alone, and as you can see, I have no weapons and no intent to harm you. I just want to ask you a few questions about this jackknife, and about a man who was lost on the Three Forks River a year and a half ago."

"What questions?" The gun jabbed into the soft tissue part of Harley's cheek.

"This knife belongs to someone who used to work at Platinum Insurance, and we need to find that person." Harley became desperate, and suddenly realized he had to pee.

"What makes you think I didn't buy this knife myself?"

"These knives were a promotional gimmick for agents to get them to sell more life insurance."

"Life insurance, eh?"

"Yes."

"You think I can help you?" Goliath looked at Harley in disbelief.

"Yes." It was all Harley could say.

"Why?"

"Because we think the man who owned this knife committed life insurance fraud. He faked a drowning death on the Three Forks River and then escaped by bike down the Big Rock Trail. This might be the evidence we need to prove it."

"Ah. I'll bet you offered a reward, and that's why all kinds of people have been invading my privacy."

"A reward? Yes!" Harley's face lit up. He couldn't believe he hadn't mentioned it. The invasion of privacy words passed right over his head. Reward said it all. Surely, the tramp in front of him could use some financial help. All he needed was a little bribe. "Yes. Yes. There is a reward of $30,000 for information to prove our theory."

"$30,000 is a lot of money."

"And the best part is you'll help justice be served."

"Justice, huh? Well that's an interesting concept." There was a long pause. "All right then. We'll go into my cabin and talk." Goliath lowered the gun and started walking toward the cabin. Harley lingered for a moment to stare at the knife, then followed some twenty yards behind. When the big man got to his front porch, Harley saw him turn and look at him.

Without saying a word, he pulled the gun up to his shoulder, took aim at Harley, and pulled the trigger.

Chapter 53

About eight o'clock the next morning, Harley woke in the big man's cabin. It took a while for Harley's mind to focus through the nightmares of violence which had chased him through the long dark night. In his dreams, a giant man hunted him, then shot him, and tied him up, leaving him to die.

As Harley came to, his neck jerked up with an involuntary snort. A blinding surge of pain bolted through his body. His lips screamed involuntarily, "Shit." Now another surge of pain bellowed. A mad bull tore through his throbbing skull.

An instant survey told him he was alone. Mud layered itself over his custom navy blue suit. His pants were ripped up to his thigh. The stench of blood mixed with urine filled his nostrils. His underwear felt wet. A blood soaked bandage wrapped around his throbbing kneecap.

Each pulse made his kneecap throb. Throb. Throb. The pain burned through him like a knife slowly cutting into his skin.

As Harley became more aware, a terrible ache spread through his shoulders, back and neck. They felt like a twisted pile of flesh. The knots covered his shoulders, and screamed for release with each throb. Like he'd been clubbed with a baseball bat. Throb again.

But there would be no release.

He sat on the rocking chair, each leg tied to a post, with his arms tied tight behind him.

"Hey." Harley hollered. The pain skewered through him. From his knee, through his shoulders. The pain twisted into the base of his neck.

Goliath came into the room with a smile on his face. "Do you remember me?"

"You're the son-of–a-bitch who shot me in the knee last night for no reason." Harley ignored the fear that rose in his heart.

The big man walked over to Harley. WHOP. His face seared

from the backhanded blow. Blood spurted from his nose. Bursts of pain radiated across his shoulders.

"My mother was not a bitch."

Harley spit blood as it flowed into his mouth.

"You don't even know who I am, do you?" The big man snarled, then began to slowly smile as he stared at Harley's bloody face.

"I've never seen you before in my life." Harley's words mixed with blood.

"I'll be back." The big man turned and left the room.

Harley's nose continued to gush blood.

"An eye for an eye." The big man now held a razor blade in front of Harley's face. "Are you sure you don't recognize me?" He cut the air with the blade, before bringing it to rest just in front of Harley's right eye.

"I've never seen you before. My name is Harley Crane. You must have me confused with someone else." For the second time, Harley pissed in his pants.

"I'll be back." The big man snarled and left the room.

Within seconds, Harley heard water running. It sounded like the man worked with a scissors, and then he heard the unmistakable buzz of an electric razor.

When Goliath returned to the room a half-hour later, the big thick mustache, the long unkempt beard, and all the dark black hair were gone. Instead a giant bald-headed man dressed in a jail uniform walked past Harley's bloody face.

"Chad Thorson, at your service."

Chapter 54

Harley sat on his throne with his hands still tied behind his back. The shoulder throb continued to pummel him. Dried blood caked itself thickly into Harley's six-day-old beard. Coagulated blood plugged his nostrils forcing him to breathe from his mouth. Every time he swallowed, a bloody aftertaste reminded him that the bleeding hadn't completely stopped.

His suit felt like it had an armored coating of blood. The red stuff spotted the wall nearest him, and the globs on the floor looked like red jigsaw puzzle pieces.

"It amazes me how things work in your mind, Crane."

The ropes rendered him powerless to do anything but listen.

"You think you can take my life and identity away, and then pay me off like it never happened." Thorson paced the room. His hands rubbed the top of his bald scalp and occasionally moved down to where his beard used to be.

"Did you know my wife Elsie left me? The last time I saw her, she told me I was the same as a dead man." He paused. "But my heart still worked, my mind had thoughts, and my soul was innocent."

"I'm sorry," Harley mumbled.

"Don't ever tell me you're sorry again, Crane. They say that the cold-hearted murderers who cry in sorrow as the judge convicts them are only sorry about one thing."

"What's that?" asked Harley.

"They're sorry they got caught."

Harley said nothing, but would have paid anything to be able to ram his foot inside Thorson's big mouth.

"Crane, I thought about you all night." Thorson paused to look at him. "If the tables were turned, you'd probably try to kill me. And we both know I could kill you. I could dump your body in the woods, at the bottom of a remote lake, and they would never find you." There was a long silence.

Then Thorson shouted, “Crane!” and feigned a jump at Harley.

Harley jolted back as much as the ropes would allow. A fresh bolt of pain shot through his shoulders.

Thorson passively watched, then continued his monologue. “But I think an even worse punishment would be to let you go.”

“Do what you have to,” Harley squeaked. He remembered how Thorson used to thump his Bible in the St. Louis County Jail.

“You put me in prison even though I’m innocent. You’re guilty of destroying my life, but I let you go free. What do you think of that irony?”

Harley never responded.

Thorson paced the floor, then walked behind Harley’s chair. He reached down near Harley’s wrists then lifted the chair six inches off the ground and dropped it. “I asked you a question!”

Vibrating pain pounded through Harley’s shoulders. The knots twisted, the ratcheted muscles tightened. His forehead shrank from the electrocuting spasms. He struggled to breathe. He tried to speak but could only wheeze.

“If you ever press charges against me for shooting you, I’m going to claim self defense.” Thorson squatted in front of Harley. “You want me to drop the chair again?”

Still unable to speak, Harley’s eyes pleaded no.

“Then I’ll hunt you down and slowly skin you like a rabbit. You understand?” Thorson pressed his face in front of Harley’s and breathed hot air on his captive.

“I got it.” Harley trembled. “I promise.” But deep down, he knew if the tables were turned, he’d have no problem putting this freak out of his misery.

Thorson radioed the sheriff, then allowed Crane to clean up while Thorson held a gun to make sure Harley did as he was told.

By the time Sheriff Crow and his four-wheel-drive Jeep finally got to the scene, Harley had cleaned up all the blood. A fire had already consumed Harley’s expensive suit and wingtips so Harley wore one of Thorson’s tattered hats, a pair of giant leather gloves, and a beat up set of wool clothes that were three sizes too big.

“I’ll be the first to say I’m surprised.” Mason’s voice sounded curious and cautious at the same time. "First I find that 'Big-foot' who lives in the woods is none other than my old friend Chad Thorson." Mason stuck out his arm to shake hands. "Then I hear that you went hunting together. I would've never thought it possible." Mason smiled like a boy who found a prize in his cereal box.

"Nice to see you, Sheriff." Thorson responded while Harley stood silently.

"You look good in sloppy clothes, Harley. You know, I thought you were lying when we first talked about the Mike Montane case."

"Lying about what?" Harley asked.

"About making peace with Thorson."

"Oh yeah. We've made peace all right." Harley wanted to make a quick sneer at Thorson, but dared not.

"That's good to hear. You're restoring my faith in humanity."

"I'm touched."

"Ya." Mason looked first at Crane and then back at Thorson trying to understand the non-verbals that flew through the air. It didn't take long for his smile to fade. "Harley, I understand that you had a little hunting accident?"

"That's right." Harley looked at Thorson's head shimmering in the light.

"Can you tell me more about what happened?" Mason asked.

"No. But before I leave, I've got to have that jack-knife." Crane ignored Mason and stared at Thorson daring him to say anything.

"What knife?" Sheriff Crow asked.

"Sheriff, I stole Crane's little pocket jack-knife from him during my trial, and now the son-of-a-bitch wants it back. What I'm saying is that Crane is still a sonnnn-of-a-bitttchhh." Thorson said the words slowly and deliberately. "It's mine, and he can't have it." He laughed in a guttural mocking.

Despite his sore knee, Harley started limping toward the tree with the knife.

"Leave the knife, Crane." Mason shouted as he headed toward

the Jeep.

"I've got to have the knife."

"I said leave it."

"I'm not going anywhere without the knife." Harley continued to hobble slowly toward the tree, and as he did so, Thorson moved to intercept him.

"You're going to leave that knife where it is, or you can walk home on your gimpy leg." Mason stood outside his Jeep with his arms crossed.

"That's it, Mason. I'll tell you the real reason I want the knife. I think that Mike Montane lost this knife when he made his escape down the Big Rock Trail, and Thorson found it. It's the missing link I need, and I'm out of time." Crane looked at both men in desperation.

Silence. For a moment the wind itself stopped.

Suddenly, Harley charged toward Thorson. Harley head-butted him in the midsection. The giant man fell backward across the cold ground. Without pause, Harley rushed for the tree. With all his might, he reached and pulled the knife free with his gloved hand.

It took only an instant for Thorson to recover. The giant man bulldozed his way through some brush and slammed into Crane with a tackle. Both men fell hard onto the forest floor.

Harley lunged to try to escape.

Thorson grabbed him, and clawed his way on top of Harley.

The sheriff unhooked the rifle strapped to the back window of the Jeep.

Thorson growled like a rabid animal as he picked up Harley and threw him back to the ground. Blood flew everywhere as the jolt ripped open Harley's broken nose. Instantly Thorson jumped on top of Harley. Thorson pinned him to the ground as he slammed his fist into his face. Still, Harley hung onto the knife.

"Stop!" Mason ordered as Thorson raised his hand. Mason fired into the sky and the sound of the gun echoed through the forest.

Then, knowing his life might be at stake, Thorson smashed his fist into the flesh of Harley's arm causing him to drop the knife. As

Thorson reached for the little blade, Mason took aim and shot at the dirt in front of Thorson's grasp. "Get off him, Thorson!" Mason screamed and moved closer through the brush.

Without a moment's pause, Thorson tore off his glove and grabbed the knife barehanded. He took his fingers and rubbed them up and down both the shaft and the blade, and then spit on it and rubbed his spittle throughout the tool.

"Drop it, mister."

"Done deal."

Chapter 55

Kelly got her check for $7,782,348 with no fanfare. An officer of the company delivered the check with sincere apologies from Platinum for the delay.

It was the final step in accepting Mike's death.

Now it was time for her to move on with her life. She called Julie Jewel and Jacobs. Together they went out to celebrate their victory over Platinum.

But for Kelly, the celebration felt empty. More than ever, even in the presence of her friends, she felt alone. Uncertain of the future, the money gave her no consolation. The people who mattered the most in her life would never laugh with her again. When Kelly got home that night, she lay in bed and stared at the empty ceiling.

That same day, Harley Crane limped into his Chicago office on crutches and had to ask for help loading all of his stuff into a moving truck. The doctors said Harley's knee suffered only superficially from the birdshot. He'd be as good as new in a couple weeks.

************ *********

After she paid Jacobs his 1.75 million-dollar fee, it took another week for Kelly to distribute the money as she once had told Harley she would. Over two million remained in the bank, but it didn't make her feel any better.

It only took Harley one day to rent a room in a house across the alley from Kelly's house. He knew she would make her move once she had the money. He still had her phones bugged, and her car had a company tracer on it so he could follow her wherever she went.

Meanwhile, Mike took another long and lonely drive, this time to Calgary, to pick up his fax messages. He hadn't heard anything for such a long time that he spent the first two hours of his journey worried that Julie Jewel might have forgotten about him.

The drive crawled on forever. At 90 kilometers per hour, the other traffic raced past him, and people gave him the finger for driving too slow. His thoughts wandered as he took the photo of Kelly out of his wallet and stared numbly at it.

When he finally pulled into the Mail-Boxes-And-More store in downtown Calgary, he was exhausted. He pushed his seat back and laid his head down for a fifteen-minute nap. The phrase "weariness makes cowards of us all" flashed in front of his closed eyelids like a repeat error message on his computer.

Two hours later he woke from his nap. He sat in the car for another ten minutes pondering for the millionth time the poor choices he had made. Then, finally, he walked inside to check his "never busy fax" line.

A short and simple message waited for him. "Kelly has won her battle with Platinum. They paid her the entire seven million dollars plus interest. I'm sure Kelly would like to hear from you. She's pretty lonely now, and the money seems to give her no happiness. She would be glad to talk to any friend of Al's. Good luck to you. Sincerely, Julie Jewel."

As Mike read the message, tears welled in his eyes and his hands trembled. He looked up, clenching the paper to his chest, and with every nerve in his body, he stretched out his hands toward heaven and prayed, "Thank you."

He sat in the parking lot for another hour as he read and re-read the short fax. His prayers had been answered. He had beaten Platinum, and now it was almost over.

Inside a folder of his locked briefcase, Mike pulled out an elaborate brochure for his adventure company he had created in Jasper. The name of his company was Adventures in Living. Only Kelly would know. He assumed Platinum would be checking her mail, so whatever he sent had to be bold enough to pass right over them. The brochure offered several different adventure opportunities, but suggested a trip to the Boundary Waters Canoe Area as a perfect place to get away from it all.

When Kelly went through her mail a week later, she habitually tossed all the junk directly into the trash barrel in her garage. As usual, the mail consisted of nothing but bills and useless advertisements. She walked into the house. Then something imperceptible pricked her memory. A vague nagging. She tripped over herself in the rush back to the garbage to see if what she had imagined was true. There it was:

Adventures in Living.

Kelly's heart pounded. Her hands turned moist. She stared at the Canadian brochure and wondered if it could really be true. She closed her eyes for a second. She had to concentrate. Breathe.

Then came the doubts. *Maybe it wasn't from Mike. What if it was nothing but a weird coincidence?*

She tore the brochure open. Her eyes raced for clues. *Adventures in Living* offered canoe trips to the Boundary Waters. Rock-climbing in Rocky Mountain National Park. Dog-sledding on Lake Vermilion. Snowmobiling Daniels Summit Lodge in Utah. Skiing at Big Mountain. Each trip offered unforgettable memories she had already shared with Mike.

Kelly wept with joy. All the hopes she had banished from her mind flooded back to her. *Mike was alive. Mike was alive! Her wonderful Mike still lived!* Harley Crane had been right after all. She couldn't believe it.

She collapsed on the cement floor. After a long moment of silence, she sat up and paged through the brochure, touching every inch of it because she knew Mike had touched it. Her eyes absorbed every detail. Everything about it said that Mike was out there waiting for her. Rock-climbing trips. Wilderness canoeing excursions. Biking expeditions. Hiking in the mountains. Paragliding. Dog sledding. Promised sunsets and "memories to last a lifetime." Her Mike was alive!

She wanted to rush out and tell the world that her man was still alive. Wanted to call her friends, her attorney, and more than anyone, wished Al could share her joy. Mike was alive!

Alive!

Kelly stopped to think for a moment. She remembered how her house had been trashed after winning some free Vikings tickets.

She never registered for any tickets, and couldn't remember a Vikings promotion at her grocery store.

Maybe this whole brochure was a trick from Harley. If anyone knew about her past trips with Mike, it would be him. *My God!* She thought. Maybe Harley had bugged her house after all.

She walked around the entire house, closed the blinds, and turned off all the lights. Whatever her next move, she knew she'd have to be careful.

The next day, Kelly drove to her office and made a reservation for a recommended canoe trip. She made a fax to a Winnipeg phone number. She checked the box indicating she was interested in joining the next group, leaving in ten days. Interestingly enough, the starting point of the trip was the North Country Retreat Center, the place that Arlen owned.

Then she drove to the airport and booked a last minute flight to San Francisco. She grabbed her carry-on luggage and made sure she was the last one to board the airplane. During the three plus hour flight, she walked slowly up and down the aisles of the plane and tried to memorize the faces of all the people who were on the plane with her. She was paranoid of being followed, and if she ever saw these people's faces again, she knew she would know for sure.

As Kelly's plane taxied down the runway, Harley was at a loss as to what to do. It took him an hour and cost over ten thousand dollars of his own money to book a private jet to follow her to San Francisco. By the time he got there, Kelly's plane had already been on the ground for fifteen minutes. Armed with some fake FBI identification, he asked the security people in the airport if he could study their surveillance tapes, and put out an alert to see if anyone had seen Kelly.

It took another 45 minutes before Harley finally had Kelly on tape. The video showed Kelly running through the airport, always turning around to see if someone followed her. Wherever she was going, she was in a real hurry.

Harley's pulse raced as the camera showed her leaving the airport and jumping into a yellow cab. He called the San Francisco Police on a conference call with the Yellow Cab Company.

"Yes, one of our drivers just reported dropping off someone with Kelly's description at the Oakland Zoo."

"Can you tell me anything else, or patch me through to the driver?"

"I'm afraid the driver says the woman had nothing to say. She paid him a $50 tip and he left her at the zoo."

Harley could hardly hang up fast enough. He bolted out of the airport with a copy of the airport video in hand and headed to the Oakland Zoo. While en-route, he called the San Francisco Police again, and they put on a three-way call with the Oakland authorities.

By the time he arrived at the Oakland Zoo, Kelly had already picked up another cab to the Oakland airport where she boarded a flight back to Minneapolis. She had no way of knowing if her plan had worked, but figured if Harley or his goons were following her, this would throw them off course for a few days.

When she got back to Minneapolis, she took a cab to an electronics store where she purchased, with cash, 1000 minutes of airtime on two new cellular phones that couldn't possibly have been bugged by Harley.

Then she phoned another cab company and had them take her to the local Toyota dealer where she paid cash for a new Sequoia, knowing it too, was not bugged.

With new wheels, a phone, and a purse full of money, Kelly set off. She guessed she only had a couple of days before Harley and his creeps would find her.

She stopped first at Platinum Insurance Agent, Zach Aabbatt's office.

"Hi, Zach."

"Ah, hello, Kelly." Zach looked surprised. "I heard you won the case against Platinum, and I'm glad for you."

"Thanks, Zach. Mike always said I could trust you, and I know how Platinum tied your hands."

"I'm awfully sorry about all the struggles you've had to go through." Zach's face and voice radiated sincerity. "Now what can I do for you today?"

"Zach, I want to sign a form to change my beneficiary, and I want you to notarize my signature."

"Who are you going to change your beneficiary to?"

"I'd love to tell you, but for your own safety, I can't. I've been told that once my policy is issued, I can change the beneficiary to whomever or whatever I want – even if they have no insurable interest in my death. Is that right?"

"You're right, although your heirs could try to contest it after you died, if they knew about it, and if the beneficiary choice seemed out of line. After all, you still have two-and-a-half million dollars of coverage, and that's a lot of money to fight over."

"Zach, I have no relatives left. And I have no idea who, besides you, would even know that I have this life insurance policy."

"Let's change it for you."

After Kelly had signed her name on the blank change of beneficiary form, she had Zach notarize her signature. Then she moved over to another table where she filled in the name of her new primary beneficiary. She took the completed form and put it in a pre-addressed envelope direct to Platinum Insurance Life Division.

"All right Zach, I need you to give me two favors. I want you to complete a change of address so my acknowledgement of beneficiary change comes directly to your office, instead of my home."

"Why do you want your Platinum mail to come here?"

"Because I think Harley Crane's men are searching through my mail, and it's essential that I keep this confidential at all costs. Sooner or later, your computer is going to tell you who my new beneficiary is, but I have to ask you to honor my wishes for confidentiality."

"I promise."

"Great. Now, when the acknowledgement comes in the mail, I want you to call me on my cell phone. I'll come by and pick it up then. Be sure to call me as soon as it comes in."

"You got it, Kelly. Anything I can do to help."

"You're a sweet man, Zach."

"What's the second thing?"

"I want to cancel this policy in ten days."

"Why would you go to the trouble of changing beneficiaries and then canceling the policy?"

"I have my reasons. I'm going to sign a cancellation notice for ten days from now, and I'd like you to notarize it. But I want you to hold this request in your files for another ten days."

"Whatever I can do to help."

With that Kelly leaned over and gave him a gentle kiss on the cheek, then turned and left.

Kelly drove to the post office where she mailed the change of beneficiary envelope certified next day mail to Platinum. Then she went to REI where she paid cash for a shiny new kevlar canoe and enough quality camping gear to last ten days in the wilderness. She had no idea what kind of supplies Mike might have with him, and this time, she was determined to be prepared.

She booked a room at the Northtown Holiday Inn on the north side of Minneapolis, afraid to go near her home. Besides, the north side of town was foreign to her and she figured no one would ever look for her there.

The next day, she had Jacobs quitclaim the deed on her house to the Dorothy Day Center for the homeless. She told him she only wanted to stay in the home another ten days, and then they could dispose of it and all of her personal possessions in whatever manner they saw fit.

Jacobs tried to press Kelly into telling him where she planned to go, but she only told him she had nothing left in the area, and wanted to get a fresh start somewhere, anywhere else.

He warned her that a sudden move might look suspicious, but she told him she didn't care. She lied to him and told him she had given all the money away except enough to buy a modest home. Saying there was simply no motive to run, Kelly told him she would call wherever she landed. In a short time, her case would be forgotten, and she wanted to remain anonymous in her new life. With that, she bid him good-bye.

After a few more days of last minute financial preparations, Kelly stopped at the cemetery, where she spent most of the day talking and praying with Al. It would be her final farewell. She kissed the headstone and told her beloved sister all that she had been through.

*********** *********

After three days of searching the Bay Area, Harley learned that Kelly had taken an immediate flight back to Minneapolis. The whole thing made him furious. Somehow, she knew he followed her. The ball hit a rock, and Harley snagged it out of mid-air. He was getting close.

When he got back to Minneapolis, he studied the surveillance tapes of her home and found nothing. No one had been to her home in the last three days. He called the credit card company, but no charges had been made. Then he called the phone company to see if any phone calls had been made from her home or cell phone. Another strikeout.

He called his buddy at the FBI and had him check the outgoing flights from Minneapolis, Chicago, St. Louis, and even the smaller cities like Des Moines, Madison, and Milwaukee. Nothing.

Harley phoned his old boss at Platinum to ask for some manpower to help him solve the case.

"Hello, Harrrleeey." The voice on the other end taunted like an eight-year-old, picking on a younger kid.

"Hello, Roger. Look I'm sorry to bother you but–"

"You're never going to bother me again, little man. I've already seen to that. For all the good you did Platinum, your attitude is reprehensible and we have no room in this company for people like you." Roger's voice turned coldly factual. He had already made up his mind about Harley, and nothing would change it. More than anything, he wanted Harley to know first-hand that it was over.

"But, Roger, would you please hear me out?"

"You have nothing to say that I want to hear."

"Roger, you know and I know that the most expensive thing in the world is a closed mind. What I have to say is invaluable to the company."

"What's this about, Harley. You've only been fired for a short time, and now you have some kind of great idea for us?"

"Yes, sir. It's about Mike Montane. I have new evidence to support my–"

"Mike Montane is dead, Harley. We've already paid his widow, and I've already told you the case is closed. Unless you can prove otherwise – on your own, with a live body – I never want to hear about him again."

"Yes. But sir."

"Did you just 'ya-but' me, Crane?"

"No."

"I think you did. How many times have I heard you condemn others for saying ya-but."

"Sir, if you'll please let me explain." The conversation was going nowhere and Harley knew it. Then the line went dead.

Undaunted, and mad as hell, Harley quickly dismissed the sudden wish for a team of men to help him. He would show the world that as a one-man show, he was better than an army.

Harley checked Kelly's office telephone log on the day before she made her sudden moves. The phone register showed nothing extraordinary. Mostly a list of calls between her and the Dorothy Day Center.

But there, the first call of the day, was also a short call to someone in Winnipeg. Only a minute long. Kelly hadn't called anyone in Winnipeg as far as he could remember, so he phoned the number himself and found it was a fax. Then he checked with the phone company to see who owned the number. They told him they had no one's name on the account, but it had been opened with a cash balance. They were told when the cash ran out, to disconnect the line. It was more than strange.

Harley didn't know where to turn next. He racked his brain on the word Winnipeg. "Winnipeg, Canada." He said it out loud. "Canada." His mind raced in overdrive. Out of the middle of nowhere, he remembered the stupid adventure brochure he had pulled from her mail. It was from Canada. It had a Canadian stamp on it. Undoubtedly, Mike had been hiding in Canada.

"Yes," Harley screamed. "I'm going to get you."

With renewed effort, Harley fast-forwarded through his hidden videos for a clue. He needed to find Kelly. It took hours of tedious watching before he finally spotted her.

Everyone had said he was nuts to hide a wireless remote video in the cemetery, but there she was – almost a whole day. "All damn day long." Harley was beyond himself with the possibilities that flooded through his brain. Why would she spend all day at her dead sister's grave unless she was saying a final good-bye?

Harley's adrenaline surged. He was heading toward the winning circle once again. He zeroed in on the light blue Sequoia parked in the background of the cemetery scene. The SUV a bright yellow canoe strapped on top of it, and the back end appeared to be loaded with gear. He stopped the tape and put it on zoom. The new truck had a bright red emblem in the place where the license plates were meant to go. The red advertisement said, "I get great service at Burnsville Toyota."

Odds were great that Kelly remained in town. He called his friend again at the FBI. "Hey, Rollie. Yeah, it's Harley again."

"Harley, I told you when you called the last time that I owed you a favor. I did it, and now we're even. You know I'm sticking my neck out for you, and you're nothing but an unemployed citizen now."

"Rollie, stop and listen. I almost have them. I only need one small favor, and if I get them with your help, I promise you that I'll hand deliver the $30,000 reward I told you about."

"What do you need?"

"I have Kelly Montane on video. She spent hours at her sister's grave talking to the headstone, and I'm certain she's making her big move. You know she tried to lose me in the Bay Area, and thinks she's home free, but I know what she's driving."

"What do you have?" The FBI man ran short on patience.

"She's driving a new light blue Sequoia, with a yellow canoe strapped on top of it."

"What are the plates?"

"None yet. It's too new. She's got a red advertisement where the plates go that says 'I get great service at Burnsville Toyota.'"

"So help me read between the lines, Crane. You want to know where a new light blue Sequoia with a banana canoe and cherry plates is parked?"

"That's right."

"And if you get your man, I get $30,000 no matter what, payable immediately?"

"Thirty grand. Immediately."

"Crane, I have only one thing to say." There was a long pause. "Next time call me when you have something a little harder than that. I'll be looking for that thirty grand."

"It's yours."

Chapter 56

Just before midnight, Harley got the call from his FBI buddy. They had located the SUV in a Holiday Inn parking lot in North Minneapolis. As Harley planted a new tracer under the truck, he couldn't help but smile. *"Is that bitch going to be surprised, or what?"*

At dawn the next day, Kelly left her hotel room. Harley was ready to follow. This time he packed his Smith&Wesson Model 2213 just in case. He stayed about ten minutes behind as he followed her electronic tracking signal.

As they headed north, Harley congratulated himself on his shrewdness. He imagined his conversation with the police, the press, and most of all, his chicken-shit boss. The racehorse spirit filled him with energy, and his visions of grandeur came flooding back.

When Harley turned north on US HWY 169, the sign said "Ely 44 miles." What a fitting place to solve this crime. Harley would capture his fugitives right in front of Sheriff Mason Crow's nose.

His blood pressure rose as he pictured Thorson holed up as a hermit for all these years. Harley knew Thorson had lied about the knife. Any idiot could see it was Montane's knife, even though the fingerprint and DNA test results pointed only to Thorson.

Thorson must have known about the Montane case all along. As Harley pondered the injustice of it, his ability to make distinction between right and wrong disappeared in a rising cloud of rage.

After this thing ended, he'd pay Thorson a visit. No one would be there to protect the giant man against Harley and his eight-round, single action cousin. Harley enjoyed the picture of taking out Thorson's knees with a couple of hollow point shells and leaving him to slowly bleed to death in the back woods. That would teach him a lesson about lying.

Harley's fist slammed against the dash, as black and white

turned gray. *I'll show the world.* His hands choked the steering wheel in a grip of death as he thought about his conservative boss abandoning him. This was no longer about Platinum. Harley Crane had done no wrong. *I'm still in the majors, and I'll always be there.*

Suddenly, Harley's mind shifted gears as he thought about Mike Montane. What kind of man would leave his wife to fend for herself in a game of insurance fraud? The fact that he had balls big enough to try to pull it off might once have impressed Harley, but not anymore. The coward played like a minor league reliever trying to wrap up a game, and now Harley would pull out a grand slam victory.

As Kelly drove through Ely she decided to get a present for Mike. Evergreen Cottage looked like the right kind of place.

Harley's pulse raced when he saw the GPS monitor come to a stop. Wherever she was, he needed to be there. He buried the gas peddle into the floorboard, pushing his car as fast as the turns leading into Ely would allow. At sixty-five miles per hour, he cruised up the main drag and ran two red lights.

The monitor showed he was close. Harley dripped wet from the anticipation. He slowed the car as he cruised up Chapman Street, scanning for Kelly. Where was Mike? Harley's heart pounded.

Suddenly, almost in front of him, the blue Sequoia appeared as Harley rounded the corner. And there, out of the little boutique, Kelly walked straight towards his car, carrying a hand carved canoe paddle.

Harley's hand shot up to cover his face. He ducked his head to the side as he drove by. Kelly could have reached out and touched his car as they passed. In his rear-view mirror he saw Kelly stop in the middle of the road. She had turned to follow his car's progress up the street.

"Shit!" Harley hoped she hadn't seen him.

"I must be paranoid," Kelly shook off the image. There was *no way* that slimy Crane could have followed her.

Kelly hopped into her SUV and continued through town. She started up the remote Fernberg Trail.

Harley smiled as he followed a half-mile behind. Fernberg dead-ended in twenty-two miles. She would lead him right to Mike. It was all going to be easy.

So very easy.

************ *********

Kelly pulled her Sequoia into the North Country Retreat Center, and saw Arlen mowing the lawn. After parking it, she handed Arlen the keys and gave him a giant hug for all his past help. She told him that he was one of the kindest and most hospitable men she had ever met in her life.

While they chatted on the lawn, Harley drove his car into the mouth of the long dirt driveway. He turned the ignition off and pulled out a long range listening device he had stolen from Platinum. He tape-recorded every word, envisioning the noose around Montane's neck.

"Why are you giving me your keys, Kelly?"

"Before I answer, can I ask you if there has been anyone here to see me?"

"Yes, as a matter of fact. A gentleman arrived yesterday. He hitchhiked here and purchased my best kevlar canoe instead of renting it. I thought it was a little strange, but I gave him a good price."

"What did he look like and where is he?" Kelly was so anxious to see Mike she could hardly stand it.

"He's a bald headed guy about your age. I let him buy the canoe and he took off. He told me to tell you that he would meet you at . . ." He paused and pulled a piece of paper out of his pocket. "He said he would meet you at this campground on Hungry Ben Lake." As Arlen pointed at the map, he had no idea he pointed to the island where Kelly and Mike had spent their last night together.

"Oh!" Kelly looked elated.

"He said he'd be waiting for you."

I hope he is. "Please keep an eye on my truck until I come back. And if I don't come back in a week, I'd like to ask you to go to Hungry Ben and retrieve my canoe. It'll simply mean that we decided to extend our trip and we preferred to canoe together."

"That's a long time to leave your canoe unattended."

"I'll padlock it to a tree, and on my key-ring, you have keys to the lock and my truck."

"I'll have to charge you fifty dollars to pick up your canoe."

"That's okay, Arlen. I know it's a bit unusual to request this, but the fifty dollars is a small price to pay for the flexibility you're providing for me."

Harley couldn't believe it. He had never canoed a day in his life. It looked so dreadfully boring he'd never been tempted to try. Now he needed to follow a girl scout into the wilderness. He waited impatiently for Kelly to take off on the lake. Although she was in the water in less than ten minutes, Harley thought she took forever.

He waited another five minutes before racing into Arlen's driveway.

"Arlen, I presume." Harley stuck out his hand. "My name is Paul Cherama and I'm Kelly Montane's brother. She's told me a lot about you."

"Nice to meet you, Paul."

"Kelly said she was coming through here to go canoeing. Has she been here yet?"

"As a matter of fact, she took off ten minutes ago."

"Oh man, I needed to talk to her. I drove all the way up from Minneapolis to find her. We've got a serious family illness."

"I'm sorry. You might be able to catch her, if you can get to her on this first lake." Arlen pointed. "Motors are allowed only on this lake, but she's just paddling."

"That sounds great. But what if she makes it to the next lake before I catch up with her? I understand she's going to Hungry Ben Lake. Can you show me where she's planning to camp on that lake?"

"Sure." Arlen pulled out his map and pointed to the little island as Harley watched. Suddenly suspicious, Arlen closed the map and asked, "How'd you know she was going to Hungry Ben?"

"Ah," Harley paused for time. "Every time she talks about this place, she mentions Hungry Ben Lake, so I assumed that's where she was going."

"I see. I'll be right back. If you'll excuse me a minute." Arlen left Harley standing in the driveway and hustled into his cabin. He ran to his phone, pounding in a number locked in memory.

"Mason Crow here."

"Hi, Mason. It's Arlen."

"How's my buddy Arlen doing today?"

"Mason, I've got some guy standing in my driveway who says he's Kelly Montane's brother. He came in a big Mercedes and he's looking for Kelly. She took off paddling fifteen minutes ago to meet a friend of hers. But something isn't right."

"What does he look like?"

"Late thirties, good looking. Brown hair, broken nose and a square jaw. Steel colored eyes."

"Kelly doesn't have a brother. It's Harley Crane, the insurance investigator."

"What should I do?" Arlen asked.

"Tell him you know who he is and ask him what he wants. Then call me back."

Arlen looked out the window to see Harley pacing back and forth. Arlen felt uncomfortable with the whole thing, but Mason was a half-hour drive away.

"Harley Crane," Arlen shouted.

Harley turned and looked.

"I understand you're not really Kelly's brother. In fact she doesn't even have a brother." Arlen boldly walked toward Harley.

"I'm sorry I lied to you. Let me tell you why I'm really here." Harley told Arlen the whole story and asked if he could hire him or one of his associates to help him follow Kelly.

Arlen remained skeptical. "I'm sorry, but I don't believe your story. I remember seeing pictures of Mike Montane when they were looking for his body, and the man I met yesterday was definitely not him."

"That's because he did something to change his appearance."

Harley raised arms stood like exclamation points.

"There is no way the guy I met could be Mike Montane."

"I'm telling you that they planned this meeting. It's him." Harley repeated in an exasperated tone.

"Listen, Mr. Crane, even if you are right, I don't have the staff to take you out. I've got a big group of boy scouts coming up here tonight, and I need all my people to take them canoeing tomorrow."

"I'll pay you triple the going rate, and there is a $30,000 reward if you help me prove Montane is alive."

"I'm sorry, but the scouts are good repeat clients. I don't have a man to spare."

"All right then, I'll give you $10,000 cash right now." Harley whipped his car door open and produced a wad of hundred dollar bills as though they were spare change.

Arlen stared in disbelief. "Just a minute."

"Where are you going?" Harley's voice raised.

"Wait a minute."

"I'll give you twenty thousand for your help, plus the reward." Harley's frantic plea followed Arlen into his cabin, where he closed the door, leaving Harley and his money standing in the driveway.

"Hello, Mason? Yeah it's me, Arlen." Arlen nodded with his ear on the receiver as if he was chatting with his friend in the same room. "It's Crane all right. He's flashing twenty thousand dollars for me to chase Kelly Montane into the Boundary Waters. He claims she's planning a rendezvous with her supposedly drowned husband."

"You do whatever you think is right, but I don't trust the guy. He's lied many times and seems bent on revenge against the Montane widow."

"What do you think he's up to?"

"I don't know. I heard he got fired. That man would rather have his heart cut out than be fired. Maybe he wants to kill the Montane widow out of spite. I wouldn't have anything to do with him. Besides, he doesn't have any authority to offer you a reward. He doesn't work for Platinum anymore, and the case is closed."

"What should I do?"

"Does he know where she is?"

"He knows she's going to Hungry Ben Lake, and before I knew what was going on, I showed him the campground where they're meeting."

"And you're sure the man she's meeting isn't Mike Montane."

"There's no way."

"I'd delay him as long as you can. If you don't help him, he'll go down to the next outfitter who will. Then you'll lose the money and he'll get what he wants anyway. Why don't you give him a heavy canoe with a small motor? He'd never know the difference anyway, and he'd think you helped him by giving him a motor."

"Can you come up here and help me?"

"No crime has been committed."

"Not yet anyway."

"Arlen, as much as I'd like to help you out, I can't leave on a hunch. I have to be at a township meeting about a major bear hunting problem in the next five minutes. The mayor, a big shot with the DNR, some guys from the NRA, and the Bois Forte Tribal Council are expecting me to be the speaker/moderator. If I don't show up, the local press will take away my fishing pole for life. The soonest I can get there is four hours."

"That's not going to help much. What about a deputy? If you think Kelly's in danger, shouldn't we do something?"

"I've got one deputy who's already in the Boundary Waters about fifty miles from you. And Deputy Anderson is on vacation in Colorado. I think if you give Kelly a two-hour head start, he'll never catch her. Do you think you can delay Crane?"

"I'll try."

"Here's one more idea. If it's not too late, you might try pointing Crane in the wrong direction. He'll never know it. Good luck."

Arlen walked back out to the driveway where Harley anxiously paced. "Harley, I'm going to accept your $20,000 offer, plus the reward. In exchange, I'm going to give you a canoe with a motor on it, and we'll outfit you with the proper gear to make sure you don't die out in the woods."

"Now you're talking." Harley wanted to be alone when he snared the Montanes.

"There's one more thing." Arlen pointed at the map. "When you get past the first lake, you can't use your motor anymore. It's a restricted, non-motorized area from that point north. I'd suggest you leave the motor at this camp to reduce the weight in your canoe, and paddle in from there."

"Why can't I use a motor there?" Harley despised arbitrary rules.

"The water has many shallow areas, and if you use your motor, you might hit a rock and destroy it."

"All right, all right." Harley wanted to get moving. He knew the real reason for the rules. It was all about a bunch of wilderness purists who had lobbied for a place to get away from it all. "Get me geared up so I can get out of here."

By the time they got Harley's tent, canoe, food, raingear, stove, lantern, and other gear together, an hour and a half had passed and Harley was mad. Then the motor wouldn't start. Harley cursed, paced and kicked the dirt. "Get me a new motor and get it now," he screamed.

With exaggerated effort, Arlen pulled the old motor off the canoe and hauled it slowly back into camp. He knew the motor was a dud. By the time he pulled out a new motor another ten minutes had passed. He carried the motor down the dock and as he set it on the edge of the canoe, the motor slipped sideways and fell into five feet of water.

"No more delays!" Harley yelled.

"I'm sorry Mr. Crane. I've never dropped a motor in the water in my life. It was an accident."

"You get me another new motor and I'll put it on myself."

While Arlen went to get another motor, one of the youth camp counselors tried to give Harley a quick canoeing lesson.

"Listen to me, sport. Any moron can row a canoe."

"I'm only trying to help, sir. If you lose your motor, and don't know how to paddle correctly, you can get stranded out there. I've heard a lot of stories about people who got stuck on an island for days before someone came to their rescue."

"I'm not interested in your lessons." Harley stormed away. "And I don't need some pimple-faced kid giving me a lecture."

Finally, Harley hopped into his canoe. At first he moved cautiously through the water trying to get the feel of the craft and the response of the motor. Canoes were tippy all right. After about ten minutes, he felt he had mastered the program, and held the motor wide open. But the speed caused the front end to come out of the water, and he lost directional control. The stern held too much weight.

Ever so carefully, Harley crawled over his gear and squatted on the yoke. He felt the canoe wobble. He tried to ignore the tipping sensation as he slid his rear end toward the middle and held his breath.

Then, slowly, he dragged his gear forward, always careful to maintain equilibrium, and piled his stuff into the bow.

With great relief, the human snake wiggled quietly, evenly, slowly back into his seat. No matter what, he knew he wouldn't stand in the canoe. "Damn canoe," he hollered for no one but the loons, certain he had wasted fifteen minutes.

Finally, he was off again. He opened the throttle on the ten horsepower motor, and the tiny craft flew across the lake. He would catch Kelly in no time.

But Harley didn't realize he was going the wrong way. While he had been moving his gear around the canoe, the wind had pushed against the bow and turned it completely around, heading him back toward Arlen's camp. All the trees looked the same, and he never noticed.

After zipping through the water for another five minutes, Harley saw people on shore near a dock. Could it possibly be Kelly and Mike? His heart raced as he slowed the motor to a crawl and pulled out his binoculars.

"Damn it." He shrieked as he saw Arlen wave to him from the dock. Out came his map and compass to re-orient himself.

*********** *********

As Kelly's canoe pierced through the water, Mike watched her approach the island through his binoculars. He jumped up and down on the edge of a granite outcropping that overlooked the water to try to catch her attention. He waved his arms in the sky, then took off his jacket and whipped it round and round over his head.

When Kelly waved back, Mike felt a lump form in his throat, and his body shook. He ran and danced along the granite wall toward his own canoe. He pulled it off the rocky shore, and pushed it into calf-deep water before jumping inside. Then he dug his paddle deep into the water as hard and fast as he could.

The two canoes raced toward each other across open lake. The paddles moved in perfect synchronization, as they reached, then pushed, then cut the air to reach again. "Switch." Mike hollered when they were close enough to hear, and their arms moved in unison as they both changed paddling sides.

As the canoes approached ever closer, Kelly set her paddle down and let momentum carry her. Mike pushed with one last powerful stroke, then dove from his canoe into the water, and swam toward Kelly. She tossed two life jackets into the water and jumped from her own canoe.

They hugged and kissed. Kelly sobbed, and Mike soon joined in. There were no words. Only crying, and laughing and holding onto each other and the life jackets, trying to stay afloat.

Their need for each other and the love they had saved was simply too powerful to hold. Mike splashed the water, then dove, and surfaced again next to Kelly and held her tight in his arms.

They continued to bob on the surface, and Mike leaned across the life jackets to kiss Kelly's face and lips. Under the water, Kelly's legs wrapped around Mike's waist and held him next to her.

Their faces parted and they stared into each other's eyes. Sparkles of love filled their quiet smiles. Between tears, laughter, kissing and looking at each other neither one said anything, until Mike finally whipped off his hat and asked, "Hey Kel, do you like my haircut?" The stubbly blond hairs on the bald head shined against the sun, and the crying and laughing started again.

They floated together, and whispered how much they had missed each other. So much needed saying, yet words could wait. They were together again. Mike had come back from the dead.

************ *********

The sun had dipped well below the trees by the time Harley got to the end of the first lake. Arlen warned him not to use a motor beyond that point, and Harley knew he needed his motor to get back to his car. Mike and Kelly's rendezvous point was only a few miles up Hungry Ben Lake, but he was too afraid to try to canoe in the dark.

So, despite Arlen's warning and the official postings, he put the motor at the slowest speed, and puttered his way toward the Montanes in the deepening darkness. He hit a couple of rocks, and both times it scared him when the motor jumped. Finally, just a little over a half- mile from the Montanes, he made camp.

Unknown to Harley, the U.S. Forest Service Campground was another 50 yards north. The darkness made it virtually impossible for anyone but an accomplished outdoorsman to navigate, and Harley felt lucky to find a place to pull his canoe ashore without scraping through rough brush.

The spot he had chosen was near a small swamp. It sat in a cove, sheltered from the wind. So, as the tenderfoot brought the canoe to shore, the first thing he noticed was the cloud of flies circling his head. They landed in his hair and bit him behind his ears.

"Son-of-a-bitch." His favorite war cry squealed from his mouth. The flies were everywhere.

He heaved the canoe onto the shore then desperately dug through his packs looking for bug juice. *They must've packed some bug juice.* The vicious flying carnivores bore down on him, and as he wiped the back of his neck, he noticed the blood on his hands. The damn flies had broken skin. They crawled over his face, in his ears, in his hair, biting into his scalp. He killed dozens of them with one hand, while he held the flashlight in his mouth and searched through the Duluth Pack with his other hand. Finally, he found the "Jungle Juice" and gratefully smeared the smelly liquid all over himself.

Now the black flies stayed off him, but they were thick like a hostile swarm of bees near their nest, and they hovered around his head. As he moved through the dark woods, he swallowed one. It lodged in his windpipe. He began to choke.

"Shit!" he screamed as loud as he possibly could.

He stumbled a few feet into the forest desperately trying to find an unobstructed place that was flat enough to put up his tent. He had to get inside the tent to get away from the bugs. He finally settled for a piece of sloping ground that was mostly barren rock, with a couple of tree roots sticking out.

He tried to hold his flashlight in one hand, while he struggled to figure out how to erect the tent with the other hand, but it was no use. Harley was beside himself to find that something this simple could be so hard. He propped the flashlight up on a log, pointing it in the general vicinity of where the tent would go. Using both hands, he laid out the tent and the poles while he fought to put the damn thing together.

Meanwhile, the flies continued to badger the would-be camper. They swarmed over and under the man. When they found an opening in his armor of clothing, they nudged their way in. They found the holes of his pant legs and gnawed away at his calves and ankles while he struggled with the tent. Here was fresh meat, and for the one week of their short lives, they were determined to feast on whatever flesh they could find.

A half-hour later, the exhausted, bleeding, and swollen camper finished putting up something resembling a gazebo. It didn't matter that several poles still lay on the ground.

He crawled inside and sat on the thin nylon that shielded him from the hard ground. With his flashlight pointed at the roof of the tent, he killed the two dozen tiny black flies that had made it inside with him.

As he went to sleep that night on the rocky, uneven earth, he cursed Mike and Kelly in a silent rage. Finally, he couldn't hold it in anymore. "Stinking shit!" he screamed with all his might. He vowed that he would make them pay dearly for what they had done to him.

************ *********

About a half mile away from Harley, a warm campfire crackled next to the water. The Montanes camped on a tiny peninsula island that jutted out into the lake. Despite the warmth of the reborn lovers, the night breeze swept over the island, keeping all the nasty bugs away.

Mike tipped his canoe upside down near the water's edge to form a table. Working together, they whipped up a gourmet meal of asparagus, wild rice, steaks, and wine. They ate at the lake's edge, and looked up into the heavens as the sky slowly filled with stars. They talked about their private ordeals of the last twenty-one months. Then they cried some more.

Suddenly they heard a distant shout. "Did you hear that?" Kelly asked.

"It sounded like someone swearing."

"That's what I thought. Sometimes I think I'm going crazy. That voice sounded like Harley Crane."

"There's no way–"

"Mike, when I drove through Ely, I thought I saw him. But it couldn't have been . . . Maybe he followed me."

"What should we do?" Even in the campfire light, Mike's face turned white.

"I think we should burn any combustible extra gear." Kelly stared into the fire.

"What about the two canoes?"

"I told Arlen, the man who owns North Country Retreat Center, that we might pair up. He has instructions from me to pick up my canoe in a week. I told him you and I might canoe together and take an extended trip."

"Have I touched your canoe, Kelly?"

"I don't think so. But just to make sure, while you burn the extra gear, I'll wipe down my canoe, then padlock it to the tree in the middle of camp."

"Good idea." They stood next to the shore and listened to the quiet. "Kelly, we need to whisper. Sound travels far at night. Let's load up my kevlar with everything else and we'll take off at first light tomorrow."

"What if Harley comes before then?" Kelly whispered back.

"We'll load my canoe first, just in case."

"He scares me."

"Me too, Kel." Mike fixed his eyes over the water. "He'd be a fool to canoe up here in the dark. Still, let's keep our eyes open, and maintain silence. On this island, I think we'd see him coming."

Without another word, they went to work. An hour later, a padlock and chain strapped Kelly's canoe to a thick birch tree in the middle of camp, and a hot fire had inhaled all their extra gear.

Mike's stash of firewood lasted until well past midnight, and slowly the fire turned into a red glow. The little breeze teased the embers into different hues of orange and red, pushing a steady spiral of smoke toward the woods. As the sound of the fire slowly faded, the gently breaking waves lulled the quiet into a rhythmic trance.

The couple sat bundled in their jackets long after the fire had died. The stars and the northern lights lit up the sky in a brilliant display. Now the night air turned crisp, and they huddled next to each other, together at last. They whispered, smiled, held each other's hands, and loved each other late into the night.

Chapter 57

By 5 AM, the rocky slope completed the job of digging into Harley's back and shoulders. A throbbing ache, and the dull roar of the no-see-ums flying around his tent woke him for the big day.

Harley squirted a shot of jungle juice all over his body, then quietly moved out of his tent and began to pack the canoe. With the sun just peeking over the edge of the horizon, Harley's sore bones screamed when he noticed the foam mattress tucked neatly under the front seat.

He raced to stuff his sleeping bag and roll up the tent. Then he jammed everything into a Duluth pack and placed it in the center of the canoe, keeping the jungle juice on top of the pack in case he needed it again.

Within ten minutes, Harley was in the canoe. As he staggered his way up the shoreline, switching his paddling from side to side in a futile attempt to make the canoe go straight, he got madder by the minute. Every bone and muscle in his body ached from the night on the rocks.

The canoe barely seemed to move. The slight chop on the water pushed the craft closer and closer to shore and Harley struggled against the wind. Without warning, he found himself on top of a fallen log and suddenly the canoe tipped to the left. Instinctively, Harley moved to the right, and the canoe followed. He swung his body hard to the left. Panic gripped him. Back to the right. His faced tensed. Left.

The canoe tipped.

Harley fell in three feet of water. His body submerged and his sore arm hit hard on a rock. Within an instant, he stood, now up to his waist in the cold water. He watched as his Duluth pack sank right in front of him.

He grabbed the canoe, terrified it would blow away, then dug through the water for his pack. With both hands full, he watched as his bottle of jungle juice floated out of reach.

Anger more powerful than fear surged through his mind as he remembered the words of that pimple faced camp counselor: *"I'm only trying to help, sir. If you lose your motor, and don't know how to paddle correctly, you can get stranded out there. I've heard a lot of stories about people who got stuck on an island for days before someone came to their rescue."*

It took another ten minutes for Harley to drag his canoe onto the rocky, shrub-infested shoreline. Being as quiet as possible, he heaved the canoe sideways and emptied most of the water. Fortunately, he had strapped the motor to the canoe's yoke, and he still had his paddle.

He tied his wet Duluth pack back into the front bow seat, then stretched against the fabric of his drenched pant leg to haul his body back into the canoe. He pointed the nose directly into the wind in an effort to stay away from the shoreline. From that point, he moved much more cautiously, silently cursing the canoe along with everyone else.

The morning winds now spit spurts of small whitecaps across the lake. Wihtout the shelter of the shoreline, the rolling waves made paddling extra difficult. Harley zigzagged, paddling as hard as he could from side to side for an eternal half hour before spotting the Montane's camp. He could see the island and make out the form of a canoe on the beach. Probably a couple blocks to go at the most, he calculated. He would get his prey.

When Mike walked down to the lake to scoop some water for dousing the campfire, he caught a glimpse of the solo canoe heading toward them. He ran back to the camp, doused the fire, then grabbed his binoculars to see who might be canoeing so early in the morning.

"Honey, come here, quick." He shouted.

"What is it?"

"I think it's Harley Crane!"

"Let me see!" Kelly grabbed the binoculars and studied the man obviously struggling against the wind. "You're right. It's him," she cried in horror.

"Let's get out of here." Mike said as they raced for the canoe.

Harley, so caught up in the struggle to go straight, never saw the canoe until they were already in the water. He pulled out his wet handgun and tried to aim at the fleeing couple, but they were too far away, and his canoe rocked and pitched with each wave.

He shot off three bullets in their general direction. Maybe the threat of death would make them stop. Instead, they continued heading away from him. They paddled in powerful, synchronized strokes. Mike on the left side of the canoe, Kelly on the right, each stroke in perfect harmony with the other. Their arms reached high into the sky and the paddles came down deep as they shot across the water in a perfectly straight line.

Watching through his binoculars, Harley recognized Mike as he turned to look back in his direction. Harley knew it! He had been right all along!

Harley screamed a fanatical curse against the wind. Adrenaline gushed through his veins as he reached for the motor. It didn't matter if they knew how to canoe. His motor would overpower them faster than a dog chasing a turtle. He still had a few bullets. He would catch them. He would triumph.

Suddenly the swelling waves and bobbing canoe ceased to bother Harley as he quickly worked to clamp the motor onto the motor mount. The bottom of the ninth. Two outs. Score tied. It was time for Harley to be the hero. There wouldn't be another inning. This was what he lived for and no waves were about to stop him.

Finally he bolted the motor tightly onto the canoe. He ripped the cord, heard the sweet, sweet whine of the engine, and immediately turned the craft upwind. It was easy to see he was gaining on them. He passed by the island campsite, each second bringing him closer and closer to victory.

Mike and Kelly looked back in shock when they heard the sound of the motor. Frantic with fear, Kelly couldn't possibly bear to lose again. With every fiber inside her, her muscles pushed. Her legs spread out and her feet gripped against the edges of the canoe. Her arms pumped like pistons as her paddle dug through the water, then gasped for air, each movement pulling them forward. Faster.

Harder. Kelly envisioned the way Al used to rock-climb. So many moves seemed impossible. But time after time, Al's fingers locked over the ledge, and she hung on.

A rush of horror flashed through Mike. A terror he had witnessed as a child came searing into his mind, paralyzing him. He envisioned a rabbit as it watched the owl's talons drop from the sky. He heard a scream as flesh ripped off the rabbit's back. The owl carried the dying rabbit away. The shriek penetrated the woods, then silence. Now the dreadful monster bore down on him, and for a moment he faltered, his muscles froze.

"Dig!" Kelly screamed, then slapped her paddle hard into the water, dousing Mike with stiff spray. Kelly's pleading face brought him back. They were together again. He loved that face, and knew he would die for her. In that sudden moment, he was reborn, and his arms came alive.

"Switch," Mike yelled as he and Kelly moved their paddles to opposite sides. Their muscles drew the canoe forward with each stroke. Arms up, the paddle sliced forward through the air, down and back, pulling through the water. Arms up, forward, down, pull. Up. Forward. Down. Pull. The motion blurred. They had to make it to the channel where the water turned shallow before Harley caught them. It was their only hope.

When Harley got within twenty yards of Mike and Kelly, he reached into his jacket to pull out the gun. He didn't care if he had to kill them both. He would show those bastards at Platinum who was right.

Mike turned and saw Harley's hard face. The man's teeth gritted in hate. His hair stood in the wind.

Harley recognized the fear in his prey. They were so weak. A rush of power surged through him. He had lived this moment a thousand times in his dreams and now he would conquer. The gap narrowed as Harley's canoe crashed against the waves, spitting water high into the air around him. Harley pulled alongside the Montanes, careful to stay far enough away so Mike couldn't lash out with his paddle.

"Stop, or I'll kill you!" Venom stung through the hate in his voice.

The Montanes kept paddling.

Harley slowed the motor to match pace, while the fear in Kelly and Mike pushed their bodies far beyond physical pain. The two canoes moved like dual torpedoes side by side, cutting evenly through the water.

Harley extended his arm, ready to shoot Mike, only five feet away. A sick smile spread across Harley's face. His eyes locked onto his target.

Harley pulled the trigger. In the exact same instant, his motor slammed hard against a rock. The canoe crashed to a sudden halt. Harley flew forward. His body heaved over the aft thwart and hammered into the yoke of the canoe, almost tipping it. The impact hurled the gun out of his hand, and into the water.

The exploding bullet ripped through the sky for about a mile, before it fell harmlessly back to the earth. In the sudden silence, Mike and Kelly continued to paddle as hard as they could.

Harley turned to yank on the cord. The motor sputtered, then died. He pulled on the cord again. And then again. Nothing.

Harley ripped on the rope as his canoe turned sideways in the waves. He pulled. He pulled again. And again. The engine didn't spurt. Didn't even whine.

The Montanes weaved through a narrow channel, then paddled out of sight.

The motor, and Harley, had both lost.

He struggled to take the useless motor off the back of the canoe. Then he stood in the canoe. With all his might, he cursed his dad's name into the wind. "I hate you, John Crane." He heaved the motor over his head and thrust it violently over the side.

As Mike and Kelly fled, Harley sat alone in his canoe and let the waves push him slowly back toward shore. There was no consolation that he had proven himself right. It didn't matter that he had masterfully called the play-by-play, because no one else had watched the game.

The waves pushed against his canoe for several hours as he sat there, blown and tossed wherever the wind took him. His shoulder ached with a throbbing pain and his back burned from pulling on the motor.

The waves pushed and tossed the small craft across the big lake, until the canoe finally settled next to the island campground. He slowly hauled himself out of the canoe onto the rocky shoreline. There, he waded through the shallow water toward the campground on the far side of the island, pulling the canoe behind him.

Softball-sized rocks hidden under the waves made the walk treacherous. Harley moved deeper into the water, somewhere near mid-thigh depth to avoid spraining an ankle. He trudged around the island, terrified of losing his grip on the canoe, all the time fighting the wave's efforts to pull it out of his hands.

An hour later, an exhausted man dragged his canoe to shore. His wet shoes slogged their way up the gravelly hill into the camp. Harley was surprised to see Kelly's canoe padlocked to a tree. A thin cloud of smoke swirled from the fire-grate. Otherwise, the camp was deserted.

And then, he noticed. There, above the fire-grate, stabbed into a tree at eye level, was a little red Platinum jackknife. It pierced the heart of an envelope flapping lightly in the wind. It was addressed to Harley's home in Chicago and had a postage stamp ready for mailing.

Harley pulled the knife out of the tree and opened the envelope. It contained a change of beneficiary form, signed, and acknowledged by Platinum Insurance. It said that Harley Crane was the beneficiary of Kelly Montane's two-and-a-half-million-dollar life policy.

A handwritten note accompanied the form. Kelly Montane's signature appeared at the bottom. "Harley. You couldn't prove that Mike lived. See if you can prove that I died."

Mark Arens has been one of the top producing insurance agents in the United States for the last 26 years.

He is an avid outdoorsman and loves canoeing, rock-climbing, snowshoeing and all quiet sports. Mark is an instrument pilot and has hang-glided in British Columbia.

Mark loves living a full life with his family, and has written a series of children's books centered on his character, "Thumbuddy." Mark says, "Just as our thumb is set apart from our fingers, our unique thumbprint sets us apart. We are all born to be ThumbPeople – blessed and destined to live unique and amazing lives. Our goal is to help parents and children embrace the truth that their child is truly Thumbuddy… Thumbuddy special, wonderful, precious, unique…
A miracle in every way."

Visit www.MarkArens.com